After the Locks are Changed

stories
by

Gary Fincke

STEPHEN F. AUSTIN STATE UNIVERSITY PRESS

Production Manager: Kimberly Verhines
Book Design: Mallory LeCroy

IBSN: 978-1-62288-260-1

For more information:
Stephen F. Austin State University Press
P.O. Box 13007 SFA Station
Nacogdoches, Texas 75962
sfapress@sfasu.edu
www.sfasu.edu/sfapress
936-468-1078

Distributed by Texas A&M University Press Consortium
www.tamupress.com

Contents

For all of the editors and publishers who have given good advice and supported my work for fifty years.

Billie Holiday, Sylvia Plath, the Weather Each Morning

April

One Saturday morning, at dawn, sixteen months after Carrie and Daniel's Christmas holiday wedding, her white German shepherd climbed on the bed and nudged its way between them. It was six a.m., and when the hundred-and-ten-pound dog lapsed into the high-pitched whine that signaled a fit of barking was about to begin, Daniel said, "God-damn-it, Duke, shut up" three times in less than a minute as if the dog might morph into stone. Instead, the dog jumped from the bed and began to nose inside the bedroom closet, but only on Carrie's side, snuffling among the dresses and skirts. "It must be a sex thing," Daniel said, his mouth half-buried in his pillow.

Duke settled inside the closet, flopping onto the rack of Carrie's shoes before squirming as if it were possible to make himself comfortable despite an assortment of heel heights underneath him. Unsuccessful, Duke scratched on the inside wall, and Carrie imagined the landlord inspecting before some future move, how their damage deposit would disappear into wallboard and paint. "Duke," she called, half-awake, "Stop it," but Duke didn't seem to hear.

"Your dog is such a pain in the ass," Daniel said. He staggered up and tried to talk the dog out, using reason, threats, volume, and curses in rapid succession, but none made a difference.

"Duke can be in there," Carrie said, "but he has to stop scratching."

Daniel turned on the radio. "This worked on my brother's dog when I was little," he said, and magically, as Lee Ann Womack and then Faith Hill sang their current hits, Duke stopped scratching. "Yes," Daniel said, but as soon as Lenny Kravitz opened his mouth, Duke pawed at the wall.

"I hate Lenny Kravitz, too," Carrie said as Daniel made a kicking motion with his bare foot that Duke ignored.

"Every sunrise will be earlier now," Daniel said. "This is bullshit that will get deeper."

"Try the Billie Holiday CD," Carrie said. "Duke doesn't care about the song. He cares about the voice."

"So you say," Daniel said, but Duke agreed. He seemed to listen. Daniel fell back asleep while Carrie lay in bed listening for half an hour. She had a box set her father had mailed to her for her birthday three years before.

That night, Carrie set one of the Billie Holiday CDs in place as if she were preparing a second coffee maker. "One for sleeping to a reasonable time, one for waking up when that time arrives," she said.

"You wish," Daniel said.

When Carrie started the CD as soon as Duke nuzzled her at dawn, the dog wandered to the closet, then turned and flopped back down beside the bed. At seven, she rose just after Billie Holiday's last track faded. She walked the dog. She fed him and ate breakfast and when Daniel rose at ten, she tried to convince him it was the music that worked, not luck. "Whatever," he said, but for two weeks, she played that long-dead singer she loved at dawn, the room going blue a few minutes earlier each day with *Body and Soul, Summertime,* and *Lover Man*. Some mornings, for the first verse or two, the dog paced and whined and scratched at the closed closet, but finally, by the chorus, settled into a corner between the dresser and the wall. "That boring shit only works until you leave for work," Daniel said. "The dog acts like a rooster at 7: 30."

May

The spring weather, at least on weekends, extended Carrie's walks with Duke. Enormous and white and led on a chain leash, he cleared wide swaths of sidewalk in Chinatown and comfortable walkways in NOLITA just below where Carrie and Daniel lived a block off Houston Street. He needed to be walked more, but Daniel shifted from grumbling about Duke to ignoring her when she asked him to help. He was busy with auditions. He needed his days to be open in order to be available. Mostly, he watched television and drank beer as if they were the paying jobs that supplemented his twice a week waiter job.

"At least," she said, "walk him once while I'm at school. He'll never make it to four o'clock."

"He didn't make it to noon," Daniel said once or twice a week when she came home to a puddle in the kitchen.

Then, for three weeks, Daniel rehearsed nightly for an off-off Broadway play he said was being kept "a secret" and watched old movies after he came home. "For acting tips," he said, and Carrie watched with him for a while before asking him to turn the volume down so she could sleep. By then, starting on his second six pack, he would turn bitter. The young men in parts he felt suited for always sucked. The Brat Pack was terrible—Judd Nelson, Rob Lowe, Emilio Estevez—and Keanu Reeves, she couldn't even mention his name.

A dog park was blocks away, absorbing time she didn't have to get there and back, and then only on Saturdays until her classes ended. The school was in Alphabet City, a few blocks from Katz's Deli, CBGBs and the big KISS mural. None of those things impressed her students. The first language of nearly all of them was Spanish. Several, she'd long ago learned, were homeless. But she taught art and mostly they were happy not to worry about language skills or algebra or American history for nearly an hour.

"The play," Daniel finally told her, "is about the fire that killed a lot of women where they worked."

"The Shirtwaist Factory."

"Yeah. You've heard of it? They had a choice—jump or burn."

"Some were girls, really young. They were locked in."

"I'm the voiceover," he said. "Like the stage manager who talks in *Our Town*. I'm the only one left on stage at the end when the fire starts. It's like the fire is talking."

"Like the women don't count," Carrie said.

"More like the fire is a character. Like it has mind enough to speak."

For only the second time, though she lived barely over 100 miles away, Carrie's mother agreed to come to New York for the play's opening. "Your place is so small," she said on the phone. "And that dog makes it smaller. I'll get a room. We'll have plenty of time to visit before and after the play."

"We can go to Daniel's restaurant. They'll comp us a fantastic meal."

"Why would they do that?"

"All the waiters are actors. If they get a speaking part, they serve a meal for two guests like a bonus."

When her mother didn't answer at once, Carrie knew she was calculating the odds of a waiter winning that bonus.

The restaurant catered to wealthy clients of a European clothing designer. The fitting room and displays were on a different floor. When Carrie and her mother arrived, the only other customers were three women who spoke French and two men who spoke German. "I always thought nobody wore those clothes the models have on in the magazines," her mother said, "but now I see I was wrong. The women look gorgeous, but the men look like homosexuals."

Daniel was charming. "Relax and enjoy," he said, and then he acted as if he didn't know them, speaking only about the food and the drinks in the same manner he used with the nearby women.

After Carrie finished her last bite of chocolate-apricot torte, Daniel laid a leather-bound folder on the table. Carrie's mother opened it. "Let's see how much the rich people pay for all this," she said. She frowned. "Of course," Carrie heard her mutter.

"What?" Carrie said.

"Never you mind," her mother said, but she was already opening her purse and extracting a credit card.

"The entrees were comped," Daniel said later. "Your mother ate the best meal of her life and now she's bitching about it? Dessert isn't included, and everybody should know that drinks are never comped."

The theater was up two flights of stairs in the East Village. Forty folding chairs. The stage formed by widely spaced bricks. "Well, this theater was perfect for that play," Carrie's mother said as soon as it ended. "I thought I smelled smoke for the last hour."

"We can go outside to wait for Daniel," Carrie said, more than half expecting her mother to mention muggers as they made their way to the sidewalk.

Instead, her mother said, "You two enjoy yourselves, I have all my things packed and in the car already. One night is enough to pay for."

"It will be Sunday before you get home. You won't be there until after midnight," Carrie said.

"This is the best time to drive. The traffic is only horrible instead of horrendous. No wonder you sold your car." The first passing cab stopped as if she'd made an appointment. "See ya," she called, opening the door.

"She's gone?" Daniel said a few minutes later. "She hated the play, right? She bitched about the venue and the crummy chairs."

"She didn't say anything about the play."

"Like everybody else. Movies are where it's at. We need to move to L.A."

Monday morning, despite the music, Duke whined and began to bark. Even after she hurried him outside, he stayed restless. From the shower, Carrie could hear the dog so clearly over the rushing water that she knew he'd nudged open the bathroom door and was standing only inches from the curtain.

That afternoon, after the principal evaluated Carrie's teaching as excellent, she asked Carrie to hold an art show. "Nobody has ever done what you have here. Some of their art is astonishing. The school might have to close, and you could help us get more funding. I'll invite everyone on our board and a few local politicians. We'll serve snacks. We'll dazzle until they reach for their wallets."

Carrie picked a piece from each student and invited a second piece from twelve students who were as astonishing as the principal had claimed. The principal sent out the invitations and ordered food.

June

One morning, between songs, Duke began to whine so terribly and so long, it seemed possible he had swallowed something sharp and indigestible.

"He's as sick of Billie Holiday as I am," Daniel said.

"We don't have any other singer's box set," Carrie said.

Instead of answering, Daniel rummaged. "When we're awake and talking, the dog doesn't start to go crazy like it thinks we're dead. It just needs voices. There's Kerouac and Ginsberg and a bunch more on this old poetry compilation. Listen up, Duke." The voice of Jack Kerouac said, "From On the Road," and began a series of long, sonorous sentences that blurred, Carrie thought, into something that would make anyone sleepy. Duke listened for what Carrie guessed was a paragraph before he resumed whining. Ginsberg fared no better.

"Try a woman," Carrie said, but Daniel covered his head with a pillow and didn't move,

Carrie rose and switched the CD. As soon as Sylvia Plath began, Duke relaxed inside the closet. "Listen to that voice," Daniel said. "I bet she was a hot fuck."

Each morning, Carrie played the spoken-word CD of *Daddy, Lady Lazarus, Ariel* and more. The dog listened like an acolyte. He sprawled in front of the small speakers after she rose at first light to start the CD. Then, after she returned to bed, Duke entered the closet and settled, still and soundless, but only for Plath's eighteen minutes.

Carrie spent a weekend hanging art in the large, all-purpose room that the principal kept locked for the Monday night show. "It starts at seven," Carrie told Daniel. "Come over around quarter to eight when the crowd is probably peaked and take some photos."

Carrie and the principal watched the clock by themselves until 7:15, when a Dominican student, one of Carrie's favorites, walked in. Four more students arrived by 7:30, but not one parent came, not one administrator from the city or the advisory board. Before eight o'clock, the students were gone, but Carrie and her supervisor waited another fifteen minutes, looking at the displays and nibbling the food.

"We'll wait five minutes and then start cleaning up," the supervisor said.

"There's my husband Daniel, at least," Carrie said. Just as the supervisor turned to look, Daniel stopped and swayed as if he'd just stepped off a boat. She watched him catch himself, then walk in a careful, practiced way to the food table where he stopped and began to scoop, one by one, seven chips through the salsa dip before devouring them. The supervisor seemed transfixed while Daniel swayed and steadied himself, wiping his mouth with one of the green paper napkins. He lifted the camera, pointed it at them, and snapped.

Instead of approaching, Daniel wandered around the room, pausing to snap pictures of the art until he reached the door and left. "Well, you have some keepsakes at least," the supervisor said. "We might as well get to work. We'll leave the artwork in place until school ends. You don't think anyone will damage it, do you?"

"Not my students, no."

"Then it's settled," she said, and walked to the table where she began by dumping the chips and salsa into a garbage bag.

July

Three weeks after classes ended, the school closed. "It was sold to a tech company," Carrie told Daniel. "I'm already looking."

When Daniel was fired a week later, he screamed at Duke until the dog showed his teeth. "I wish I could fire this dog," he said when Carrie told him to shut up and explain just how, unless he was stealing or dumping food on customers, he could get himself fired without any warning.

"They said I was late a couple of times."

"Were they right?"

"Were they right? You sound just like those pricks."

They were home together all day now. Near the end of the month, Daniel began working Tuesday and Thursday as a caterer's assistant, six-hour shifts of deliveries. "Like being a pizza guy," he said. "The food is more expensive, but it's still delivery. Fucking humiliating."

He catered in the Trade Center, once all the way up to the offices of Cantor Fitzgerald, just below Windows on the World. "It's incredible up that high," he said.

"You could apply at Windows," she said. "You're such a great waiter."

"You know why I can't. You know exactly why."

"Actors have to be available," Carrie said as he nodded. "But it's not that far away. You could even walk to work on a nice day if you made time. For the exercise."

"Like the dog? Jesus, it's cab distance away, and the dog doesn't have a six-hour shift on its feet after walking all the way down there. It comes home and lays around waiting for food and water." He turned on the television where a movie she didn't recognize was on.

"I got a job at another school."

"Just like that?"

"I sent a resume. I interviewed."

"Like an audition?"

"What's that mean?"

"Pretending."

"No. Not like that."

Daniel waved at the screen. "These two guys suck in this movie, but whoever that woman is dominates this scene. She's fantastic."

"Her clothes are doing the acting," Carrie said.

After Carrie turned on Plath the next morning, Duke barked at the CD player. He clawed at the closet as if Carrie's clothing softly whispered the secrets of happiness on a frequency that could only he could hear. "I'm sick of that bitch, too," Daniel said.

August

CDs had limits, Carrie and David agreed. "Other than that, all we have is the TV," Carrie said. "There's a woman on the weather channel early every morning."

"Who watches forecasts before six a.m.?" Daniel said.

"Farmers. Baseball players, pilots, people who walk to work."

"The remote is right beside you," he said, placing it on her side of the bed. "You and Duke will be the first to know if there's clouds, and I'll happily stay ignorant and asleep. And thank Christ the days are getting shorter again."

The temperature in the city settled into a run of ninety-degree days, each more humid than the one before. The forecasts grew dire. A violent thunderstorm warning for three days, the rain arriving around four p.m. as if it were keeping a regular schedule. The weather-woman's voice was soft no matter the forecast. Duke, each morning, lay on the floor on Carrie's side of the bed. Daniel slept in past their walks, all of them completed before clouds began to build up.

The remote made it easy to calm the dog, but more and more often, Daniel left it by his chair. She stayed up on those mornings, six a.m. becoming a habit. She began to paint in the kitchen after she walked the dog. When Daniel was finally on his feet, she walked the dog again, the clouds beginning to threaten, but the rain, she discovered, always another couple of hours away. During one of those storms, Daniel had a callback for a movie.

"Friday, for the male lead," he said, then paused. "Or maybe not. Auditions are tense, but callbacks are hell. The failure is way worse when you have hope."

"We'll celebrate when hope is rewarded."

"Things are moving fast. They plan to start shooting late next week, so there's that."

"Any time but this weekend. Mom is coming. Remember? We're going to my college friend's wedding."

"Why would I remember that? I don't even know your friend."

"That's what you said a month ago, so Mom agreed to go along with me so you didn't have to be bored. And she's staying over Friday night just this one time and never again, ok?"

"Never again needs to be a promise kept."

Carrie buzzed her mother up at ten o'clock. "Daniel's at a callback," she said at once. "It must be running late."

"You don't have to make excuses. I'm so beat from the trip that I'll go right to sleep no matter what."

Carrie woke before Duke and turned the weather on. In the faint light, she saw that Daniel wasn't on the couch. Duke didn't stir.

An hour later, as soon as Duke nuzzled her, she rose and clipped on his leash. They walked for an hour, giving her mother and her questions more time to sleep. Carrie called three of the guys Daniel hung out with, all of them with places a few blocks above Houston, but no luck. She called Anita, her best friend. For comfort, not information.

"It's not a first time, right?" she said. "He'll turn up."

As soon as she hung up, shaking her head, her mother said, "How long before we leave without knowing what he's been up to? An hour or two? We can watch a movie while we wait. New York must have more stations to pick from."

"It doesn't work like that anymore, Mom. There's cable everywhere."

"I don't have cable. I watch the stations from Binghamton. Sometimes they're fuzzy, but enough reach our town for anybody unless they're too picky."

"There's a lot of picky people, Mom."

"If you lived in a better neighborhood, we could walk somewhere."

"It's not dangerous."

"It looks like somewhere is dangerous with us waiting here like this nearly noon." When Carrie didn't answer, her mother whispered a short laugh. "Speaking of picky, we sure weren't. Your father used to do this." Carrie thought she sounded almost giddy, like they were close now, best friends.

"I thought you were worried."

"I was until the heavens opened and that voice I heard years ago said, 'You're a goddamned fool, honey.' I'm afraid I taught you how to drown instead of swim."

"Nobody's drowning here."

"That's what they said on the Titanic."

"I have a new job."

"Good for you. You'll need it. And now that it's officially afternoon, we're calling the police. That wedding of yours is up shit's creek, I'm afraid."

Carrie called hospitals first, the three closest. The police promised to show up, but didn't sound like they were in a hurry, so she walked Duke for half an hour of R&R. Another hour passed before the police arrived. A minute later, as if he'd been staking out the apartment, Daniel appeared. "Hi guys," he said.

"You the missing person?" one policeman said.

"I went to a party and fell asleep," Daniel said. "It happens."

"I'm sorry for troubling you," Carrie said, the policemen already out the door and starting down the stairs. She followed them outside to apologize a second time.

"That dog of yours?" one cop said. "It didn't even perk up when it heard his footsteps on the stairs. That speaks volumes."

The other cop nodded, then laughed. "I bet it has stories it could tell."

By the time she was back in the apartment, Daniel had disappeared into the bedroom and closed the door. Duke nuzzled against her until she rubbed his head. "Your father bought you that dog to keep you safe and give himself a clear conscience without ever showing his face to do that himself," her mother said. "I should have given you a big bottle of common sense to go with it." Her face softened. "Don't you dare settle for. Please."

"You don't know as much as you think you do, Mom."

"Your father didn't leave," she said, "until one of his sluts turned out to have money."

"It's not like that."

"You'll think that's true until you work things down to the lowest common denominator."

"Jesus, Mom."

"He's got nothing to do with it. Sleeping Beauty in there will divide and divide what he does for you until he's not even like a church-goer tithing, not even 10% give-back for all you do for him."

"Mom."

"That dog knows. He gets it, crawling into that closet and pretending what he doesn't see doesn't happen."

Carrie recognized her mother's tone, the one her father claimed drove him away. "The flinty bitch voice," he'd called it.

"The one you deserve," her mother had always replied.

"I wasn't sleeping," Daniel said after her mother was gone. "I was always going to stay over somewhere until you were off to the wedding. Christ, the police and all that. Why didn't you just go when the time came?"

"Think about that for a second," Carrie said. "It'll come to you."

"Your mother fucks me up. It's like she casts a spell. I was happy and didn't want her to ruin it. The director said he loved the chemistry between me and Jackie. You know she's on *Six Feet Under*. It's all over HBO. She's doing him a favor because they went to high school together or something. Damn. This movie can get a distributor with her name on it if she breaks out, and the buzz says her part is scheduled to be enlarged if it gets renewed. And there's a guy in it who you've seen in a dozen movies. A character actor. You'll know his face as soon as you see him."

"So, the director is really young?"

"Yeah. That's a good thing. Once he gets famous, I'll have an in." He took a deep breath, the kind Carrie imagined someone taking as rising water was about to reach the ceiling of a locked room. "I'm not going to tell you anything more. They talked about still making script changes. Maybe my character will get more scenes."

September

Labor Day came and went. Because the caterer called, she knew Daniel was late for work on Tuesday. "They'll fire you, too," Carrie said, yet he left at the same time again on Thursday. Carrie walked Duke all the way to her new school and back, wearing herself out, so she could fall asleep while Daniel bitched about the director dragging his feet on hiring him, drank beer, and cursed movies past midnight. Friday was a rerun. And Saturday.

When she came out of the shower late Sunday morning, Daniel was busy making breakfast—omelets, bacon extra crispy. "I'm in," he said.

"I'll get Anita to dog-sit. She loves Duke. She's on night shift, but I'll leave her money for pizza. She has to eat before she goes to the hospital."

"Filming starts next week. I quit that fucking delivery job while you were in the shower. It was fucking great telling them to fuck off."

"You could have done another two days. Kept that door open."

"Let the tourists enjoy the Trade Center. And all those men in suits. And those women who look like they're auditioning for something."

"Tell me all about it at dinner," Carrie said. "Tell me when we're someplace special."

Carrie dropped their flip phone into her purse before she hugged Anita at the top of the stairs. "You're a lifesaver," she said.

"It's just a few hours. You're not one of those moths that live for one night."

"Be good, Duke," Carrie said, and when the dog barely stirred, she relaxed and followed Daniel down the stairs. The restaurant was so close—three and a half blocks—that she was able to keep from asking about the movie until they were seated and they'd ordered drinks. "All right," she said. "Start with the title."

"*Poisonous*," Daniel said. "The drinking water in this town gets tainted and almost everybody dies."

"A disaster movie?"

"Sort of, but the dead people come back to life."

She wanted to say, *A religious movie?* but stopped herself and waited him out. "There's zombies, sure, but it's more like eco-horror. It's about the environment. This girl and me and a couple of others drink only bottled water, so we're alive when the zombies come after us in this medical center. We're all scientists. We're the ones who could figure out how to fix things if the zombies just left us alone."

Daniel ordered a meatball parmesan sandwich and fries; Carrie asked for a strip steak, medium rare. They ordered another round of drinks. "So, you get eaten by the zombies?"

"I save Jackie. I'm the last one to get eaten."

"That's something good, right?"

"For now. Maybe the script will be rewritten."

"*Poisonous* sounds like a snake movie. Maybe they should change the title."

"They already did. It was *Biohazardous,* and then they found out there's a movie that just came out with that name. It went straight to video, but still."

Their meals seemed to take forever to arrive, and when, at last, they did, Daniel stared as she forked bites of red meat into her mouth. "You don't act like you're excited," he said.

"I'm excited. Really. I'm glad you're happy, but I'm concentrating on this steak for a while." Daniel ordered another drink. They both refused dessert, but Daniel tapped his drink glass and nodded. *Like something he's seen in a movie,* Carrie thought. *Like he's in character.*

Another hour passed before they left the restaurant. Daniel walked in front of her out the door, a sign, Carrie knew, that his mood had changed. "What's going on?" she said as they walked.

"Your steak cost more than three times my meatball parm."

A little boy's voice, Carrie thought. "I had two glasses of wine and a steak; you had six mixed drinks and an Italian cheeseburger you didn't even finish. It's the same cost and anyway, we're celebrating."

"I'm celebrating. You're criticizing." He glanced at her purse. "Answer that. They might want me tomorrow or something. Almost nobody else knows the number."

"Anita does. I told her just in case."

A block from their apartment, still walking, Carrie mouthed "Anita" to Daniel and began to talk. "This has to be short, but I had to call. Duke is missing. You guys were running late and I had a shift to do. I had to go. I'm sorry. I looked and looked and now I'm calling on my way to work."

Carrie stopped, but Daniel kept walking. "What do you mean? Duke's out somewhere?"

"All I did was go downstairs to pay for the pizza. I couldn't believe it. The dog's too big not to notice passing by me."

"Maybe it came half way down to the landing and you didn't see it with the pizza and Pepsi up in front of your face going up."

"No way."

She agreed. No way unless Anita had chatted up the pizza guy or stepped onto the sidewalk to listen to the carillon from the cathedral half a block down, the pizza arriving exactly on the hour. Anita, Carrie knew, was still a real Catholic who went to weekly mass and confession. "Did you leave the doorway?"

"You think I took the pizza for a walk?"

"Just to the curb, even just a step or two to look at something or listen to the bells from St. What's-his-name's."

"Two steps aren't enough. The dog is huge." Carrie could hear Anita start to cry. "I have to go. I'm inside now. Personal calls are taboo. I'm so sorry."

Carrie crossed the street and shouted ahead to Daniel. "Go up and take a look. Make sure before we start searching."

Daniel shook his head, but disappeared up the stairs. Carrie heard two doors slam shut. "It's outside for sure," he yelled on his way down.

"Look in the bathtub before you come all the way down."

Daniel seemed to hurry. "First place I peeked," he said, back on the sidewalk.

"We have to look," Carrie said. "As long as it takes."

"The dog will come back. Where else can it go?" Carrie saw he had a beer in a paper bag.

"He might be hurt somewhere. He might have been hit by a car on Houston. He wouldn't go far. You go that way, and I'll go toward NOLITA."

She waited for him to move. "Go ahead," and watched until he turned the corner. *He'll walk until the beer is gone*, she thought. *Ten minutes. A couple of blocks and back.*

She hurried along every side street for nearly an hour, all the dark places, then back to the well-lit and busy, returning to the apartment in tears. An empty can on the floor, another in his hand, Daniel was watching television, his feet on the coffee table, his shoes, she noticed, still on. He looked so happy to be alone that she stayed in the kitchen, sitting on the floor with her back against the refrigerator.

Except for some of the old movies, she never watched television. That and the stereo were Daniel's from before they were married. Every one of the books on the shelves by the CD player were hers. Half of them were art books, expensive ones with color plates her father mailed for her birthday and Christmas and the wedding he'd dubbed "Y2K-Eve" on the gift-wrapping. None were from her mother. "That's the country he lives in," she'd said once as she examined them. Since the wedding, her mother had bought her gift cards to women's clothing stores. "So I can count on the cards staying yours," she'd said. "So he won't touch them."

She should leave, Carrie thought. Pack some things while Daniel slept until noon or later. Stay with Anita. School started on Tuesday. Because Anita's apartment was below Chinatown, there was only three blocks to walk to her third-floor classroom that looked south and east from a corner of a converted building. Daniel didn't know Anita's last name or where she lived. He wouldn't even call her mother for a few days. Until he needed something. He'd never asked the name of her new school or where it was. He'd call her old school, and when he'd ask if they knew where she worked now, they would refuse to tell him. It was like thinking in her mother's voice.

When a woman spoke louder from the television, talking earnestly at length, Carrie heard a noise from under the sink, a scraping and sigh. The door was so slightly ajar it was as if the dog had closed it behind him.

Soundless, she watched the tiny crack for a few seconds. She needed to call Anita, but not now, when she was at work. "Wow oh wow, who knew?" she would say. "That dog loves you, for sure, you're lucky that way, you know," and Carrie would tell her she didn't blame Anita for anything.

When Carrie opened the door, beginning to cry, Duke snuffled and settled deeper among the soaps and cleansers. Daniel had disappeared into the bedroom, but the television still played. Another woman was speaking now, then another, all of them so intense that Carrie strained to hear what they were saying. It sounded important.

Roustabouts

THOUGH IT HAD BEEN ten years since he'd worked on an oilrig and he'd held half a dozen jobs since, my stepfather Ray Ressler always told people he met that he was a retired roustabout. Said he worked out of Galveston, a town that was as rough and ready as any you'd ever see. "I was coming up for roughneck when my accident finished all that," he told me right off. "That's the real deal. Somebody call you a roughneck, you tell them there's such a thing that's worth a good goddamn."

I liked the sound of roustabout, but roughneck was even better. "All right," I said, though I was imagining gangsters or bandits or even the high-wayman we'd read about in a poem in my eighth grade English class. You had to be a tough guy who could take charge, somebody, though I was far from it, I thought I wanted to be.

My mother, as if she could read my mind, told me that roustabout jobs were "at the bottom of the pile out there in the Gulf." When I asked how big the pile was, she shook her head. "Big enough to smother you if you don't get out from under, but Ray says it paid good."

"Wet and dirty" is how Ray put it when I asked. "Unloading crap. Carrying it around. Cleaning up after everybody. Maybe fix a few things if you're handy that way. But it was two weeks on, two weeks off, the way to do it. Like one of those regular puny vacations most get only they come around every month." He was standing outside smoking like he always did because my mother wouldn't put up with it inside. He took a long drag and grinned. "There's no sissies stay long out there," he said. "You need to have some balls, Wayne, that's God's truth. And there I was a few days, maybe a few weeks, from being promoted to roughneck and my car wreck ended all that."

RAY WAS ABOUT FIFTY when he married my mother, which would have made him fifteen years older than her, but still a young man when it came to all his retirement talk a year after their wedding and I turned fourteen in Front Royal, Virginia where we moved at the end of April 1962. Because we lived outside of town and I didn't own a bike, Front Royal didn't seem to be much except a place where tourists passed through on their way to the Skyline Drive and the Shenandoah National Park. I had a month of junior high school to finish, so short a time nobody paid much attention to me, but it wasn't so bad in the tiny four room house with no basement, a sight better, at least, than Ray's crummy apartment in Hagerstown we'd moved into when my mother married him, three rooms with families on either side always loud with radios, televisions, and angry voices. And it was way better than the two rooms and the shared bathroom my grandmother let us live in at her run-down house for the six years after my father got killed because of what my mother called a "misunderstanding."

What I hated about the new house was the water that came out of the spigots. It stunk like rotten eggs. Sulfur, Ray said the first time I complained. Like he was letting me in on a secret. "It don't hurt you, so get yourself used to it," he said every time he saw me making a face. "It tastes the same as what comes from that fountain you love at the A&P."

He'd seen me go back to that fountain three times while my mother went up and down every aisle loading up a cart with all the things we needed to get us started in the house Ray told us he'd gotten "for a song." It was the only time he ever came along to the A&P, but he seemed to know I drank my fill every time I kept my mother company when she shopped.

Because it was the only refrigerated fountain I knew of. Because it wasn't room temperature like the school fountains that, by second period, were clogged with gum wads that encouraged puddles that showed globs of mucus-laced spit. For the five weeks that I attended after we moved, I never took a drink except before my first class of the day.

Ray, it turned out, was on disability, a monthly check my mother called small but steady. He was still doing maintenance at the Kmart in Hagerstown when we met, but by the time they were married and we were settled in his place, he said he was on his way out and was looking around for a new start for all of us. "Thank the good Lord for my disability that comes regular," he said as if God had a plan for us.

"Your new Pop's too banged up to work at anything he's good at," my mother said a few days later.

"What hurts him?" I asked.

"Everything you need to do a man's work—shoulders, knees, back. Don't you be bellyaching to him about anything that ails you unless it's deep inside."

So by the time school ended, my mother was cleaning houses three afternoons a week, all she could manage because Ray had to drive her to and from, and her back, she explained, was starting "to go south." Ray chipped in by being a paperboy. He left the house at six a.m. and was home by nine. "If folks wasn't so scattered out this way, you could deliver too," he told me. "If they had lawns they loved, you could babysit them, but we'll figure something before too long a fourteen-year-old can do to help out."

I had plenty to do for a while. We had a yard that looked huge because the lots on either side were vacant, but all of that space was over grown from a spring of being uncut. Ray set me to work with a rusty scythe and a pair of old gloves to get all the lots presentable. "Good, honest work," he said every time he came outside to smoke. Right before school ended he brought home an old power mower he said he'd found along his paper route, the thing laying across the back seat like he'd told it to keep its head down. "You keep that all cut and you got yourself a park to play in," Ray said. "Baseball, football, you name it. Just make sure the mower's under that there tarp when it's not running."

Which I did. I wanted that grass and weeds as short as I could keep them. I had a couple of old golf clubs my mother had kept in the back of her closet since I could remember, and now, she said, there was room for me to give them a try. Right away, Ray noticed that one had a wooden shaft. "Antiques," Ray declared. "Maybe worth something." But after he showed them around, he stopped imagining any windfall out of the two of them. No luck either with the burlap sack full of balls my mother fished out for me like an early birthday present. Eighty-six balls in that sack, half of them cut, which meant Ray couldn't get a quarter for them or even a dime, what he marked the cut ones down to for the yard sale he put together in June to get rid of anything worth a damn that we didn't need laying around. "Go ahead then, all yours to waste your time with." I almost agreed with him about the waste of time because all I did, mostly, was smack line drives that hooked left if I swung any harder than half speed. There was a secret to those clubs that kept me coming back though, and I had forever to learn before ninth grade started up at Warren County High School.

Ray was short and wiry. A banty rooster, Mom called him when she was upset. "You settle down, you banty rooster," she'd say. More like Jack Sprat and his wife, I sometimes thought. I loved Mom enough to keep that to myself, but Ray was all the time acting like skinny was something to be proud of, explaining his side of things like the one time in July when he called out, "Your Momma was a looker when we got hitched, just a little extra meat on her bones, but she's taken to forgetting about herself." He was smoking out back like he always did, and I gave him distance, but soon enough he waved me closer and started in on roustabout, acting like that was all there was to talk about besides finding some work for me to do that paid.

Ray moved his neck around the way he always did, acting like his t-shirt collar was too tight. I'd never seen him in anything but t-shirts, almost all of them the white underwear kind. My mother had told me he'd let slip that his first wife had broken him of forever tugging at his shirts because it ruined them. "But now he wears that crick-in-the-neck habit," she'd said.

"Your Momma says you're one of them that's scared of being up high," he started in.

"A little," I said, as far as I wanted to admit. Right about then I didn't have anything particular enough to be doing except listening.

"A little's too much out there on the rig. Lots of working up high when you're a roustabout, and for starters you're way up over the water to begin with. You go out on the walkways and you get yourself a good look down to where hell's waiting for the careless. You fall in the water and it'll kill you fast with cold most of the year and kill you slow with it the rest."

It sounded like something I'd never want to do, another reason to be a roughneck, somebody in charge, somebody with enough of a reputation he'd get to keep his feet right up close to the ground, even on an oilrig. "I'd get used to it," I said for something to say besides admitting I couldn't even climb the ropes in gym class without thinking about wetting my shorts. I wasn't ever going to mention that to Ray. Sissy was just about the worst thing there was to be this side of getting paralyzed or going blind. I knew Ray thought golf was a sissy game, that if I was going to end up being friends with boys who were on their way to being real men that football was what I needed to try, and practice was starting in a couple of weeks.

"Get used to it or get the fuck out," he said, and then he added, "You want to try one of these here smokes?"

"That's ok," I said, but Ray tapped one out and handed it to me like he knew I'd started stealing one almost every day since school had ended.

"It's like being up high," he said. "You get used to this here too."

A FEW DAYS AFTER that, my mother out cleaning, Ray returned with a trunk and back seat full of plants. I watched from the kitchen as he emptied them onto our scraggly lawn, and then he called me outside. "Your Momma laid down the law about all this here," Ray said, his hands motioning toward the base of the outside of the house. I counted eight bushes sitting nearby, their root balls snug and moist looking. I recognized four rhododendrons; the others looked like they were related to pine trees only smaller and rounder. "We got work to do."

I had to admit that with the plants sitting there, the house looked even uglier than usual, like it might pick up and sail away in the wind because nothing held it to the earth. Ray dug in with a shovel, turning up mostly rocks and clay. For a while he looked like someone else, a man concentrating hard on doing things right, somebody who had planned this out and had thought about improving the way the house looked in ways that I never would.

There were bags of topsoil so dark and rich it looked like it came from another planet. There was peat moss and fertilizer. We had never done any work together, but now I cut open the bags and dumped part of their contents into the first three holes Ray dug. I carried cans of our smelly water and poured it into each hole. Ray set two of the rhododendrons on each side of the front door and one of the bushes farther along the outside wall.

After that he stopped to smoke, lighting one for me off the first. "You do the next ones," he said. "Build you some muscle." When I hesitated, making what he called "my beat-dog face," he added, "and maybe you find yourself some fancy rocks to read about," because I'd shown him a brochure for the Skyline Caverns I'd picked up at the A&P and told him about the anthodites in one of the pictures, crystals you could only find right there in the Skyline Caverns and a couple of other caves in the whole country.

I started in on trying to dig a hole then, showing him it wasn't about being weak and lazy, but he disappeared into the house like I was on my own for the next five bushes. I was down about six inches into the dirt when he came back with a beer and a soda for me that he set on the front stoop. And then he watched. "Get used to this roustabout business," he said. "It's coming right on down the highway."

A half hour later, I'd dug five holes and raised blisters on both hands. "You oughta put on them gloves I gave you first," Ray said as he lit a cigarette and inspected the holes. "And you think on this while you're wishing you had your hands back--all these here stones you have in a pile, they bring you nothing but sweat and blood. There's no cash money for knowing their names. For goddamn sure, nobody cared if I knew geology out there on the rigs." I waited, keeping my hands on the shovel, until he said, "I'll finish this here, and you find that whisk broom your Momma has and get to work on the inside of the car. She'll have herself a fit if she has to ride home on filth."

Instead of handing over the shovel, I leaned on it, imagining I looked like somebody who was used to work. "There had to be some men out there who knew all about geology," I said, and for once Ray looked thoughtful, like he was considering on whether I might have learned something about drilling for oil.

Finally, he said, "That's them, not us."

"I could go to college."

Ray took a drag and let the smoke out slow and easy. "I seen your grades."

"It's just high school that counts."

"Right now, it's this here that counts. You get that bitty little broom now and bring me out another of these cold ones on your way back."

When I handed him the beer, he nodded. "That's the stuff," he said. "You know what science they should be teaching you?" but me not answering didn't slow him down. "You don't need chemistry and physics and geology, you need to know the ins and outs of what's happening to you."

"That's not science," I said.

"Yes, it is," Ray said. "Don't you be fooling yourself."

"My boys," my mother said when she saw the shrubbery all in place, neat and green. "Thank you." She fished around in the fridge and came out with a beer for Ray and a soda for me. Ray grinned and tapped his can against mine.

"Right about now I feel just a little bit like I did after we rode out the big one in the Gulf back a ways," Ray said.

"Hardly," my mother said right off, surprising me.

"You oughta be up in among the scaffolding looking down. Skyscraper window washers got nothing on that all harnessed in and back inside as soon as the weather turns."

"I meant the other way around, Ray," my mother said. "This is nice; that's something else entirely."

Ray downed a big gulp and touched cans with me again. I thought he was going to hug my mother, but he started in with "You damn betcha" and kept right on going. "This beauty of a storm blew across the Gulf and was working its way up to hurricane force with just me and a few others stuck out on a rig. There was nothing to do but ride it out. Ready to keel over, it was. The whole shootin' match. There wasn't none of us wasn't cursing Texaco for a few hours. But Wayne, let me tell you this about that—there ain't nothin' like it, knowing the next minute you might be done for. There's nothing like it you'll ever feel for yourself anywhere near here."

He slapped my back, drained his beer, and tapped out a cigarette, but he didn't take another beer out to the porch with him as he stepped outside to smoke. My mother followed him with her eyes and stepped closer to me, lowering her voice to say, "Before you go on and think your stepdaddy lived through a hurricane out in the middle of the Gulf, you should know that was a tropical storm he was stuck in. That don't make light of it, but there weren't any big ones around where he was that summer. His old rig buddy told me that at our wedding reception. I thought he might take his fists to his friend, but all he said was, 'Anybody think it's a joy ride out there should go out and wait his turn.'"

"It would still be a big deal," I said. "The rig would still feel like it could collapse."

"Maybe so," my mother said, "but Ray is all the time wishing it was a full-fledged hurricane he could have ridden out, one with a name. Back then the big ones were named like how the army does it—Abel, Baker, Charley, Dog." She picked up Ray's empty beer can and tossed it into the trashcan beside the sink. "Dog," she said, that had to sound dumb for a hurricane even at the start. And Easy. Imagine those that went through that hurricane and how they felt." She walked over to the window and looked out as if she thought Ray might be listening at the door. "Look at him out there. A regular chimney, he is." She turned back to me and smiled. "You know your step-daddy smokes more than he drinks. Trust me, that's a blessing. Some have it the other way."

"Like my real Pop?" I said, and she laughed and brushed her hand in front of her face like she was fanning herself.

"We had ourselves some good times."

"And bad?" I started, but when her smile disappeared, I didn't know what came next.

"Nobody wants to be alone," she said. "You settle for what comes your way."

A WEEK LATER, FOR my birthday, my mother gave me two tickets to the Skyline Caverns. "I know you've been looking at that pamphlet you grabbed at the grocery," she said before she added the real surprise: "And Ray's ready to take you whenever you're up for going. He's been underground and can tell you stories."

Ray moved closer to me and punched my shoulder just hard enough to make me grimace. "And one to grow on," he said, like we'd turned the corner onto Good Buddies Street while my mother beamed. Right then I was sure my mother had told him to make nice if we were going to be under the same roof from now on.

JUST LIKE THAT, BEFORE the week ended, Ray and I were on the way to the caverns, him talking the whole way about how his Daddy was a coal miner. "My Pap took me down just the one time to show me why I should never grow up to be him," Ray said. "He already had the cough that comes with the dust. He took me to where they were working a seam, sometimes on their knees where the ceiling was so low you'd be better off being a midget. He turned off my helmet light and his own, and we were in the dark all hunched over like that ugly fucker who rang the bells in the big church. Never ever work underground is my advice. Pap was dead at forty, almost twenty-five years down there is what killed him. I was in the Navy by then, so I was used to being out where you can't see anything but water except right there where you're standing. It made it easy for me to go out on the rigs in the Gulf."

"I bet they turn out the lights when we get way down under," I said, and Ray snorted.

"I bet they do, too, boy. I bet some tourists squeal like pigs when the lights go out."

It turned out about a dozen of us followed a guide for a while where stalactites and all that were lit up by colored lights. Nothing looked real until we were in plain old white light and the guide said, "See the eagle?" And there it was, a feathered wing formed so clearly in the rock I wanted to reach up and run my hand over it. "Isn't it wonderful," the guide said, "this formation right here and it being so close to Washington like we are?"

Ray leaned over and whispered, "They want us to feel like God made this just for the good old US of A."

The pretty, crystal-like anthodites were bathed in white light, too, but I knew enough not to ooh and aah over them around Ray. The rest of everything interesting was all in color. A chandelier. The Fairyland Lake. It reminded me of the wheel of three-colored cellophane that circled a light bulb every year near the base of the silver artificial Christmas tree my grandmother put up. A little thing about four feet high she stuck on her coffee table after she moved it into a corner. "Just right for a growing boy," my mother said every year, even when I was taller than it, table and all.

Our group walked about a dozen steps away from the Fairyland Lake before the guide said, "I want everyone to stand still for a moment like you're getting your picture taken. Ready?" All of the lights went out, and I heard Ray clear his throat, spit and whisper, "Now we're talking."

I waited for my eyes to adjust, but nothing changed. The guide didn't speak. A woman's voice went "Ohhh," startled and nervous like she'd felt a hand on her. And just about the time when I thought of the nearby lake and how somebody in a panic might walk right into it trying to get above ground, the lights came on and a ripple of undertone went through everyone but Ray and me. The woman who had called out looked like she was brushing something off her blouse. A woman beside her watched, and I wondered, for a moment, whether the nearest man had brushed her body as he reached out to steady himself in the dark.

After we came back out into the sunlight, Ray tapped out a cigarette and held it up as if he needed to inspect it. "You been sneaking these again?" Ray said.

"Not since."

Ray chuckled. "Already a liar," he said. "Your Pap must have been a pistol. I bet we'd a been friends. Here, take one. Let's talk about ways I've been thinking to make spend money."

I inhaled and held the smoke like I'd been smoking for a lifetime. "You're fourteen now," Ray said, "starting at the high school in a month. Maybe you want something special, save up for a car you'll be driving soon enough. Maybe you want real golf clubs for next summer. You want to putt on those carpets at the golf club you're always staring at when we pass? Well, there's nothing you can do at fourteen to make any part of that happen."

"I don't get it then," I said.

"You will," Ray said, "but first let's learn you how to drive. All that's anywhere tricky is learning the stick shift. We're not going out in heavy traffic. It's thirty-five tops and just a little coming and going up there on the Skyline where what we need you to be doing is waiting for you to show up and be ready."

A WEEK IT TOOK me to make Ray believe I could be trusted not to stall his car or over steer it into a ditch. All that time he put me off about what he had in mind. It was like I had another birthday coming, a surprise I couldn't quite imagine. Finally, he drove into the national park and started up the Skyline Drive a few miles before he pulled off at the first overlook and told me to show the road who's boss. "Easy as pie, right?" he said after a couple of miles. "Speed limit like we have here suits a beginner and keeps the hurry-ups from boiling over."

I nodded, happy not to have any trucks or horn-blowers on my tail, but I kept my eyes on the road, and Ray laughed, short and almost a cough, before lighting up a cigarette like he'd done all week about the time I'd driven a couple of miles without anything going wrong. "Let me show you something right up around here. Pull into that there lot coming up."

There were three other cars, plenty of room for me to swing in ten feet from the nearest one. "I've been sniffing around and know not many stop here to do their hiking because it's so close to where the park starts. They figure there's better up ahead, you know?"

He had me walk into the woods with him, passing, five minutes in, a man and a woman who were taking pictures and a family with small children.

"Down here," he said at last, "there's a little bitty path you can barely see the start of that looks to be going nowhere. Folks going that way know right off they made a wrong turn and give it up, but you set your mind to it, you can cut back through the woods here and go straight to the road without making the big loop they have marked on the signs."

I peered down the narrow path like I might learn something worth remarking upon. "I don't think anybody would think this was the way they were supposed to go," I said.

Ray slapped me on the back. "Yessiree, boy, that's just what this here doctor ordered. Follow me."

Two minutes of scrambling over downed trees and through briars got us to the road. "Just us and the animals come that way," Ray said. "It's a half-mile hike up the hill back to where we parked, but we can use the time for me to tell you exactly how me and you are going to be a team."

Ray talked as we hiked along the shoulder. "Listen. Here's the plan. You drop me off up ahead at that lot and then drive back down this way ten minutes later and pull off where we was just standing. Anybody passing will think it's some animal you're seeing in the woods, but any kind of good timing will make it me coming out like I've been on bathroom break. I can't be prancing around in that parking lot after, that's for damn sure."

I felt my heart racing, but I said, "I don't get it" to buy some time before I knew for certain what Ray had in mind.

"I thought you was smart," Ray said, "but I'll lay it out for you. I've had me a pistol since my roustabout days. I ain't never fired it and don't intend to now, you can be sure of that, but I aim to scare a few rich people shitless. It'll be easy. They think being in a park means there's nothing could hurt them here. Like the bears are toys. By the time they follow that trail back up here and find a phone, we'll be back to Front Royal. They ain't none of them going to miss what I take. It'll end up like they paid to have a story to tell back home and we'll be a step ahead of wishing."

Instead of "count me out," I heard myself say, "Don't you need a mask or something?"

Ray smiled like he knew secrets. "I got me sunglasses and a ball cap like a tourist. You saw that outfit your Momma bought me when she thought I needed something besides jeans and a t shirt. Bermuda shorts and that shirt with a collar like I was fixing to play golf. I'll look like nobody I'd ever be and that's good." He looked me up and down, making sure I understood what he thought of my own khaki shorts and raggedy polo.

"And I'm driving getaway?"

"All them that hands over their cash will be scrambling back to that parking lot we just left behind. That trail loops big and bendy so they'll never know where I've been or where I'm gone to. Meanwhile, you're picking me up like a taxi driver." Ray pulled out two cigarettes, but he kept on walking and didn't light them. "I bet you like that fella Robin Hood. It's no different right here. We're poor as all get out."

"I don't think so."

Just then the parking lot showed itself as we came around a bend, and Ray lit both cigarettes, handing me one. "You don't like spend money, you don't have to do more than the once, but you got to drive like I told you so we learn how good this can be before you make up your mind."

Ahead of us, after getting out of a car, two women in shorts put on sunglasses and visors. Ray whistled softly. "I've seen women up in here by themselves while I was doing the look-around, but I ain't that kind of man. What we're doing is strictly business."

"One time only," I said.

Ray laughed, full-throated this time. "That sounds like a boy about to spark up his first cigarette." Then, before I could open the car door, he stepped up close and his eyes went to slits. "We're on for tomorrow. I don't need my partner mulling things over so long he gets hisself religion."

THE NEXT AFTERNOON, RAY not saying a word all the way to the park kept me quiet too. Just as well, since all I wanted to say was "Let's not do this." I felt like I did every time I had to start over in a new school, only worse. Like maybe how I'd feel in a couple of weeks when some senior would pick me out of a crowd because I'd give off some kind of fear smell. Maybe, I started hoping, Ray was thinking along those lines, but when he pulled into the lot and there were two cars, both station wagons, he said, "Good, families," and I started concentrating on doing things right.

Ray handed me the keys and put on his sunglasses and Oriole's cap. I had to admit he didn't look like Ray Ressler the roustabout. In his getup with those dark glasses, he looked blind. "Ready, hoss?" he said. "I'm counting on you."

"Ready," I said, and he disappeared down the trail.

Three minutes to the second I was out of the car because I couldn't think of a reason, if anybody drove up, I could give for sitting by myself in a hot car in full sun. I walked just far enough to be in the shade and checked my watch, waiting for the sweep hand to announce four minutes. I kicked an old pinecone around the lot and checked my watch. Kicked it some more and saw eight minutes had passed, close enough to let me get behind the wheel, start the car, and wait a full minute before pulling out.

I thought I'd be early, but there was Ray stepping out of the woods as soon as I eased the car to a stop. "Jackpot," he said, climbing inside. I got to do a two-for-one."

I didn't say anything, concentrating on the road, but Ray didn't need any prompting. "Both families were down the trail aways and together when I come up on them. One fella was taking a picture of the other family, kids and all, by some tree they must have thought was special. Who'd a thought there'd be a traffic jam up in there, but a break for us, just double the cash, no trace."

I drove slow, glancing down at the speedometer to make sure I wasn't going over the limit, but no cars caught up to us and only one passed going the other way. "Pull in here," Ray said when we got back to the first overlook. We switched, Ray getting behind the wheel and lighting a cigarette and offering me one, saying, "Here you go, partner" before he pulled out, both windows rolled down to ease the smoke, me having the time to wonder if I was already acquiring that smell Ray had of sweat and cigarettes.

"Damn," Ray said as he looked at me and smiled. "Damn!"

Back at the house, my mother not needing a ride for another hour, Ray showed me $320. "See? What did I tell you? Easy pickings. And here's sixty for you," he said. "Driver's pay."

"I don't want it," I said.

"You too good for it? You all high and mighty now?"

"I was just helping out."

Ray took my hand and laid the bills on my palm. When I didn't let them fall, he said, "That's it. Take it. You and all your bellyaching, but I knew you was cut out for this here."

Ray was so sure of me I started thinking of alibis and denials, but what I knew right then was that I was afraid this was something like smoking, that once this guilt and fear passed, I'd look forward to it. When he left to pick up my mother, I put the six ten dollar bills, spreading them out every twenty pages in one of the set of Chip Hilton books my father had given me for Christmas just before he was killed, the only book where Chip's high school sports team doesn't win the championship. Ray was right. We were partners. He thought he'd seen something in me that I'd grow into. I was just the bellyaching one who worried all the time about what other people would think and then acted high and mighty.

My mother looked tired when she walked in with Ray, but she settled in on making dinner. Ray sat down to watch the six o'clock news, but nothing came on about the Skyline Drive. "You getting interested in where we live now?" my mother said.

"Yeah," I said, and Ray snapped me a look like I was introducing a confession.

At eleven that night, my mother asleep for an hour by then, Ray switched to the news, and there it was, a report about armed robberies in the Shenandoah National Park, a few seconds of footage taken from the parking lot where I'd dropped Ray off. "Ok," Ray whispered. "Now we wait until nobody cares anymore that this ever happened."

FOR A WEEK I spent all my time outside, staying away from Ray and trying not to smoke. I'd changed my grip on the clubs, getting rid of holding them like baseball bats, what felt good at first but led to all those low line drives that hooked, or just as likely skittered and bounced if I swung as hard as I could.

Once I moved my hands, I loved hitting with the pitching wedge. It didn't seem that hard to loft most of the balls into high arcs that the angle of the club provided. My best shots carried the length of the three lots and scattered just short of the road, and when, the few times a ball carried to the road, it bounced high and ended up in the yard across the highway, I pretended I'd made a hole-in-one on a real course.

"You're getting so good at that," my mother said one afternoon. "You could show the rich boys a thing or two about their game." I was using the sand wedge, which, even though it had a metal shaft, looked older, and the club face was thicker and heavier in a way that made it harder for me to loft the ball unless I placed it on a tuft of sparse grass like I'd just done while my mother watched.

"Maybe so," I said, half-believing her. It didn't seem that hard and surely would be easier hitting off the perfect-looking grass at the local course.

"Remember when we used to live by the Bon-Air Golf Course? Your Daddy found those clubs after men left them on the course. He told me he expected to find a full set like that after a spell, and there might come a day when you had a use for them. I never saw him even swing one. And all those golf balls in that dirty old sack, most of them all cut up and scuffed like somebody wanted to murder them. And now here you are."

"I was too little to do much except slap the balls around the yard."

"Speaking of swinging, do you remember how scared you were of that bridge they had up there on the course?"

"Sure. I always thought it would throw me off into the creek when it moved."

"The golfers would walk across that with their clubs and nobody ever fell."

"I didn't know that. Back then I was small enough to fit underneath the railing."

My mother picked up the pitching wedge, and for a moment I thought she wanted to give it a try, but all she did was hand it to me like a caddy. "You know what your Daddy said hurt him most in his life?" she said. "Being fingerprinted. He was a prideful man."

It's hard for me to remember anything about how he felt," I said.

"He told me it all come about after a fight with a man over his first wife. He couldn't abide a man taking her clothes off with his eyes." My mother seemed out of breath as she talked, but now she relaxed and spoke evenly. "And it cost him dearly the second time," she went on. "You should know how much a woman is floored by such a devotion. One important thing like that matters more than a fistful of flaws."

Ray stepped outside like a man who'd been listening to every word. "Having a problem?" he said, and my mother's expression changed.

"I know Wayne's been smoking," she said. She looked at Ray and me like she was adding up the sum of her disappointments.

"I'm sorry," I said.

"You're so smart," she said. "It's what fooled me for a while." Ray grinned like he was about to do a little dance.

"I'll leave you to it," he said, and he got into his car and drove off.

My mother watched the road for a few seconds before she turned back to me. "Such a filthy habit. I have to believe that brains are stronger than desires in the long run. Can I believe that?"

"Yes," I said at once.

"You know Ray's not perfect by any stretch, but he's never laid a hand to me. Don't you think that of him."

"I've never thought that," I told her, which was true.

"He keeps his filth outside our house." She sounded so awkward that I knew this was about sex.

"You don't have to tell me."

"Yes, I do, or I'm going to burst." She took a deep breath. "Whores," she said, the word a near whistle. "There, now you know. He spends his money on their privates. A paper boy, and that's where the money goes."

"How much does a paper boy make?" I said, but instead of answering she began to cry.

I didn't mind her not saying. I was sure a paperboy made next to nothing. What I really wanted to know was how much a whore charged, how many days Ray had to deliver to pay for one.

LIKE RAY EXPECTED, THE park robberies disappeared from the news after two days. He waited another week before he drove into the park to sniff around for stakeouts, and then he waited two days more before he said, "By now the cops think the bandit was just passing through. And we need to do this before Labor Day when the traffic starts to thin."

"No," I said. "I've had enough." I felt committed. I hadn't even smoked a cigarette for two days.

"Hard to get, huh? You took that stash of bills after acting the saint. Like some cunt saying no until your balls deep in her."

I pulled myself up straighter and said, "Your whores always do whatever you want, don't they?"

I thought Ray would look embarrassed or angry, but his voice stayed even. "You want to spend some of that loot to find out?"

"No."

"Maybe you're wishing you could charm some young thing. You're going to be in ninth grade. All you'll get is something to imagine from while you play with yourself."

"Last time," I said then. "For absolutely sure, and anyway, school's starting, and I won't be around when Mom's out working."

"There you go," Ray said. "We'll reconsider on everything when the time comes."

SO I WENT, DRIVING slow after I took the wheel in the first overlook, looking like I was wishing for deer or bears to wander out along the road. Ray smoked and said nothing, his window closed, I thought, to punish me for acting like a sissy. There was just one car in the lot, perfect for what we were up to. Ray put on his sunglasses and ball cap and got out without saying a word, dropped his stub and stepped on it before he hiked into the woods in his Bermuda's and golf shirt.

I wound down Ray's window and lit the cigarette I'd stashed under the seat, telling myself I was creating a reason to be sitting in a parked car. I didn't want to get out like I had the first time and show myself as a kid who had no business driving. When I finished, I let a few more minutes pass before I drove back to the meet spot, but Ray wasn't in sight, and every time a car passed I thought it was a park ranger or an unmarked police car.

I started thinking of how stupid it was to go back to the same trail and all that. I pulled out and drove a mile, turned around and drove back, but Ray still wasn't there. I told myself I was being smart, smarter than Ray at least, and when I turned again, facing the right direction to leave the park,

I checked my mirror and saw nothing behind me so I could go really slow, school zone slow, I saw a bear slow, until, from a quarter mile away I could see Ray standing on the shoulder.

With the late August sun nearly behind me, I thought Ray might not be able to make me out for sure, and I pulled off to the side and stopped like I could be the police. I saw him light up, turn, and go back into the woods. I wanted him sweating in there, maybe scrambling up that narrow path like he was a lost tourist, his eyes off the road. When I thought he was deep enough, I drove up to the meet spot and parked like I was just late. It took him a minute to come out, so I was pretty sure he didn't see it was me sitting back up the road.

"Jesus Christ, where were you?" he said, flicking his cigarette onto the road.

"There was a car parked up there," I said. "I thought this place might be staked out."

"I saw it," Ray said. "Just a minute ago. I was waiting for it to pass." He looked back. "It's gone," he said, "but I never saw nothing go by."

"It u-turned. It went by me going the other way. I was worried whoever was in it might be wondering what I was doing pulled off the road up a ways."

Ray looked puzzled, like he was working out the scenario. He laughed then, short and air-filled, like he'd made up his mind that I was somebody who understood so little about the science of experience that I could believe in heaven.

"Step on it," he finally said. "Christ. I thought two weeks would put them to sleep about this." I drove right at the speed limit for a minute, Ray glancing around like he thought the trees were full of eyes. "$78," he said then. "I had time to count it back in there. I was ready to hide it and just walk out clean as a whistle. It's practically nothing that guy had on him."

"You keep it all," I said. "You earned it."

"I should have kept that card I saw in that fellow's wallet, you know, what some people have nowadays to buy things without handing over their money."

"I think a lot of people have credit cards," I said, though I had no way of knowing that for sure.

I slowed when I saw the first overlook, but Ray said, "Keep going." He was breathing hard. "I should burn that little box we live in and let the insurance company buy us a new one." He seemed to be talking to himself now, making plans he'd never put into any kind of motion. He'd gone out and followed through on one crazy idea, and here we were leaving the park with $78 and him all panicked about the police knocking on our door. "Get ourselves a place where the water don't stink to high heaven, right?" he finally said.

"Sure," I said.

"You damn betcha," he said, but I knew Ray was scared. Adult scared, like what he was afraid of was here to stay, and I understood then that Ray had done a lot of talking to himself to come up with the robbery plan, that he'd coached himself up the way Mr. Glass, back in Hagerstown, got our junior high basketball team to run out onto the court believing we were better than we were, and now he could see he was losing this particular game.

"Your Momma never knows about any of this," he said then. "Understand?"

"I get it," I said, suddenly happy I had something Ray had to depend upon.

"I love your mother. Don't you forget that. She told me all about giving you the lowdown, but that other stuff is just entertainment, like going to a ball game. Understand?"

"I think so."

"You will. Just wait half a lifetime and it'll come to you."

Ray, for once, didn't light a cigarette. It seemed like he'd forgotten his habit because he wasn't driving on the way out of the park like he always did, that he was out of sync with who he was. Like he's a boy, I thought, and then dismissed it when he grabbed my thigh hard and hissed, "You keep your damn eyes on the road. No fuckups allowed."

I didn't say anything then. We were out of the park and I was still behind the wheel. Ray said, "Take us home, you know the way," and I did, though I was sweating so much the whole way that I thought if I had to turn the wheel hard my hands would slip off and we'd end up going straight ahead until we ran into something that wouldn't budge.

From the Heart

May

Dale

Dale's dog, an all-white Spitz named Blizzard, had thrown up three times the night before and had diarrhea during the day. "Maybe she'll pull out of it," he told his wife.

"You hoped for too long," Cilla said.

When Blizzard began to whimper and cry, Dale thought the dog sounded just like Cilla, who, in her nightmares, made a whining sound that extended into a wail that raised gooseflesh on his body. Something about that sound—its pitch set exactly to terror—made Dale lie in the dark and listen, trying to somehow eavesdrop.

He'd never learned what was happening in her dreams. That wail never turned into a scream. He never touched or shook her awake. She never remembered what she had dreamed. He didn't argue with Cilla. He wished he'd called the vet before his office hours ended. Or yesterday or even the day before. The office didn't open again until eight a.m.

Because the forecast was for a perfect, late-spring evening, Dale carried the dog outside and laid her gingerly on an old bed spread under the backyard weeping cherry. Though he knew she could barely stand, he tied the leash around the trunk, clipped it to Blizzard's collar, and said "Goodnight."

"That won't help," Cilla said.

Just after midnight, Blizzard began to wail. Each time she quieted, Dale held his breath and hoped, but soon she began again, extending the terrible, pain-infused cry. When Dale opened the back door as it first grew light, the dog was unable to rise to her feet. He laid a bowl of water beside her and sat on the damp grass, but Blizzard began to wail again, making the sound of helplessness.

On the deck next door, his neighbors, an elderly couple, were out early to sit with coffee. Dale held his breath, afraid they would shout accusations. Maybe they had even called the police, Dale thought, and he carried Blizzard to the car inside the blanket, carefully circling his house on the side opposite where his neighbors were perched.

He drove for over an hour, the radio turned down to a murmur for a few miles, then muted. Blizzard, at last, drifted off with the motion. Just before eight, he arrived at the vet's. When Dale slowed and parked, Blizzard whimpered, but she lay quietly on the blanket as he carried her to the front door.

Another car was parked farther away, but now the driver's side door opened and a woman swung her legs out to allow a small, lively leashed terrier to scramble past her. "My God," she said. "Whatever have you there?"

Dale turned to face the door. He heard the woman's footsteps on the gravel. The terrier yipped twice. As soon as the attendant, wearing a pink-and-black striped mask, unlocked the door, Dale stepped past her. He kept his eyes on the receptionist, softly starting an apology, not looking back at the attendant or the woman with the terrier as Blizzard, without lifting her head or stirring, began to wail.

Cilla

As everyone at Cilla's Zoom book club meeting began the odd goodbyes of isolation, May's host said, "Would you like to see our butterfly collection?"

None of the eight face-filled panels blacked out. The host tilted her laptop so the camera showed the dining room wall behind her was nearly covered with hung boxes of butterflies. Cilla counted twelve, nine in each box. 108 butterflies that looked identical to her.

"It's our best wall," the host said. "They come dry in the mail, then my husband moistens them and fixes them in place. He builds all the boxes himself." While Cilla searched the faces in the panels, looking for a match to her wonder, two panels went dark.

The host stood, the room swaying through her camera. She carried the laptop closer to the wall. All of the butterflies seemed to have the same deep blue with golden specks in a simple, consistent pattern. "They have names," she said, beginning a slow pan across the boxes. "If I turned these frames over, you'd see them on the back. They're all the same species, but more like cousins than brothers and sisters."

Cilla noticed four panels were dark. "My husband is in self-quarantine," the host said, "but so far, he's fine. He has a new set to keep him occupied. He is so incredible with the tweezers and pins and the syringe."

She moved her laptop closer to the wall and held it steady. Cilla thought of an atlas she and Dale once owned, how the biggest cities were enlarged in panels. "We have so many walls," the host said. "Eventually, we'll be surrounded. Don't these look well-cared for? Don't they look as if they could fly?"

By now, Cilla was alone with her. She vowed to look up the species. To ask her now seemed taboo, an interruption of worship. She imagined the woman's husband busy with a new specimen, carefully restoring something dry and fragile under a brilliant light. While she stared and stared, all that was left was the woman's breathing.

June

Cilla and Dale

Cilla told Dale that there were nights when he screamed aloud during a nightmare. If he remembered them, those dreams always included him or Cilla or their daughter Kayla about to be killed—bombs, madmen, head-on crashes, falls from great heights. The screams always began while he was asleep. The ones he remembered continued long enough for him to hear himself make the sound of hopelessness.

Now, after months, they'd settled under the virus, night and day. They were quieter. More careful. They wondered aloud how long a virus remained potent on frequently touched surfaces. After the grocery store delivered, Cilla sanitized their produce—oranges, tomatoes, an eggplant, two variates of squash. She disinfected as if they were hospitalized. They were riding this out, she told him, as if they'd paid in advance for a season pass to next year's normal when everything would reopen.

"Japan is already reopening its amusement parks," Dale said. "Their parks were on last night's news."

"They don't have cases anymore?" Cilla was busy with a scattering of her election stuff. When Dale had said it was summer, months yet, until voting, she hadn't mentioned whether or not she was working on her re-election campaign. She'd reminded him it was never too soon to help oust that fool who lived in the White House.

"Fewer than last month. Enough for people to take a ride," he said, trying to keep her attention. "To prevent the spread of the virus, the government is telling all those riders, 'Please, scream in your heart.'"

"Like that old ice cream song," Cilla said. "I scream, you scream, we all scream in our hearts." She shoved the list of phone numbers and addresses to the side and stood. "And we do, don't we?" she went on, her voice rising, nearly bitter. "Even with the safety bars of distancing and isolation and masks."

Since the last borough council meeting, Cilla seemed constantly angry. "You asked for this," Dale reminded her. "You knocked on doors. Paid for signs."

"There are people on the board who are more afraid of thinking than they are of the virus."

The argument had been about the cost of recycling, how the price of each pull and haul had been raised yet the majority resisted adding a small assessment on each property owner. "If people have to pay, more might actually do it," Cilla said. "Even a few of the ones who still have burn barrels in their back yards, right in plain sight as if they know they won't be fined."

"You could quit."

"Impossible. I think they'd vote for a landfill on that vacant lot near the grade school if I wasn't there. It's terrifying what some people are capable of."

"Tell those people about the glacier that's completely disappeared in Iceland. They held a funeral for it when it was about to vanish. Mourners gathered, and there were old photographs, you know, like some people have at viewings."

"That's more like it," Cilla said. "They were thinking local. That's where terrifying lives. They were making sure they were remembering what indestructible had been said to look like. Winter is going extinct."

Since it was Friday, they stayed up late to make sure their daughter Kayla and her two girls were finished with dinner in Los Angeles before they called for their weekly Face-Time. In early January, as if she'd made a resolution she needed to keep, she'd kicked her husband out. Her daughters were nearly ten and just-turned-seven, young enough for Kayla to shoo them to the room they shared so she could have "private time" at the end of each call.

This time, Kayla barely waited for the door to close. "Teddy sends texts almost every night," she said. "He drinks until he can type how much he wants to get back together. How he wants to see the girls."

"Don't answer," Cilla said at once.

"I tried that," Kayla said. "Then he gets angry and sends ugly texts, mean and full of name-calling."

"Never respond," Cilla said. "Some things are unacceptable." Kayla nodded, then vanished. Cilla closed the laptop and said, "The older one looked so sad."

"She seemed fine."

"It's all over her face. Even the way she sits. She's the one who's screaming in her heart." Until she'd retired three years ago, Cilla had been an elementary school teacher. Every year, in September, she reminded him that teachers learn how to read their kids or else they're the wrong persons for the job. "She looks like somebody who's been forced onto one of those Japanese coasters."

"I always closed my eyes as soon as we were half way up the first hill," Dale said. "Even buckled in and barely moving, I gripped that safety bar. It was scarier than toxic waste half a block from the playground."

"You should have screamed like everybody else the very first time you rode. You might have surprised yourself."

"Like Janet Leigh in *Psycho*? Even with the screeching violins added, that scream didn't change a thing."

"Now middle school kids watch stuff like that." Cilla didn't sound angry. She sounded bored.

"Hitchcock's first idea was no soundtrack at all for the shower scene. He wanted Janet Leigh doing nothing but screaming in her heart."

"It's still just a movie," Cilla said. "You know what else? This next biopsy of yours will show benign just like the other ones. Then we'll get a Spitz puppy when this is over. Something to hope on."

Dale

At the door, Dale was asked for his name and birthday. His temperature was taken while he submitted to a brief inquest about recent contacts, shortness of breath, and persistent cough. Whether four months of stay-at-home had, by now, seduced his restlessness and made him reckless with indoor crowds.

Because he was a veteran of imaging, Dale recognized that two women, socially distanced, were struggling to finish the milkshake that would highlight their lower GI Cat-scans. The man who limped to the chair farthest from him would be investigated by MRI. Dale felt more mysterious, unmarked, arriving for the cell extraction that would name the future.

When his glasses fogged, he slowed his breathing. He had been summoned before by tumors left and right on the thyroid, a best-call location according to the algorithms for survival. For years, they had kept their uneasy truce, but now one had swollen like a militia covertly arming. Already, the biopsy had been delayed three months by the pandemic.

Intimacy so recently rare, he nearly welcomed a doctor's blue sheathed hand, his throat softly touched and swept sideways for a needle so thin the myth of "only a pinch" comes true. He recognized extraction's pressure, the impulse to swallow throughout each attempt, five without success this time, as if the pandemic had complicated biopsy, the aisles in his tumor designated one-way, the cells reluctant to emerge from lockdown because everyone was dangerous.

The doctor and the radiologist apologized while the technician carried his last sample to pathology. Slowly deep-breathing, Dale told himself that all three of those medical faces would be as unrecognizable as his if they accidentally met, unmasked in the open. His throat would look so common they would never remember the mayhem of his small, ambiguous illness.

Cilla

Her younger granddaughter's letters from Los Angeles always end with butterflies. One of her drawings, this time, was half a page large, and Cilla was sketched inside both of its wings. Like a species pattern, she thought, blue-masked, with red and white dots along her arms and legs, the butterfly a blaze of orange and yellow, the antennae green.

Cilla Googled "Butterfly Farms" and discovered one was an hour's drive away. Tours were available by appointment. There were presentations about Monarch butterflies and their life cycle, a "dress-up demonstration representing the anatomy of the butterfly." The perfect gift for Darcy when she visited, as always, in August, if it was safe to fly.

The butterfly farm also offers butterfly releases for special events, including weddings, anniversaries, birthdays, graduations, and memorials. Besides the ones from "mass release boxes," the farm promises special releases from individual envelopes that can be personalized with writing and a small picture.

The butterfly farm web site noted that although butterflies know when they are touched, it was thought that their nervous system did not have pain receptors that registered pain as humans know it.

July

Dale

Most often, the old died. The overweight. The already sick with something else. But so far, all the experts were puzzled that among the young and healthy, some people barely knew they were infected with the virus while some died. Dale wasn't surprised. For his whole life, he'd believed that being healthy was the mystery. There were thousands of ways to sickness. Thousands of reasons to die. It was astonishing, with all the hidden, complicated parts inside the body, that things lasted as long as they did.

Dale's doctor's office was across the street from a nursing home that was shuttered, its parking lot secured from traffic with crime scene tape. He parked and called the office number to announce his arrival and waited as instructed, by his car. After ten minutes, the midday sun brought up sweat, and he called again, this time from inside the car with the air conditioner running.

He was startled when the receptionist rapped on the window, and he stepped outside, unmasked, so close to her that she retreated.

The doctor, minutes later, said, "Non-diagnostic, but statistically safe." Despite that assurance, he was ordering a second biopsy. Though during these times, scheduling was difficult. Though weeks would likely pass. When Dale returned to his car, the nursing home, emptied like a glacier, seemed capable of becoming airborne.

Cilla and Dale

"They've moved everybody from that home," he told Cilla.

"To avoid disaster," she said.

"Not really. The disaster has already happened."

There were rumors of multiple cases in the large nursing home near their grocery. Talk of collective memorial services and a refrigerated truck for bodies. "Thank God we still live at home," Cilla said. "No visitors allowed at those places. Danielle Owens, who retired only three years before me, is in there all by herself."

"She's not alone. She's surrounded," Dale said. "She'll be sick for sure stuck in that crowd."

Cilla pressed a finger against his lips. "Call Kayla and the girls. Let's do some visiting we're still allowed to do. We can wish Renee happy birthday."

After they sang "Happy Birthday," Carrie said, "Thanks," but she didn't smile.

During "private time," Kayla explained. "Teddy sent Renee flowers." Dale and Cilla held their breath until Kayla added, "Renee threw them out." Together, they exhaled.

"You need to start remembering your lip seal better," Cilla said afterward. "If we're stuck for months aging on FaceTime, the girls will start noticing and wonder if there's something wrong with you."

"I think I forgot because I was concentrating on trying to read Renee's face. Mostly, she just looked tired."

"She looked heartbroken. Think like a teacher. Listen and look."

"The girls always seem to talk right at you. Like they know you. I bet all those kids you had in class will remember you even when they're as old as we are."

"A tiny part of them. Or no part. Aren't there lots of teachers you can't remember at all?"

"No. I remember everyone. Their names. What they looked like. Things they said. Mostly, how I felt about them then."

"You don't even own a yearbook."

"They were too expensive. My mother said, 'You'll remember everybody who matters without their pictures.' She was wrong. I remember the ones who didn't, too."

"That's why you're a scientist. Physics--you remember what everybody else never learns."

"I ended up running data. I analyzed. I gave business people statistics that helped them make money."

"You make it sound trivial."

"Some people see physics as a search for God. I searched for profit"

Cilla

Even though their plans to sell the house had been delayed by the virus, Dale tried to act interested in her planning--who could repair the deck, who could reseal the driveway. When he asked if she remembered who used a specially-designed extension handle to repaint the cathedral ceiling, Cilla said, "Of course, I do. He was disgusting. A week later, he called and said he wanted to rape me." She saw him hesitate. Surprised. She didn't wait for him to ask how she knew.

"He tried to disguise it by deepening it and sounding hoarse, but I recognized his voice," Cilla said. "He had just been inside our house. I can quote him exactly: 'Lock your doors because I'm coming to rape you.'" She paused for his apology. When he said nothing, her voice rose. "Absolutely, I'm sure about that one. And I had to see him a few more times. At the post office. In the grocery store. It made me sick every time."

She remembered what that man looked like—his thick muscular arms, his protruding belly. He'd been squat. A toad. He'd been recently retired, twenty-five years older than they were. The housepainter was, give or take, the same age she was now. He had been dead for more than ten years, whatever punishment she wished upon him impossible. From the balcony, that housepainter must have looked down at her going through the movements of an ordinary late afternoon and early evening. He must have stared, the track lights on the wall below the balcony railing brightly illuminating her body as she passed beneath him. His gaze must have had time to cover every intimate area of her body each time he paused while perfecting the paint on the difficult-to-reach ceiling.

Every time she pictured him stabbing their number into his phone, she imagined it exploding when he pressed the final digit, erasing his face with fire.

August

   Cilla and Dale

"We did everything right and yet here we are," Cilla said.

"A few trips to doctors' offices and one haircut each, first thing in the morning, washed ahead of time, masked." Dale's voice trailed off.

Cilla thought she'd been infected at a council meeting. They had all been masked. The meeting had been streamed to whoever cared to listen in, but Cilla remembered that the two conspiracy nutcases on the board were in the bathroom together before her. "They were laughing in there," she said. "I could tell they weren't masked. I should have just held it instead of following them so soon after they left."

"It wasn't them," Dale said. "It was from that time I stood in line at the drug store instead of waiting in that traffic jam for outside pickup. When I turned to leave, I saw this fat guy behind me wasn't wearing a mask. He'd been wheezing so loud I didn't want to turn around. The clerk hadn't said a word while she took her sweet time hunting for the prescriptions."

Dale was light-headed but barely feverish. Unsteady. Even dizzy. As if he'd had a stroke, not come down with the virus. Just one more way for the body to break. He felt older. That's what he told Cilla. Tired and achy and resigned to waiting for his body to signal improvement or further decline. What he had dreaded was coughing and breathlessness, pneumonia or some hybrid complication because of his asthma, but Cilla was the one coughing, like the virus had a mind. Like it had arrived in the dark and settled upon her by mistake.

"I'm the same age my mother was when she died. Sixty-seven."

"You're not going to die from this," Cilla said. "You're not even coughing like I am. You're breathing just fine."

"I feel like I'm ninety, like my father when he died."

Cilla dialed FaceTime. "Keep that to yourself for half an hour," she said.

"We both tested positive, but here we are feeling well enough to talk." Cilla coughed, turning her head as if the virus could spread through the Internet. "So far it's a bad cold for me and the regular flu for Dad. In a week, we'll be over this and feeling better and glad we've gotten being sick out of the way."

Dale kept his lips pressed together. He listened and looked for twenty minutes. When the girls were gone, Kayla said, "What's up with you, Dad?"

"We can barely get up and down the stairs these last two days. This is like the way we're going to feel all the time in eight or nine years," Dale said, picking seventy-five as the age when something awful would be chronic instead of imagined.

"Always the optimist," Kayla said.

Cilla

Darcy, when Cilla called for their weekly face-to-face, complained that she and Renee had to begin school online. Cilla kept her cheery teacher's voice to tell Darcy about the butterfly farm and promised to take her next summer. Afterward, to distract herself, she weeded around the yard's shrubbery. Because Dale had forgotten to prune for the second consecutive year, the butterfly bush Darcy loved towered far beyond repair, its leaves, in a dry August, gone uniformly curled and brown. Cilla sat to do the weeding, but after ten minutes, she was exhausted. When she shuffled inside and sat, she told Dale that it was like her body hated her. "In physics," Dale said, "sometimes the theories hate each other."

"You say things like that all the time," she said. "I thought you were the smartest person I'd ever met. Sometimes, I think you fell in love with my admiration, not me."

Cilla and Dale

In the morning, after Cilla lapsed into an extended coughing spell, Dale drove her to the hospital. A woman wearing a mask and a face shield escorted them to a room marked PRIVATE, NO ADMITTANCE. They sat for an hour before the same woman returned to lead Cilla away.

"I'm not sick enough to be admitted," Cilla said when she reappeared. "My pulse-ox reading was 95. That's a good thing, right?" She coughed in a way that turned the face-shielded woman's head as she escorted them through a side entrance into the half-empty parking lot.

Late in the following afternoon, Cilla shared a text from Kayla. Teddy had shown up drunk. He'd pounded on the door and shouted to the girls until she'd called the police, but instead of arresting him, they'd sent him away when he hadn't resisted. "In a car he'd borrowed from somebody," Kayla wrote. "Drunk. Calling me the ugliest things."

Cilla was already dressed for bed, sitting up with a book. "Unacceptable," she said. "If Kayla had a place to go, she should just leave so he never finds her."

"There are worse ways to be unacceptable," Dale said.

"Like hitting her? Like hitting the girls?" A spell of coughing began. As if it would help, she sat up straighter. She pressed her hand on her forehead and reached for the thermometer.

"You know what I mean."

"You mean you? There's only one thing that made me so angry I wanted to leave."

"To leave?"

"Yes. It was when you called me an idiot," Cilla said. "You did it twice. The second time was worse because I said, 'Never again' after the first."

"Go ahead," Dale said. "Tell me."

"You always asked me to call people to make appointments for you," she said, "doctors, dentists, mechanics, you name it. I didn't know any better back then, but you told me once that your mother even dialed the phone for your father for social calls, even said 'hello' like a receptionist."

"She did," he said. "Right up to when she died."

"I forgot to make one of those calls, and when you complained, I said, 'I'm not your mother,' and you said, 'No, you're an idiot.'"

"That's it?"

"Let's stop," she said. "Let me take my temperature and finish this book."

"With a cliffhanger?"

Panting, she shook her head. She concentrated on catching her breath. Dale counted nearly to sixty before the gasping slowed. He hadn't felt sick all day. Whatever she might say could wait.

When Cilla was asleep at last, Dale went through the stack of books he was supposed to return to the library for her. All four of them were memoirs. The one lying on the bottom was about a boy who was lobotomized at his father's request for being unruly. Dale read the last chapter to find out how the story turned out, the boy a bus driver as an adult. And now a memoirist. He slid it back into its original spot before deciding to sleep on the couch.

Just after dawn, Dale woke to the sound of her gasping between coughs. She was sitting up when he entered the bedroom, her face pale. "It's like I'm drowning," she said. She went limp against him as he helped her stand. Her slippers shuffling slowly, he guided her to the bathroom and sat her on the toilet before he walked to the kitchen to call for an ambulance.

It took seventeen minutes for the ambulance to arrive. Cilla's pulse registered ninety-seven; her pulse-ox number was eighty-eight. Adding the book beside the bed to the suitcase Cilla had prepared two days before, he followed the ambulance in his car.

At the hospital, he was stopped just inside the door. "You don't have a temperature, but you were exposed," the nurse said.

"I had the virus," Dale nearly shouted. "I'm over it."

"You've been very lucky then," she said. "I promise either a doctor or I will call within the hour." A masked security officer shooed him toward the door. By noon, the promised call included a pulse-ox of eighty-two and an explanation of how a ventilator was helping her breathe.

Dale tapped Kayla's phone number. "I don't want the girls watching me and listening," he said at once. "Your mother's in the hospital."

"How bad is it?"

"It's like asthma when you're locked inside a used book store without an inhaler."

For a few seconds, he heard nothing but his daughter breathing. Then she said, "And nobody is coming with a key?"

"They are if you think a ventilator is like a locksmith."

"I know what you're doing with the similes. Mom is critical, right? She's in the ICU."

Dale

Only another three days it took before Dale's phone buzzed just before seven a.m. "I'm the one who promised to call if things changed," the woman's voice said. "Unfortunately, it's for the worst." By seven thirty, Dale was escorted to a window by a nurse in full protective gear. By seven thirty-seven, he understood that Cilla's lungs could never recover, that the machinery did her breathing.

That Cilla wanted to be cremated seemed horrible now. He'd expected her to outlive him and yet now the CFO of their marriage was dying. Removing the breathing apparatus guaranteed it. He was about to be someone he'd never imagined--a widower, a walking absence.

Aloud, he repeated endearments that included the word "love" as if declaring it would breathe life into the cells of her lungs—like antibodies, like white cells that rescued the body. He mouthed compliments and wishes. When that wasn't enough, he began to tell lies about where she was going, how he looked forward to reuniting, throwing out the old bromides he'd been raised with by his parents, all of them full of light and happiness and forever, saving that impossibility for last before he turned away and nodded at the nurse, walking back into the brilliant, cloudless morning, mouth breathing to keep from suffocating.

He sat in the car with the air-conditioner running. He needed to call Kayla. He tapped on her number, listened to it ring twice before he realized the time in Los Angeles meant he should wait. Her phone would be muted. She was like her mother. Nothing would stir her at 5:46 a.m.

Dale thought of his recurring dream about falling up, how levitating was a wonderful sensation until he kept rising, going higher and higher until he screamed silently in his dream as he disappeared. There was nothing in physics to account for that. None of those heartless formulas took into account his terror. Not then and not now as he remembered:

Cilla had left her camera at an overlook on a weekend trip. The camera was new and expensive, a birthday present from him less than a month before. They were a mile away when she remembered, less than two minutes for the drive back. There hadn't been another car in the small lot when they'd stopped. "It will be there," she said, but it wasn't. "We need to see if it fell," she said, and he followed her to the railing. Just below them was bare mown grass. "Five minutes is time enough for a thief," Dale said. "Who thinks like that?" she said, and he blurted, "Only a fucking idiot wouldn't."

Not drunk, but sober when he'd said it. That's what terrifies, Dale said to nobody. Not Hitchcock—he entertains. Not those roller coasters in Japan. Everybody knows what happens when the coaster gets moving and when the camera watches a woman in a shower. Now he was entering silence. Years of it without forgiveness. He pressed his lips together and concentrated on breathing through his nose.

Gun Comfort

A thousand times by now Cassidy's daddy had told her, "You live out here, gun comfort comes automatic as breathing." Sometimes he made it end with "as your beating heart," but she believed it either way. A gun in her hands was second nature.

Her Uncle Walt, who'd put himself through the state college to be a teacher, said, "You take to a gun early, it's like growing up knowing a second language."

"And he's never forgot hisself," her daddy said, as if a brother could turn uppity and leave like a wife. Though mostly, she knew it was Daddy wanting to be alone and answering to nobody, like he'd tried the world's ordinary ways and decided they weren't meant for him. She already could feel him waiting for her to leave in another year after she graduated from high school.

It didn't hardly matter, she wanted to tell him. He wasn't going to be by himself, not with the cell phone tower already close by, the rumors of the big tire burner plant getting built less than a mile away, and the gas drillers all the time looking to buy somebody out. He should be fretting about all that, not the little problem of the detour sending traffic past their house night and day while the bridge along County Road 213 was under repair.

Cars and trucks times ten, according to Daddy when he cursed them for speeding, but what was worse, nearly all of them were being driven by strangers. "Who knows what those people do with themselves," he'd say, standing at the front window however long it took to smoke one of his generic cigarettes down, using an empty Blue Ribbon bottle for the ash. It was how he paced his drinking and smoking, one then the other, then on to the next pair, maybe twenty minutes a cycle, sometimes less when he got going on some itch to scratch, nothing else to do once it was dark and outside work was shut off. Most nights, he just settled on drinking himself to sleep. He didn't read or watch television or even listen to the tiny clock radio that never played except for the ten seconds, every morning in the dark, it took for him to shuffle to the kitchen and find the button to shut off the talk radio station he had on at nine out of ten on the volume control. If she was anywhere nearby while he opened the refrigerator for a fresh beer, he'd tell her she should keep an eye out when she had the chance because with more than a hundred cars coming by every hour of the day and night, hardly a handful carrying any kind of neighbor, there was trouble so close you could smell it.

Lately, with the weather warm, he'd taken, after two Blue Ribbons, to leaving the window behind to sit on the porch like he was riding shotgun on a stagecoach. Like their house was a target for bandits who thought he had treasure of some sort even though there wasn't anything about the property or the house that suggested that could be true. When she sometimes joined him, bringing a fresh bottle as a ticket to the other porch chair, he'd say something like "They're all married to their gadgets and things. Next thing you know we'll be hearing all those whistles and bells going off right in our ears and then we're in for it."

"They can't see anything they'd want here," she'd said that time.

"Some of them want everything, what we have included," he'd said, and she'd known he'd meant her.

His other subject was work.

"You going to live on your own, you best be ready for it," he reminded her about keeping a steady job every time he thought she had "that look." Like seventeen was old maid's age. Like she didn't have a year of high school to finish plus this summer season of work at the Tasty Creem. Or like he thought she was playing around in some boy's car on her breaks.

"Your Momma had your brother Ricky at eighteen and Rafe at nineteen," he said in June when her job turned full time. Her brothers were in the service, safe from becoming daddies, signing on together right after Rafe graduated from high school, but Cassidy could see him counting backwards until he was right beside her age. And then, as if she'd asked him the details of what he was remembering, he left those years behind. "You snuck up on us when she'd turned twenty-five, and she skedaddled at thirty like there was something only she could hear, calling her like she had the ears for some kind of dog whistle."

What Cassidy repeated was "You've never even come to the TC to take a look," but there was nothing on the porch for her to do but listen and think about how, in the morning, she'd be on her way to work at ten o'clock and on her way home at six to make dinner for him while he worked outside or worse, when it rained, sat in the kitchen and watched her.

She had to ride her bike the two miles. The shoulder was narrow and rutted, so she rode on the asphalt surface, facing traffic like she used to when she walked. It didn't make sense to have her back turned to the traffic that might hit her, no matter what the bike safety people said and now, because of the traffic, she had to keep a look out the whole way instead of just the last half mile. But what she hated most was having to ride the bike in the tan and brown uniform that made her feel ugly. "Don't you worry about ugly,"

Daddy had said the one time she'd brought it up, "a thing like that don't stop imagination."

Selling dessert had sounded like fun once upon a time when she was fourteen and could only work short shifts because of her age, but by her second summer she dreamed about the soft ice cream machine, waking up at two a.m. and thinking it was already time to fill it, or worse, to clean it. Soon enough it was time to empty that goop into sugar cones and the big waffle ones that cost extra. The rest of the day was a few hot dogs, bags of chips, and being bored. There was a gallon jar that had once held pickle slices on the counter for tips. Boys didn't tip anyone except Sarah Kantz, but men almost always at least tossed their change in the jar, especially if she flirted. Fathers with children waiting at a table or even just hovering behind them would smile and make a show of it if they folded a dollar or two and pushed it through the slot.

She wondered at that, because she'd never considered herself what her Daddy called "a looker," only one boyfriend in all her years and just a few months of that and never alone for more than a few minutes, Daddy reminding her all this summer, "I wish to hell you had one over here to keep company sometimes, a boy around the house discourages the rest from their ideas. Your Uncle Walt sees girls like you every day. He tells me how the men go on and on about them, what they imagine those girls are asking for what with all their teasing talk."

When she thought about Uncle Walt claiming he knew what was in the minds of teachers way older than Daddy, she remembered the men who sometimes ordered ice cream and stared at her while she worked their chocolate or vanilla or half and half into a cone. At school she knew which girls the boys had eyes for, but at Tasty Creem, even when she worked the counter with Sarah Kantz, she felt eyes touching her.

"That's cause they're all pigs," Sarah said. Back in May she'd shown Cassidy the bruises her daddy had made on her fleshy upper arms where she'd said he'd gripped to shake some sense into her. She'd come to school a week later with the traces of a slap left on her face.

Cassidy had told Sarah her daddy had never touched her, no matter the best moments or the worst. "Cassidy Heimbach, you are the world's worst liar," Sarah had said, and when Cassidy shook her head, Sarah had stroked her hair with her fingers and said, "Next you'll tell me you never touched yourself."

"Your pop is somebody who likes to be alone so everything's his way," Uncle Walt said. "He'll never be happy until you're out of the house, too."

"That's a terrible thing to say."

"That doesn't mean he doesn't love you, sweetheart. He just loves his all-alone more."

"He's never cooked or cleaned. He made the boys when I was little, and now he has me."

"Your cleaning up after him be damned, there's just the getting used to is all."

When her brothers were still at home, they and her daddy left their dishes on the table after she cooked for them. "It's all yours in here from now on," he'd said when she'd turned ten. "You're the woman of the house." Her daddy had bought a dishwasher for her thirteenth birthday. "There she sits," he'd said, like it was a prize for cooking for three years by then, her brothers clapping as if she'd sung or danced.

Once, when she was sick the past February, he'd opened a can of baked beans and eaten them cold. She'd found the can in the garbage. For all she knew, he'd licked it clean and was proud of saving her the work.

IN THE MORNING, EVEN in summer, Daddy would wake her and tell her coffee would be ready in five minutes. He'd come back with two cups, expecting her to have used the bathroom and "be decent." "I don't have all day," he'd say, or "While it's hot," until she took the cup and began to sip.

"Can't have you sleep through work," he would add as if that was any sort of explanation. As if he was ashamed of saying what he meant, that he wanted her awake and alert and on her feet if anything that might happen in a house by herself began to unspool like an old movie reel. It wasn't about getting to work on time, it was about her being safe from things he couldn't say out loud.

"You leave the house, you have a place to go," he said. Work, he meant. And going outside meant she was on the way to it. Straight there, no dilly-dally. Not anywhere that he called "just out the door." Not the woods where her brothers spent all their free time growing up, where she watched them run off to like they were in a story as soon as they disappeared. Not, at least, until she thought there might only be the choice between going crazy and going into the woods.

Awake with the sun barely up and Daddy gone, she was left with hours that didn't amount to anything but time. She hated those hours between Daddy leaving and when she had to ride her bike to work. She needed voices, and the television, without cable since her brothers had gone, didn't show anything but two fuzzy channels and the old movies Daddy had bought when the video store was going out of business five years ago and he brought home twenty of them for twenty dollars. "Enough to last forever," he'd said, not hardly accurate, but what she watched sometimes were the ones on television, their stories being told by actors and actresses who must be older than even Daddy by a long shot.

The people in those old movies were, after all, doing things before she was born, when she was absent. She watched the black and white ones that were shown early in the day and tried to imagine how the world worked without her, their hair and makeup and clothes before Daddy was born, too. When she asked him what his favorite movies were, he told her he hadn't gone to one "since your mother dragged me."

"How about TV shows?" she asked.

"There wasn't time for television when I was growing up, and then came all of you kids and there wasn't any time for it being a man."

A week ago, when he'd started in on the way time was different for men and women, she'd said that couldn't be true, and he'd opened the closet in his room and stepped back like a game show host presenting a prize. "Look at all this she had time for. Your momma left half a closet-full of things because she had more than she'd ever need, and here they all sit forever maybe."

"They don't belong to me," she said, and then waited for him to go on about shopping and television being like life on another planet, but he kept looking at the clothes as if he was thinking hard on something.

"Your momma had her eye all the time on wearing what turned a man's head."

Or yours, Cassidy wanted to say and settled on, "We're not scavengers. We don't live up some hillbilly hollow with no running water or electricity. There's paved road right outside our front door."

"Most days I wish the hell we was."

"It's four miles to Taylorville."

"It's not the same as when it had to be walked."

"Nothing is, Daddy, not even you."

"This is where your momma picked to live," he said. "Somewhere between a farm and a packed-tight place."

She knew the house was planted on a six-acre plot, but to look at it wouldn't make anybody see but an acre, tops, the rest spreading into the field behind the house, what Daddy mowed less of each summer, and less often on top of that, the rest going to sumac and locust and all sorts of brambles that were nearly into the back yard now.

All they had that looked like room was the raggedy, weed-choked lawn that her brothers had mowed with the small tractor and the twenty-yard setback from the road with its long gravel driveway to plow in the winter and repair every spring. But last winter Daddy had parked down by the mailbox when it snowed, leaving the driveway untouched and slogging up to the house like someone who'd broken down on the road and needed help. Mornings and afternoons she'd tried to step in his footprints going and coming to where the school bus picked her up, the driveway untouched in a way that shamed her.

"Your momma thought she'd garden flowers and such all around and found out it was work." There were still patches of iris and hostas scattered in the field, roses and mums close by the house, and the lamb's ear and coleus that had spread into the lawn like a bad case of acne.

Except for the large picture window in the living room, the windows in the house were small and cross-hatched into smaller sections of glass, the kind, she'd said once, that nobody could get out through in case of a fire that blocked the doors. "Why you all of a sudden worried about fire? There's just the two of us. You know what happens when you have big glass in the windows like the one we have out front. You get yourself a slew of dead birds from them breaking their necks on it. Just the one so we don't hardly get them dead in our yard and both of us standing here not all burnt up."

"I hear them hit sometimes, but I never see them dead."

"I get after them, save you the looking." He turned and pointed. "You see that tower for everybody's damn phone? That's how you hunt birds without lifting a finger." The nearest tower was part of the Kratzer farm, twenty acres of corn and a plot of vegetables, but the old man had sold off an acre to the phone people five years before. "You wait for a foggy night and follow me in the morning."

When that foggy night had come on a Thursday, he'd told her to throw on whatever was handy and walked her out first thing Friday morning to show her twenty-six dead birds, all the same. "All these beauties got led right to slaughter. These monsters are serial killers for things that fly."

"You can't stop what everybody wants," she said. Daddy nodded like he agreed for once, but his lips set tight, and she could hear the suck of air as he inhaled through his half-clogged nose as if he was inflating himself. "I feel sorry for you having all this nonsense to live with," he said. He tilted his head slightly as if he was reluctant to give any more acknowledgment to the nearby towers.

She wanted to tell him the tower was twice as ugly when you didn't have a phone to carry around. That if those towers were going to be planted everywhere, you oughtn't be left out of their magic. "So there it is," he said.

"The half of you listening without both ears." She felt his eyes on her chest. "Ready yourself up like you know how the world thinks because every day there's more shit spreading every whichawhere." He stared at her then until she tugged her blouse together.

He'd walked off straight to the car and driven to work, and before she showered, she opened her blouse and slid her jeans to the floor before she lay back on her bed, imagining a boy's hands sliding up her thighs to where she began to touch herself, inserting one finger, then two, until she gasped with joy.

Afterwards, she was afraid it might be strange that it took her only a few minutes to get off. And lately she wondered if Sarah Kantz enjoyed herself as often as she did, but sometimes she just remembered Daddy telling her that dreaming during the day was cursing yourself.

IN JULY, BEFORE SHE even ate breakfast, she walked into the woods for the first time and came across two chairs, one overturned as if the owner had walked away angry, and farther along, a Phillies shirt and black hooded sweatshirt soaked and faintly rotten as if they'd wintered there. She righted the chairs and sat on one until she began to shiver, listening like a schoolgirl as if someone would return, months later, to retrieve his clothes.

She set that chair up, sat down on it, and waited like she expected that somebody until she began to shiver and the trees turned flint-colored, her Daddy's favorite shade. He was all the time telling her how there are more plants than people, how it was intended by God. She touched a rock at her feet, but in the early morning, it felt cold and damp. Nothing here was like the road with its gradual curves, with its straight lines, everything able to be measured.

A few minutes later, on the way out of the trees, she stopped twice, listening for footsteps, but each time she thought she heard the sloshing of her heart murmur, the little squishy sound the doctor had said she'd grow out of, but she hadn't been to the doctors for six years.

AT TASTY CREEM THE next day, Uncle Walt brought her Taco Bell. "You're all the time saying you only get the hot dogs and the cones and those god-awful slushy things."

"There's microwave," she said. "And we chip in sometimes, but for sure, I don't want to see another hot dog for a while."

"Your dad wants me to come shoot with him Saturday. He thinks I'm turning into a town boy."

"He has his ways of looking out for people."

"Your dad thinks a man without a gun in his house is a man who looks and wishes more than he does. Hah!"

Cassidy smiled like she always did when Uncle Walt added "Hah!" at the end of his opinions that had a hint of sex in them. Like he meant her to know he was just being funny, that right then he wasn't explaining exactly how small-minded his brother was, but it sounded like a period to her, not an exclamation point. "That's a lot of lookers," she finally said.

"Half the men I work with. Your dad wouldn't do well among them."

"I thought every man looked and wished, to hear Daddy tell it."

"He's only right five times out of ten, but that there's plenty of miserable men working themselves into a fret. Hah!"

When she didn't answer, squinting at him the way she'd seen teachers look at boys who hadn't done their homework, he laughed. "Stupid, right?" he said. "Don't tell your dad I said so."

She heard Sarah laughing at something a boy at the counter was saying. Uncle Walt smiled. "Who you know that likes you serving him?"

"Nobody."

"That can't be true."

"I don't mind," she said.

"I know you know better than that. Hah!" When she didn't smile, he added, "Just you wait," and after he left, she imagined herself living in her daddy's house alone, a woman in her forties, as old as daddy now, who would be dead by then, she thought, and her brothers with teenage sons and daughters living somewhere far away. "Impossible," she said aloud, and thought she sounded like a crazy person.

BEFORE HER BROTHERS LEFT, when they called her into their room, Cassidy had been excited. A surprise goodbye present, she'd thought, something handed down like the cable bill paid for a year in advance, because for weeks they'd been teasing her about how, twelve days after they boarded the bus, the television would turn to snow. "What?" she'd said, the two of them grinning. "Come on, what?"

They'd showed her their porn magazines. "We know you've been looking," they said. But she hadn't been. She hadn't even known they had those magazines, but they were so sure she'd been peeking, she knew it had to be her Daddy doing the looking.

That day she'd looked at the pictures of the naked women, wondering which of them excited her brothers most. What she'd done, at last, was examine the expressions on the faces of the men and women, and she'd shuddered when none of them looked like they cared about anyone else in the picture. No matter what they said, calling her inside, she hadn't gone back in their room until they were gone to the army for a month.

Now, when she looked for those magazines, they were gone from any place in that room where somebody would hide anything larger than a postcard, and was left without knowing whether her brothers had burned them all or whether her Daddy had moved them to his own secret location, a place she didn't want to find.

FOR A WHOLE WEEK, she went into the woods and sat on the same chair until she could feel herself growing so excited she hurried to her room to undress and lie naked on her bed. Afterward, each time, she told herself she wouldn't go back in the woods, but all she did differently, by the third day, was lie on one of her brothers' beds, first Ricky's and the next day Rafe's, putting the face of a boy from school on her memory of each brother's body.

Pushing herself up from Rafe's bed, she remembered Uncle Walt telling her once, "You'll know when you're in love. You'll give up your secrets nobody else will ever know." She'd nodded then, polite, but now she shuddered, imagining the words.

Sarah Kantz told her all week she looked pasty. "You know," she said, "like you're sick. Nobody looks pasty in the summer except old people."

The next Monday, the weather turning hot even at eight o'clock, she lay out in her two-piece bathing suit, choosing something besides the chair in the woods.

All those cars with somebody's eyes inside. What they did after she lay out three days in a row was tell her how many would never stop. She wanted to tell her daddy that nobody noticed, not even a horn blowing. She'd bet nobody would remember even passing by, even after using the detour for weeks. And nobody would even remember her on her bike in her stupid, ugly uniform.

The third morning, when the sun moved behind a set of thunderheads, Cassidy walked through the house in her bathing suit looking at photographs. There were dozens of photos of her in frames and albums. She smiled when she saw that in three of them she was wearing a bathing suit. But it was the most recent one, from last summer, where she was wearing the bikini she'd been wearing three straight mornings, her breasts in the picture lifted by the bra, and she remembered being surprised by the camera, that the surprise made her look like a stranger, like a girl her father might be looking at, imagining. "See there," her daddy had said when he'd first set the picture out. "See how somebody could see you wrong?" as much as he could get out of his mouth except, a minute later, like he'd expected her to be standing there waiting, "I don't ever want you outside like that."

"Like what?" she'd said. "Like what?"

And he'd managed, "Half naked."

"Like every girl I know," she'd said.

"You cover yourself before you leave your room when I'm gone. You don't flounce around just because nobody's around."

"Nobody means empty."

"There's never empty," he'd said then. "Not when you're showing yourself off."

Like always, Uncle Walt had his cooler in the truck when he parked it on the back grass the next Sunday. The only mystery about it was how many cans of beer he had on ice and how many he'd already slugged down before he arrived so he could slow down to match her daddy's pace and still have that head start to keep him. It made no sense at all. Daddy was so set on safety, and yet they finished one after the other. "You can drop the sour face," Daddy said. "When our six packs are gone, we stop."

She kept her mouth set exactly the same, counting to ten before she said, "Until you're back on the porch."

"Hah!" Uncle Walt said, starting with the period before he added, "You're getting sassy as that hottie, Carrie Bradshaw."

Her Daddy snorted like he'd just heard a fart. "I know who that is." she said. "Just cause we can't see her here on our TV doesn't mean I don't know. Anyway, that's not who she really is."

"Make believe," Daddy said, looking at Cassidy. "The TV keeps him wishing."

"It's not from watching," Uncle Walt said. "It's teaching teenagers keeps you in the know. And it's the girls who tell me, so there you are." He headed for the cooler.

"Ten years ago, by the sound of it," Cassidy called after him, and her daddy laughed out loud.

"Here," he said, handing her his rifle, "show Walt how it's done."

Cassidy hesitated. Not since teaching her to shoot when she was twelve, had Daddy put one of his rifles in her hands. A weekend he'd spent with her, and on Monday morning, at breakfast, he'd given her a Remington 700 just like the ones he'd given to her brothers when they'd turned ten. Like always, it was loaded right now, one bullet in the chamber, but locked above her bed just like the two still displayed in her brothers' room.

"The clip's full," Daddy said. Cassidy thought about saying she wasn't used to the Savage 99, her daddy's favorite that he'd had forever, but she knew not to make an excuse. She swung it up and readied herself.

"A girl looks so sexy when she's shooting," Uncle Walt said.

"That's no kind of talk," Daddy said, but Uncle Walt didn't apologize and he didn't crack open his fresh beer or hand its partner to Daddy.

"The truth is always the right talk," he said, and she felt her daddy's eyes on her as if Uncle Walt had given him permission to just outright stare like some kind of contest judge.

"All the time with the fear of God," Daddy said slowly, like he was trying to make the words out on a page.

"Sunday sermons," Uncle Walt said.

"And all week long," Daddy said. "There's worse than God to fear."

She steadied and squeezed and a jelly jar a hundred feet away on the stone wall exploded. Walt whooped like she'd done something hard. She shot again, shattering another. "That's enough," Daddy said.

"Your pop can't let go of his antique for more than a minute," Uncle Walt said. "They haven't made a new one of those since when you were born."

"A gun proper cared for lasts forever," Daddy said.

"Truth in that," Walt said, "but a girl who shoots like that ought to have herself a beer. Hah!"

"A man old enough to have hisself grandkids ought to know when he talks too much."

Walt whistled. "Listen to Warren the proud poppa."

"Exactly," Daddy said. "Do that."

"All right then. I know my place, but it's a powerful thing to watch a girl handle a gun like that."

After they ate the hamburgers she fried up for the two of them, Uncle Walt hugged her and whispered, "Remember—what you see," before he drove off in his truck, but Daddy kept his eyes on it as if he intended to follow it the six miles to Uncle Walt's apartment. "He keeps his learning to hisself, that's for sure," he said, still watching the empty road.

"It's just the beer talking," Cassidy said.

Daddy spit off the porch. "Walt teach you that there bit of wisdom?"

"He just talks."

"In a circle, how he goes."

"No different than other teachers."

"Then they should be looking to hire more women at that school."

"Uncle Walt has a girlfriend, Daddy. Miss Davis. She's as old as he is, the way you like it."

"The way it's s'pose to be." He tapped his empty bottle of Blue Ribbon, the one he'd pulled from the refrigerator and sipped while he was eating, against the porch railing. "Some Sunday Walt can play house with Miss Davis and we'll shoot, just the two of us and leave the drinking until after."

THE NEXT MORNING, THE coffee sounding its alarm as always, she had to pee after Daddy left. When the flushing stopped, she was left looking at herself in the mirror, a minute, no more. Her shift was hours away, and already excited, she came down the hall in her nightgown, wanting to lie down on one of her brothers' beds, undress completely. And then she listened hard because she thought she heard the slow rhythm of careful footsteps downstairs.

When the footsteps stopped, she glanced over the railing to make sure she wasn't imagining. A man was standing at the base of the stairs, one foot on the first step as if testing it to see if it would squeak. He didn't have anything in his hands that made him look like a thief, and so she knew he had come for her. Someone, maybe, who'd watched her in the yard, who'd learned when her Daddy left every weekday morning. He looked young, maybe not even thirty. Just a ball cap pulled low so she couldn't make out his face as he started up the stairs.

There was time to back up to her room while those footsteps took the stairs slowly. Whoever it was, she thought, expected her, a high school girl, to be sleeping at six a.m. He figured her to be in her room, that maybe he could watch her for a while lying in her bed in her flimsy summer nightgown. He didn't know her daddy brought her coffee before he left, that he drank his second cup with her in the half-light to make sure she was up, all last summer and now this with her brothers gone, no argument from her that he would abide.

She stepped into her room and closed the door before she lifted the rifle from its rack. She had it down in a second. She waited. The man took his time, maybe ten seconds, before the knob turned and he stepped through the doorway, a ski mask over his face now, and stopped. She felt his eyes on her nearly bare thighs, and then she brought the gun up and his head jerked as he stiffened. A detour man, she thought, like Daddy expects, or somebody from the Tasty Creem or even some teacher friend of Uncle Walt. Because up close, she noticed the would-be attacker had the soft stomach of an older man.

She let the safety off so he could hear. His eyes went to the gun rack and back to her hands. He was deciding, she knew, whether she was someone who could fire a gun at a man. He said nothing, and neither did she. The room was in full sunlight now, the drapes open the way Daddy always left them year-round when he said goodbye. "Fuck you, bitch," the man finally said, but he took a step back. "Fucking cunt," he said, and he retreated into the hall and she listened with the gun still pointing until she heard him on the stairs. She went to the window then and watched him walk to the car he'd parked out front, facing away from the house. The car was at the road before she thought to look at the license plate.

She kept the gun with her as she went down the stairs. She saw that a screen had been popped out. It was propped, slightly bowed, against the dining room wall. They didn't have air conditioning, the windows open day and night all summer except during thunderstorms.

Still in her negligee, she carried the rifle into the back yard, walked to where Daddy had started that stone wall years ago, getting it waist-high for fifty feet before it stopped. She brought along two of his beer bottles, both of them full, and placed them there, the slippers she'd pulled on before coming downstairs crunching the crust of broken glass. She backed up and stood ten feet away, the distance to that flabby man in the ball cap and ski mask, and fired, exploding one bottle and then the other, beer spraying in a quick arc.

She stood in that spot for a minute, her eyes scanning the edge of the woods. She had all day to decide whether she would tell Daddy, but she knew for sure she wasn't calling the police, standing in her room in her tan and brown Tasty Creem uniform while they inspected her weapon and asked her to hold it just the same as she was telling them she had—as if that were some sort of proof her story was true.

She wanted to call Sarah and tell this story so it would do some good maybe, but it was so early, not even seven yet, that a ringing phone wouldn't set well in anybody's house. She knew Sarah's house didn't have any guns inside, and then it didn't seem as if it would do a bit of good to tell her anything.

The urge passed. She hurried into the house and locked the door behind her. She checked every ground floor window. Back in her room, she dressed quickly in her uniform without taking a shower. As alert and focused as she'd ever been firing the rifle, she felt just as tired now. Exhausted. As if she'd worked an eight-hour shift at the Tasty Creem from right after school to eleven at night the way she had in April and May when customers, on those first hot days, stood in line for cones and sundaes and shakes. In a month, when school began, she'd feel that way every Monday, Tuesday, and Wednesday until the place shut down for winter.

If she told him, Daddy would ask, "Were you dressed?" and he would know she was lying. He'd look at her body like it belonged to him. "What did I tell you?" he'd say, and she'd hate him for it.

Maybe it was enough to have lived through this, to think that she was glad the man had entered the house, that he looked as soft as Mr. Hartman, the old biology teacher who had just retired. Now she knew one more thing about herself. She began to clean the gun, plenty of time to do it right. She had another year to live with Daddy, not too long to keep one more thing to herself.

Something like the Truth

NO MATTER WHOSE VOICE is speaking, when the phone rings at seven a.m. on a Sunday, there's need on the line. This time it was Roseanne Metz, the public relations officer, saying, "Jack, we had a student die on campus last evening." Because I was being called, I knew the student she was about to name was an Admissions Office intern, and I thought, before she went on, of Ellen Volpe, who seemed capable of suicide, someone who could swallow a bottle of pills and lock the door behind her. "The student's name is Jolene Hirsch," Roseanne finally said. "I'm calling to let you know because I've been told you were her assistantship mentor."

Not suicide then, I thought, and murmured, "Thank you for calling" and waited, stepping into the living room where Jolene Hirsch, Ellen Volpe, and six other interns had stood or sat the night before.

"Her parents are already here. Jolene died early this morning from a fall on a flight of stairs near her dormitory. A memorial service is planned for tomorrow for the entire campus community, and it's hoped that you would be willing to speak."

I crossed into the kitchen, my bare feet moving across the floor's cold tile. Roseanne sounded like a press release. How many others had received this call? Jolene Hirsch had been intense, but shy. She'd been the kind of student who might not have had many friends. But when Roseanne added, as if she wanted to sound more candid, "Unfortunately, Jolene was drinking before the accident," I felt myself turn hot because Jolene, while she'd nibbled on crackers and hummus and raw vegetables I put out for her and three other vegetarians, had sipped continuously on wine coolers.

When I was stuffing a slice of chicken quesadilla into my mouth, she'd made a face and taken a swig from her bottle. "You might be eating clones," she'd said. "I read that they're in the food supply now. Doesn't that make you sick?"

I'd smiled, keeping my lips together so the mess in my mouth didn't show. After I'd swallowed, I'd said, "I think there are vegetables like that now, too."

"That's not the same," Jolene had said. "They don't have nerves or brains," and she'd laughed, taking another drink before turning away.

AS SHE'S BEEN DOING for six years now, my wife Stacy was spending the month of April three times zones away in California with one of our three daughters, so I waited until noon to call her.

"I don't remember her," Stacy said. "Have you talked about her?"

"Probably not."

"And yet she was just at the house for your party?"

"She was an intern. There's eight of them. They don't all get talked about."

Stacy was quiet for a moment, but I had nothing else. A girl was dead. Talking on the phone about her felt like gossip. Then she said, "There's wildfire in the area. We're worried here."

"It's on the news," I said. "It looks to be six or eight miles away."

"That's close for a fire like this. They started evacuating in the development that's four miles from here. If it moves there, we're next. All there is between us and them is brush and forest. I thought it was so wonderful to fly here when the weather was still chilly at our place, but this fire has us worried."

"I'm watering all your stuff," I said. "It hasn't rained here since you left. It doesn't feel like April."

"You don't know what dry is, Jack," Stacy said.

"I'm speaking at the memorial service," I said. "Fire or no fire, I wish the hell I was in California."

Though it was 12:15, as soon as she hung up, I opened one of the beers left over from the party and took a long pull. The phone rang thirteen times during the afternoon and evening. Only Roseanne Metz, calling back for confirmation around four o'clock, left a message. By then I was so deep into drinking, working on leftover wine coolers, that I was afraid to answer.

ON CAMPUS MONDAY, STILL wearing my black, gold-striped sweat pants and college-logo t-shirt, I slipped into my office half an hour early and closed the door. I read emails, three of them from other interns saying they were too upset to conduct tours, not a big problem in late April with fewer tours scheduled. Another was from Roseanne Metz, who still wanted to confirm my part in the memorial service. I scrolled through a dozen more before I sat staring at the intern schedule posted above my desk, trying out first sentences for condolence in my head until I heard voices and stepped out to listen to the staff compare rumors.

The stories, it turned out, were consistent. The outside steps where she'd fallen were concrete and led into the student center basement. She'd taken the first three one at a time and then jumped to take the last four of them at once, catching her heel on the bottom one. "It doesn't seem that far," the receptionist said. "She must have been drinking way too much to have that happen." What everyone seemed to know was that when Jolene had lost her balance, she'd flown backwards instead of being flung forward, her head striking the edge of a stair.

I didn't add anything. None of the interns who had begged off were scheduled until one o'clock. I told Marsha Walsh, my secretary, to get a few subs for the afternoon. "I have an appointment to talk about the memorial service," I said, and she looked as if she wanted to remind me to take a shower first, but she nodded, and five minutes later I walked by the accident site. I wanted to stop and examine, but there were students milling around, and I felt embarrassment wrap its thick arms around me the way it did when I slowed down for a house fire. Gawking was permissible if I kept moving, but it was taboo to park.

I drove the mile and a quarter to my house, stopping first to pick up two six packs at the convenience store. I bought warm to keep myself from opening one, but then there was nothing to do but sit in front of the television and stay away from the refrigerator for an hour and a half before I had to shower and change. At noon, while I ironed my only white shirt, I sealed wrinkles so deeply into the sleeves I reminded myself never to take off the jacket of my dark suit no matter how crowded and warm the reception afterwards might become. Three times I wove a gray tie into a Windsor knot before the wide end reached close enough to my belt to keep me from shame. I tugged it tight at my throat and pulled a beer from the refrigerator.

Just the one I had, but between the beer and the suit, I was sweating when I arrived at the service. I took a seat to the right of the President and the chaplain. *Eulogies*, it said in the program, my name listed the first of three. When Jolene's parents were escorted to the front row, Mrs. Hirsch looked too old to have a twenty-year-old daughter. I'd turned fifty-six a month before, and she looked older than I did. Even more unsettling, her husband walked with a shuffle that said fear of falling had become a priority.

"It is difficult," I began after the chaplain offered an opening prayer, "to find the words that preserve us, keeping the stories of those we know and love from turning into secrets again . . ."

I spoke about talent and promise, how the short stories by a college junior predicted, not necessarily a life of literary fame, but certainly one of richness and achievement. It felt like the truth. Jolene had showed me a few of her stories, and they'd seemed ordinary. I praised her discipline--"sticktoitiveness," I called it, citing my father's constant use of the word as a form of praise.

And then I sat down and had half an hour to think about how Jolene had finished at least three of those wine coolers at the end-of-the-semester party I hosted twice a year, that her evening had started at my house where, since I'd taken my job, I'd allowed students of any age to drink. When the President, after the service ended, said, "We should talk," I imagined defending myself by saying all of those students walked over a mile back to school because I didn't allow cars. And when the President's wife moved so readily alongside Mr. and Mrs. Hirsch as we left the chapel, I estimated the disgust he was already feeling.

The President slowed, and I kept pace until we were half a block behind his wife and the Hirsch's. "What can you tell me?" he said.

I swallowed but kept moving, afraid, if I turned to face him, my fear would be transparent. "What do you want to know?"

"Something like the truth," he said, and I had to force my feet forward in order to stay beside him.

"Well," I started, pressure building in my groin. I glanced up, squinting as the sun reflected off the windows of the library that stood a block from the President's house.

"We don't have much time here, so let me put it a different way," he said. "Give me three details about this young woman that I can use this afternoon."

"Ok," I said. "Her favorite writer was Alice Munro. She could name every organization on campus. She was a vegetarian."

"Good," he said, quickening his pace. "Now let's get to work."

DURING THE RECEPTION, I met Jolene's three sisters—seventeen, fifteen, and thirteen, ages that seemed even more improbable for how old her parents looked. All of them looked frightened. "Jolene was the smart one," the thirteen-year-old told me. "She could be drunk and sit down with Mom and Dad at dinner and they'd never know."

She hugged me like I was her brother, her arms half extended. "That's why she was such a good writer," she said before her sisters took her hands and backed her away.

A moment later, I felt a hand rest on my forearm, pressing tightly through my sleeve. "Mr. Elser," a voice said from the side, and then Jolene's mother was there in front of me. "Thank you for speaking."

I lifted her hand and clasped it as I considered what to say. "This is awful," I managed.

"Worse than that," she said as Mr. Hirsch shuffled toward us.

Jolene had told me he was fifty-seven, but his hair, what remained of it, was near white, and he carried himself with the slight stoop of the elderly, the sort of posture that suggested a future of creep to cane to walker, and finally, to wheelchair. He was one of those men who turned seventy on his fiftieth birthday and subsequently never aged except through the legs.

Hardly anything worse could happen to a man, I thought, a conviction I was ready to defend. "Hello," I said, "I'm Jack Elser."

Without speaking, Mr. Hirsch took my hand and fixed on me, the room shrinking to the pinpoint of his face like an old television picture diminishing to a centered dot.

"George, this is Mr. Elser," Jolene's mother said, speaking as if she'd just returned from getting a glass of punch. Mr. Hirsch squeezed my hand and let go, but his expression didn't change. "Jolene's mentor in the Admissions Office."

"I'm sorry," I said, "I should have something to say here, but I don't."

Jolene's mother smiled. "Some things have no words for them," she said.

I wondered if both of them had looked younger two days ago, whether grief could crease a face, draw moisture from the skin. Or anticipation, I thought then. Three more daughters to send to college. I felt nauseous, as if I were catching her despair like a disease.

"Thank you for being kind to Jolene," she said at last. "To her work."

What I had sensed when her husband had touched me returned. This woman had read my once-a-semester evaluation comments. I wondered if she'd read any of the stories Jolene had written over the past three years, what she might say to Warren Zale and Cynthia Waxman, the fiction professors who were standing together across the room. "She worked hard," I said.

"Of course, she did. But now that's all past, isn't it? Now she's done with working." Her hands twisted my suit coat. "I'm fifty-three years old, and now my daughter is a story."

I watched her face for the first sign of rage, but only resignation settled upon her. "I want to do something in her memory," I blurted, a fresh burst of sweat breaking out on my forehead. "I'd like, if you're willing, to begin a scholarship fund in Jolene's name."

She kept my coat in her hands and drew closer. "You're so kind," she said, and I thought, for a moment, she was inspecting my sweat, gauging something.

"I'll pledge $5,000 to get it started," I said. "It's the least I can do." I thought I might throw up, that she might tug my coat off to evaluate the sweat stains and wrinkles on my shirt. She leaned up and kissed me on the cheek, releasing my arm and stepping back beside her husband who was staring at me as if he'd just entered a class reunion after forty years of separation.

I made an excuse about using the bathroom, and though there was one on the ground floor, I climbed the stairs that led up from a hall that divided the house to search for another one. For five minutes, I sat on the edge of a bathtub behind a locked door, willing myself to relax. No one tried the knob or knocked. No one was in the hall when I stepped back out, but when I glanced through the doorway of the bedroom across the hall, I saw suitcases sitting open on the bed, and I pulled the door shut, steadying myself against it after the bolt clicked into place.

As I started down the stairs, I saw Mr. Hirsch standing in the hall near where coats would be hung if it were winter. Now, there was just the long, polished bar and a few dozen wooden hangers bunched together at the far end where Mr. Hirsch stood holding a drink half-filled with ice cubes.

I paused on the landing of the two-tiered staircase, looking down at the pink crown that showed through the wisps of white hair combed across Mr. Hirsch's head. Suddenly, without turning, Mr. Hirsch tilted his head back until his eyes found me. His throat was so arched I could see his Adam's apple working as if Mr. Hirsch was swallowing something before he spoke.

I waited while Mr. Hirsch swallowed a second and then a third time with his eyes rolled up at me. At last, he spoke. "I know how endowments work," he said, his voice steady. "You have quite a long way to go." I glanced down the stairs to see that no one else had drifted out of the two large reception rooms. I walked down the carpeted stairs without looking back at Mr. Hirsch. When I reached the bottom, I headed directly to the front door, hearing the President's voice say, "Jack, how wonderful of you" as I stepped off the porch.

I didn't pause. I followed the brick path until it ended at the sidewalk. Let him think, for a while longer, that I was modest. Or generous.

Hours later I sat outside eating tortilla chips with bean dip while I drank beer. Dinner seemed impossible, but the chips and dip and beer gave me something to do while the sky darkened.

When I heard knocking on the front door, I blew out a breath and stood. "Ok," I murmured, but there wasn't a car parked along the street, and I went around the corner of the house to look. A boy who looked to be college age pulled his hand back from the brass knocker and stepped off the porch. "Brett Helms," he said. "Jolene's boy friend. I wanted to talk to you at the reception, but you were up and gone before I could reach you."

"Let's go sit on the patio," I said before I thought about how I hadn't cleared the table, but Brett Helms sat down as if he didn't see five cans clustered there. I took it as discretion. Nearly offered him a beer. Instead, I nudged the bag of chips his way. "No thanks," he said, and he rose from his chair and stood by the low wall that angled up to meet the back of the house.

"Jolene always made herself throw up when she was drinking," he said. "She barfed right before she left the room on Saturday. Skinny was important. Even when she was drunk she remembered to throw up."

Brett Helms seemed determined to say something terrible, but then he went silent and looked around at all of the plants that surrounded the patio. "It's like a jungle out here," he said.

"Somewhat," I said. "for sure. My wife buys a potted plant for our anniversary each year, but these seventeen are the only survivors."

"Fuck," Brett Helms said, maybe letting me know how stupid anniversary talk was.

"Sorry," I said. "I just wanted to explain about how they do better now that we live in North Carolina and they can stay outside nine months a year."

"No lie," he said. "A fucking jungle." Brett Helms, I realized, was drunk. "She cried, you know," he said. "She'd show me the things Zale and Waxman wrote on her stories, and she'd be crying, but she never cried when she showed me your evaluations."

They were generous, I almost said aloud. "She was a good guide," I said, and when Brett Helms backed up one step, he nearly smacked his head against a pot hanging from the cast iron bar Stacy had had put in the summer we'd moved.

"You have characters here that aren't seen at all deeply," he said as if he was reading Zale's and Waxman's comments from a page. "Let them stay in a scene more than momentarily and see if that pressure might give them something that suggests complexity."

Brett Helms recited another half page of comments before he came out of his trance and switched back to conversation. "I tried to call you last night, but you weren't picking up. I knew you were there. I could feel it." He took a deep breath and let it out between his pursed lips. "Jolene read your evaluations over and over. I think she was trying to memorize what it was that pleased you so she could do more of that for somebody else."

I looked from one plant to another, willing to hear Brett Helms out. "I don't know what she saw in that fucking job of yours," he said. "It's all so canned over there. Did you ever walk along on one of those tours? And here it is she's like somebody in one of her own stories. There's always somebody dying in them." He paused, fingering the rope that held the hanging pot. "Fuck," he said, "if I had any balls, I'd call you out for serving her drinks on Saturday and see what happened."

"It's ok," I said. "I'd deserve it."

His eyes locked on mine. "You just think you do," he said. "You're just imagining you had something to do with Jolene's life." He pivoted and punched the large flowerpot. It rocked up and back, but didn't fall. I thought he might have broken his hand, but his face showed no evidence of physical pain. "See you around," he said.

He cut across the back yard, heading, I figured, back to the college. Not once, while I watched, did he touch his hand. When I laid my hand on the flower pot to assess how hard it was, I discovered it was made from something like rubber, that it was so light it gave against my fingertips.

An hour later I lay in bed holding a notebook. Without Stacy around, I had all of my paperwork arranged where she slept, and I thought, despite the beer, that I could sketch out a proposal for extended travel into territory where the college had never recruited heavily. All I had to do was make a case for generating name recognition more than three hundred miles away.

While I sat there, the phone rang three times at exactly ten-minute intervals, but no one left a message. When twenty minutes passed without another call, I told myself whoever it was had given up, but the notebook had turned foreign, like one that might be filled with calculus formulas or history notes from decades ago. One of the student interns was sure to have mentioned the party at my house. It didn't take Brett Ellis.

Showered and shaved by 5:30, I went to the office at six a.m. I finished everything necessary for the day by nine o'clock, and then I turned off the lights and locked the door. When someone knocked, I held my breath and waited two minutes before I let myself shift in my chair.

The day before the party Jolene had turned in a rough draft of a story about new roommates on the first day of college. She'd brought a copy to the party and handed it to me. "I know it sucks," she said, "but there's Admissions in it, and I want you to read it and tell me if it sounds real."

"Making the ordinary new is hard," I'd finally said, thankful that the words seemed to surprise her.

"Ordinary," she said, using the index finger of her right hand to brush her hair from where it swept in front of her eyes. "That's me, all right."

Standing in my living room, a beer in one hand, I curled her manuscript into a cylinder, and for a moment I thought of raising it to one eye and peering at her like a pirate examining a passing ship. Instead, I let it uncurl, glanced at it, and tapped it against my hip, and when she stayed quiet, I laid it on an end table under a lamp. The first line had read, "I felt sadder than I'd ever been when my parents got in their car and left me in my new dorm room."

As soon as I looked at her again, I saw that she had been watching me read. "That's all bullshit," she said. "I should have just started with the truth. My roommate thought I was weird because I didn't follow my parents to the parking lot when they were leaving, and then I didn't even watch them get in the car from the window." She waved toward the top page of the rough draft. "My roommate did. She watched my parents and waved, and I thought she was pretending to be me standing in the shadows like she did."

Jolene had hesitated then, as if she expected a suggestion for revision, but I'd remained quiet. She'd looked at the pictures of my three daughters lined up on the nearby bookshelf. "They're older here than in the ones in your office," she said.

"What?"

"Your daughters," she said, but she'd pointed to the manuscript. "You know what my roommate said, Mr. Elser? 'Your Mom and Dad both looked up here. I thought you'd want to know.'"

"Good," I said. "Now we're listening," and she'd looked puzzled.

"That's not good," she said. "That's ugly."

"That's why I want to know more."

"I don't know why," Jolene said, yet she promised to revise.

ALL YEAR I'D NOTICED Jolene in the fitness room at six a.m. every Tuesday and Thursday, the mornings I worked out, going early because I was supposed to be in my office at 8:30. She came by herself like the other half dozen skinny girls who were always on the elliptical machines, all of them churning the pedals for an hour. I'd never seen one of those girls leave except the times I'd arrived late, 6:30 or 6:45 to do twenty minutes of pedaling and twenty minutes of free weights before the football players arrived for weight training at 7:30.

The heavy girls always came in pairs. They chose the treadmills and walked them on "level" in silence, looking straight ahead through the glass wall as if they were afraid of passersby. They exercised in sweat pants with baggy shirts. The skinny girls all wore earbuds; they wore shorts that showed their boyish thighs.

Once, when I went at 6:45 on a Friday, trying to make up for three consecutive nights of drinking, Jolene was there, and I realized she worked out every day, grinding out hundreds of miles per week.

MY OFFICE PHONE RANG fifteen minutes after the knocking. *Marsha*, the display read, so I picked up. "I knocked, but you didn't answer," she said.

"Sorry, I was in the middle of something."

"The President would like you to come to his house for a few minutes during the lunch hour." She paused, and I looked at the door in expectation. "To say goodbye to the Hirsch's. They want to thank you for everything."

She paused again. "$5,000, Mr. Elser. Everybody's heard about it. Do you want me to set it up for ten years at $500 annually so you complete the donation by the time you retire?"

"I'll take care of it," I said, hanging up before she could offer something less per year until her estimation of when I would die.

I checked the news on the Internet without turning on the light. The wind had shifted in California, and the fire had stalled. I'd call Stacy at five after I made it home. For now, there was plenty of time to go to the campus center.

I'd had knee surgery at fifty and recovered, but after I took the first three concrete steps one at a time and jumped, I felt a shock of pain right up from my ankles through my knees and hips and into my shoulders. And then, except for a persistent ache in my repaired knee, it dissipated and was gone. I'd cleared the bottom step by more than a foot.

I walked back up and stood on the landing a second time. Nobody was watching. I chose a spot to aim for three inches from the base of the first stair and jumped the last four steps again. This time I felt more pain, but I'd landed less than six inches from the bottom step and barely swayed. An ending had rushed up to meet me but blown right by into the past.

IN EARLY APRIL, JUST after Stacy had flown to California, a consultant had come to campus to evaluate admissions and financial aid. During the first of his two-day visit, I'd arranged for him to speak individually with Jolene and three other interns.

The day ended with dinner and preliminary talks, but the consultant said he was happy to stay at the restaurant for drinks, that he wanted to stay out of his motel room as long as possible. "Jack's your man," someone said, and I laughed. "I know what you mean," I said. "I have an empty house, and it's only 7:30."

Two drinks later, the consultant leaned my way at the bar like a conspirator and said, "Those girls you had me talk to this afternoon were the kind you might risk your job for."

"Once upon a time," I said, playing host.

"They're so fuckable," he said. "It's a good fucking thing I don't work your job or I'd be out on my ass."

The words followed me to the President's house. The consultant had expected me to say something like "Fuck, yes." As if he had a reason for such confidence. As if he knew me.

JOLENE, THREE DAYS AGO, had drifted back into the living room as the other students were leaving. After she'd looked at the photos of my daughters, she'd said, "You're so young to have children so old."

"Not so young as you think," I'd said.

"You're just saying that. What are they, thirty or something? Did you start having them when you were still in college?"

"No," I'd said at once, hearing in her tone that thirty was the brink of middle age.

She'd smiled. "But right after, for sure."

Right then fifty-six sounded like something terrible, and I remembered joking with Stacy about going over the speed limit on my birthday. The crowd had thinned to four, and she'd moved from picture to picture so slowly that I began to feel myself stir as I studied her thin, toned body, the way her breasts sat high on her chest and swelled the tight blue blouse she wore. The way I could see the definition in her calves and thighs through her snug, beige slacks. The way, on the wooden floor, her small heels tapped as she moved. And when I heard voices from the kitchen say, "See you, Mr. Elser, thanks," I answered, "You're welcome" in a voice that shifted higher.

The door slapped shut to silence, and Jolene laid one hand on my arm then, just above the elbow and nearly whispered, "You're not that old" before she clattered across the kitchen calling, "Hey, wait up."

THE HIRSCH'S YOUNGEST DAUGHTER was standing outside the President's house, waiting, I thought, like a child who had been promised punishment if she came back inside to ask when they were going to leave. "What a house," she said. "You ever stay overnight here?"

"No," I said. "I work here. I'm not a guest."

"Isn't it kind of like being a guest when you work some place? You're there for a while and then you leave."

"In that case, the President's a guest in his own house."

Her expression turned guarded, but then she gave a short laugh and said, "You still remember when you were in eighth grade?"

"Sure. Algebra and junior high basketball and chasing after Nancy Jarvis."

"Was she hard to catch?"

"I kept trying."

"I mean did anything happen? Did you catch Nancy Jarvis?"

I glanced around the spacious yard, trying to figure what she was seeing—the perfectly weeded flower beds, the carefully trimmed shrubbery, the flight of stairs built into the hillside where the lawn ended, twelve flat stones that were ornamental now that a row of forsythia had grown in so thickly above them that no one had used those steps, I imagined, in years.

"No. Not really."

"Then how could you stand it?" she said, sitting down on the lawn and drawing her knees up to her chin. "Take care," I said, already moving toward the house.

"Yeah, whatever, right?" followed me inside where Mr. Hirsch seemed to cower as I approached him and his wife in the large living room. It was a look I hadn't seen since college, when there were fights every weekend in my fraternity house. It came to me that fear became anxiety when it aged.

"I'm the one who asked President Hoy to call you," Mrs. Hirsch said. "You've been so generous I'd like to give you something in return."

She led me into the dining room where a folder lay on the table. "These are all of her stories," Mrs. Hirsch said. "I want you to have them."

"No, they're yours."

"I want them to be somewhere else than a box under her bed."

I thought of the revision Jolene might have made to that story that turned out to be about a character so like herself grieving over lost love for her parents. Only Mrs. Hirsch would have glanced at it, and she may not have read past that early desperation to the redemption Jolene would certainly have wished for her narrator without earning it.

"At least let me Xerox them and give you the originals," I said. "After a while you might be glad you kept them."

"No, I'm certain of this. Knowing someone who cared for her has her stories is like they've been published."

I stared at the manuscripts as she undid the loop of colored string that tied the folder together. She fanned them out, and I counted nine stories altogether. My eyes went directly to the new one, scanning the beginning. "I didn't follow my parents to the parking lot when they dropped me off at school. I stood in my room and imagined them turning around at the bottom of the stairs and looking back up, waiting for me to appear." Either before or after she'd made herself throw up, Jolene had changed the first paragraph before she'd left her dorm room.

I gathered the stories together and retied the folder, slipping it under my arm. I let Mrs. Hirsch hug me like a mother, silently and extended, her breath on my neck, the sadness of her arms around me so unbearable I thought, for a few seconds, I was earning something.

The Probabilities of Timing

Monday, Wednesday, and Friday, my second period seniors read the city newspaper for credit. Tuesday and Thursday, I read the newspaper for myself during my free first period. This morning, before I finished, the school was evacuated. A bomb threat. My walk home was twelve minutes, more time than it took to empty the school.

When I entered the house, Wendy was lying on the couch with a magazine. She sat up fast and covered her mouth as if suppressing a scream. "You scared me walking in like that when there's no good reason." She laid her hands on her slightly swollen stomach, listening, I knew, for the kicking of tiny feet. "It's viability day plus four," she said. "Half way through week twenty-five."

"Good," I said, "but better when it's May, and minimum is behind us."

She'd had two miscarriages, one and three years before. We'd become experts on gestation. The doctor had cautioned that twenty-four weeks was the first realistic milestone, that twenty-six was when the odds weren't set at longshot for a baby without defects, but Wendy had read about a couple of twenty-three-week babies surviving. I didn't blame her for fudging. I'd just said "May" when I'd really meant "the end of May," but for now, here we were at the beginning of hope.

                                                      •

"Yesterday was better than a snow day," Larry Wertz said, "because once roll is called, the day counts. We're not making that one up."

Wertz had once passed along the advice never to use a sick day when sick. "What's the point of a day off if you're sick and can't do anything?" he'd said. "Tough it out when you're feeling like shit. The day's wasted anyway. Use sick days for doing something you like."

He worked in a trailer parked behind the elementary school teaching remedial reading in a state-mandated program, a couple of students at a time. No discipline issues was its best feature, he'd said, but the down side was there wasn't much hope, so I tried to give him a pass. I'll admit that having an absolute free day in mid-April without facing a late spring makeup day was exhilarating.

My second period senior history class was what I called Life Skills and the students—18 girls, 9 boys, like they'd been scheduled according to a recipe—called Dealing with Bullshit.

Mostly, we role-played: bankers, employers, landlords, school officials, and whoever else I thought they had to deal with. They weren't going to college, not one of them. But they needed to keep their heads above water in order to graduate, and the newspaper days got them talking and writing while maybe teaching them something that would help them cope. Once a week, they had to compose a letter to the editor reacting, with evidence, to one of the articles. They all needed to know what might make somebody listen.

They carried their papers home, and they were good about it because none of them wanted to do what the seniors in other history classes did—something called Problems of Democracy. POD—Pieces of Dung, the farm boys called it.

Now we had a dealing with bullshit example right in front of us. The bomb threat caller was probably someone they knew. The headline story ran down beside a picture of the building where they were sitting. Everybody wanted to role play our principal and the local police.

"We're famous," a girl said.

We didn't discuss any other stories. During the last minute, while they gathered their books, one of the pregnant girls said, "I wish there was a real bomb and my old boyfriend was the one person who didn't leave when he was told to."

"But then he'd be famous," her friend said as the bell rang, "and that would suck."

Monday, April 21ˢᵗ – *Iran Gives OK to Family Visit*
The principal held a faculty meeting at 7:30 a.m., all the teachers and staff crammed into the school's double-sized classroom for an early morning unpaid overtime. He sputtered outrage and guaranteed the hoaxer would be caught. He asked us to have "ears on the ground" for "scuttlebutt."

An hour later, as first period wound down, Wertz said, "Come on, bomber, do your thing."

I kept reading. Wertz didn't seem to notice. "He'll call soon," he said. "He's a student who can't wait to do it again. Count on it." As the bell rang, he sighed. "Maybe tomorrow then," he said.

Life Skills labored through the hostage crisis. The students unanimously voted for a full-scale invasion. "But it'll never happen because Carter's a pussy," one boy said. "My Dad hates him."

"Watch your mouth," a girl said. She was another of the eight mothers-to-be. Years before, I'd learned that early spring was pregnancy season for these seniors. Most girls would deliver late summer or early fall. It seemed as if they'd spent Christmas break in bed with boys who pledged their love daily in between looking at brochures for whichever branch of the Armed Forces they most wanted to join. Since late February, one by one, each of the pregnancies had been signaled in class by a girl crying "for no reason." None of them mentioned worrying about complications.

Wednesday, April 23rd – *Boston Marathon Investigates Possible Cheating*
When the class voted like a jury, every boy said Ruiz had cheated. Every girl but two voted "innocent."

Friday, April 25th – *Hostage Rescue Mission Fails—8 Killed*
Carter had given rescue a shot, but now there was disaster. "We left the bodies there," the Carter-hater said. "My father was in Korea. He said that's never supposed to happen. Not ever. He says Carter's a pussy."

Nobody told him to watch his mouth. "My father yells at Carter when he's on the news," said a girl who, as far as I knew, wasn't pregnant. "It's like Carter is my older brother, the way he swears at him."

The most visibly pregnant girl said, "My Mom says yelling is a good thing. It means you care. You should yell more, Mr. Arbus. When you never yell, it sounds like you've decided that we're worthless, that you'll let us do anything because you're out of caring."

For the first time since October, Wendy and I ate dinner on the back porch, but even though she'd wrapped herself in a sweatshirt half way through, a chill swept in from the west and drove us inside. In the kitchen, the shades pulled as if she needed privacy, she said, "Those pregnant girls of yours, the seniors. I bet some of them don't even go to a doctor until the last minute."

"It's possible," I said, "but they have mothers of their own, someone who sees to things."

"What about fathers?"

"At home? Some must."

"I meant the real fathers. Some might be sitting right there in front of you."

"Maybe."

"The selfish young pricks."

Monday, April 28th – *Is Economic Embargo Enough?*
Wertz posted a calendar for May and June. Eight weekdays near the end of May were already marked by an X and sets of initials. "You in?" he said. "Five bucks, winner-take-all."

Wertz ran a yearly pool for picking the day when Don Gaskins would use the last of his twelve sick and personal days. Gaskins had never failed to use them all, not once in the twelve years since he'd gotten tenure. With the most likely days x'd out, I chose the first Friday in June, my X, for now, the only one in that month. Wertz took my money. "Good luck with that," he said.

When the principal walked in to fill his coffee mug, Wertz pointed to the calendar. "You in?" he said, but the principal used the grimace he'd repeated a few times during his get-the-bomber speech.

The class wanted Carter to use bombs, not sanctions. Mostly, they wanted to talk about Terry Fox. They loved the story about him running across Canada after he'd lost a leg to cancer, but that headline was two weeks old now. On April 12th, he'd dipped his artificial leg into the Atlantic Ocean in Newfoundland to start his Marathon of Hope.

There was a map of North America that scrolled down across the front blackboard. On April 14th, a girl, pregnant but not yet showing, had stuck a small gold star on the edge of Newfoundland, and we'd started following Fox across Canada, planning to add a star every week until the end of the school year. Half the girls had written letters of support to the newspaper editor. Most of their evidence was based on experience with grandfathers who struggled with crippling diseases but didn't ever complain. "Next fall he'll be close," the star-placer had declared. "I have a sister who will be in this class. She can finish the stars." Three stars touched each other, some of the points overlapping, but it was way more hopeful than talking about hostages, inflation, or Carter's boycott of the summer Olympics.

The first time she was pregnant, Wendy bought a book about the Lamaze Method. She signed us up for a session at the community center, and sometimes, in the car, she would tell me to choke her thigh just above her knee. She would startle, then pant until I relaxed, watching the highway with one hand on the wheel before gripping her again, the interval a sign of urgency, contractions close together for imminence. She would close her eyes for the darkness of realism, riding tensed and blind in the passenger seat.

The miscarriage occurred three days before our official instruction meeting.

The second miscarriage happened even sooner. Wendy threw the Lamaze book away. Once, when I laid my hand on her thigh as I drove, she said, "Don't touch me. Don't you dare."

Wednesday, April 30th – *Terrorists Seize Iranian Embassy in London*
Before she opened her newspaper, a girl said, "How many terrorists are there?"

"I can't wait to join up and shoot as many as I can," a boy who was late said as he sat down in the back.

"This newspaper sucks," the girl said. "There should be a newspaper just for baby news so all of ours would be in the headlines instead of terrorists."

"The hospital sends the notices to the newspaper," I said. "Babies are local stories."

"Unless there's like four or five at a time," the boy said. "Or something happens to it like it's stolen or something."

"Yes," I said, "nobody wants their baby to have a headline."

Wendy was asleep at 3:45. I ordered pizza to be delivered. When she woke, she began to cry. "Your teenagers have normal babies without even paying attention. This is your eighth year. You must have taught a hundred like that by now."

"Their problems come after, and they last a lifetime."

"Miscarriage doesn't ever end, Jerry."

"That's not what I meant."

"Yes, you did. Like it's nothing more than a nuisance like a broken arm."

"This one isn't a miscarriage anymore. It's premature."

"Fuck you, Jerry Arbus. Seriously, fuck you for saying that."

"Sorry," I said, though I thought it would be something worse if it was stillborn, something even worse if it was damaged and lived. I knew the baby's chances by the week, the probabilities of timing. It was all about the lungs now, survival likely, but disabilities at 20%. Next week, would lower that to 10%. A month more to be ordinarily premature.

Thursday, May 1st – *Juliana, Queen of the Netherlands, Abdicates*
After the second bomb threat came in, Wertz cheered and hurried out, but twenty minutes went by before I slipped out a side door. Some students stood under the small roof outside, deciding whether or not it was a good idea to wait for the drizzle to stop. My walk home was mostly full of wishing it didn't begin to pour.

I made sure to call out when I opened the door. "Everybody knew it was a hoax, but we had to leave." I expected silence, a reminder of what I deserved for being an asshole.

Wendy said, "It's May" and left it to me to deal with guilt. She was nearly to odds-tipping, but still plenty of reason to tiptoe past surprises. The calendar was like Valium.

While she finished breakfast, I settled into a chair with the newspaper I'd been reading while Wertz muttered. "Come on, bomber."

Wendy gathered her dishes. She leaned over the sink and stared outside. "The first time was the happiest I've ever been," she said, "but the second time it was different. It wasn't joy, it was anxiety. And now it's fear."

Friday, May 2nd – *Tito Dies*

The newspaper used two paragraphs in "Regional" to summarize the bomb threat. "It's not news when it happens again, is it?" a boy said.

Before anyone else spoke, there was a fresh set of tears, this time from the girl who had moved to town just after Thanksgiving. The girls shared their empathy. Even the boys observed silence while the girls who had been consoled in March provided comfort, hugs and tears. The girl wailed that the father, though he knew she was Catholic, had offered abortion as the only solution.

Settled, the crying girl asked how old I was before I got married. When I said twenty-three, she said, "That sounds old. I thought I could finish high school before I had a baby, but I'd never make it all the way to twenty-three. I'd be forty when she was in high school. My mother's thirty-three."

The girl who had just hugged her said, "I bet you got married and she wasn't pregnant."

"That's right."

The crying girl said. "You two must have been really lucky."

"There's pills. And other choices, too, but they're the easiest."

"Aren't you afraid of hell?" she said, as if bringing up birth control had never crossed her mind after she'd already broken one taboo.

There was nowhere to go except into controversy. When a girl who had yet to cry in class waved her hand, I called on her. "I heard there's a McDonald's coming to town," she said. "It would be fun working there. I love how McDonald's smells, don't you?"

"Yes, I do," I said, and everybody laughed.

"Who's Tito?" a boy said just before the bell.

After school, in front of all the teachers and staff, the principal announced, "The authorities believe they have a way to catch whoever it is. If there is another bomb threat, we'll put an end to his fun. And there will be no mitigating circumstances that will affect appropriate punishment."

Wertz poked me as we walked out of the building. "You know what mitigating circumstances are? They're what puts people in front of me in the trailer."

I kept walking.

"You know what I'm talking about," he said. "You have seniors. They never learn to read because they've been too busy fucking."

"We have a doctor's appointment," Wendy said the moment I got home. "In case you forgot," she added, her tone still brimming with accusation.

"Another girl confessed today," I said. "She only moved here at the end of November. She's knocked up and strict Catholic. I felt like a priest."

Wendy made a face that reminded me of the principal's. "You're no priest. You think you know those girls because they tell personal stories, but they only give bits of themselves away so the rest can stay secret."

"That sounds like what everybody does," I said.

"Does it? Then it's working."

Monday, May 5th – *Siege at Iranian Embassy Ends*

I scrolled the map down, and the new girl added a star. Everybody clapped, but the four stars had formed a solid line that was farther across Canada than Terry Fox. The girl who loved McDonald's said, "Canada is so big. This will take him forever."

"We saw you," the girl beside her said. "My mom and me at the doctor's on Friday. Your wife's pregnant, too." The class clapped, even the boys. That girl had entered the waiting room as we were leaving. She'd smiled and stared at Wendy, and now everyone in Life Skills knew I was going to be a father, and none of them thought anything could possibly go wrong. "How come you didn't tell us?"

"We haven't told anybody."

"For what? Five months?"

"Six and a half, closer to seven now."

Everyone was doing the math. I could hear them thinking "Thanksgiving."

"What names you pick out? Mine's either Tammy or Tommy. Isn't it weird how one letter makes somebody so different?"

"We have a pretty long list yet, from Anais to Zach."

"One for every letter. For real? No wonder you're a teacher."

"My Grand Ma's in the paper," another girl blurted. "She died. There's a thing all about her because she moved to the city when I was little."

The obituary said the woman had worked at the Jello factory until it had closed. "They made Jello here," the girl said, looking at the new girl. "We used to be famous. My Grand Ma worked at the Jello her whole life. My mother grew up believing that's what she would do, too." The girl became animated, the class quiet. "Imagine that," she said, "being a little girl and already knowing what you wanted to do. It was like living in a town where Willy Wonka had his candy factory, and then it wasn't. She quit school when she got pregnant. They wouldn't let you go to class once you started showing back then, so I'll be the first girl in my family to finish high school."

She looked at me. "Another month to sit here, right?" she said. "Hardly any time at all."

"Yes," I said, "but we need to talk about something besides babies." When she didn't speak, I watched her expression shift to what I thought was contempt.

"Your students ever mention they get the Sunday paper at home?" Wendy said. She kept the Sunday edition on the kitchen table until mid-week, when she finally finished every section. "Those girls would see this then," she said. "It might make them think. Take a look."

"*Lactaria* means places of milk," the article began, "the Roman columns, once, where babies were brought by mothers, sometimes for the milk of a wet nurse, but more often, abandoned. The mothers had to trust pity's power. Its time may have come again. After a newborn was discovered in a city park, surviving one night's exposure to a late March freeze, a local church has offered itself as a modern-day "place of milk.""

When I looked up from the paper, Wendy said, "That church should be on the front page."

Tuesday, May 6th – *Kitty Hawk ready for Flight across the Continent*

We were going to study a lease, what all that legalese might mean when the landlord didn't fix things or raised the rent or didn't want to renew you as a tenant. We were five minutes into trying to understand any of it when the new girl walked in crying. "What?" three girls said at once.

The girl didn't look up. She folded her arms on her desk and laid her head on them. "I lost my baby," she murmured. The girls surrounded her. The boys watched, as paralyzed as I was. I wondered if a few of them might envy whoever had escaped being a father. None of the girls seemed anything but sad.

When, one by one, the girls returned to their seats, a boy said, "Sometimes that happens because the baby isn't made right."

"That's a terrible thing to say," a girl said, but he didn't let it go.

"It could mean the baby was going to be crippled or retarded."

All of the girls looked so outraged, I thought a few of them would rush at him. "Or worse," I said.

"What's worse?" two girls said.

"Missing something the baby needs to live after it's born."

"Like a fish out of water?" another girl said.

"Yes."

"You're always so calm, even about something like this that's so terrible," she said. "What's wrong with you?"

Doubt swelled up in my throat like phlegm I couldn't swallow or cough loose. I had no faith. It was a secret I needed to keep from them. Wendy already knew.

Wednesday, May 7th – *Tito to be Buried*

Five minutes into first period, the Principal stepped into the lounge. Without looking at Wertz, he asked me to fill in for Don Gaskins. "Don has a family emergency," he said. "He's half way out the door already."

Wertz gave me a thumbs-up and mouthed, "You lose." There were nearly four weeks left, and Gaskins' real emergency had just slimmed my odds to a million to one.

"Get them settled and keep them occupied," the principal said as he stopped ten feet short of the open door of Gaskins' room. Noise flooded the hall.

I imagined the principal standing outside the door to listen, comparing me to Gaskins. The class was 8th grade social studies. Four years from now, the survivors would be in Life Skills. "Let's talk about bomb threats," I began. Ten hands went up. "One at a time," I said. If the principal was listening, maybe he wouldn't leave as soon as the class volume lowered. Maybe he'd hope to overhear a clue from a room full of the sort of students he expected to make prank calls. I chose a boy who looked big enough to threaten me. When he started to speak, everyone shut up.

The Life Skills class wanted to talk about Mt. St. Helens, the volcano that was showing signs of erupting. They liked Harry Truman, the old man who refused to evacuate.

"He sounds like my PopPop," a boy said.

"That's so sweet you still call him that," the Jello girl said. "I know what you mean. It's cute when he says, 'If the mountain goes, I'm going with it, but the mountain ain't gonna hurt me.'"

"Harry Truman should be President," the boy beside him said.

"Harry Truman is stupid," the new girl said, and the room filled with groans. "He thinks he knows more than anyone else. He sounds like a teacher."

"He wants to die." A boy who never talked interrupted without raising his hand. "He doesn't want to move and be like a hostage stuck in some place where nobody thinks like he does."

The class went quiet. "You're so smart," the Jello girl said. "Why are you in this class?"

Friday, May 9th – *Smallpox Eradicated*

Even my great-grandmother couldn't get smallpox when she was a kid," a girl said. "It's been gone since forever. What took so long?"

Nobody cared about smallpox. It was one problem they weren't going to have. They found a quote from Harry Truman to write on the side blackboard that nobody ever used. "That mountain's part of Truman and Truman's part of that mountain."

"Current events are interesting now," the girl at the board said. "People like feelings way more than science."

"Write your letter to Truman this week, if you want," I said. She clapped, but the rest of the class was still.

"Writing's writing no matter who you do it for," a boy said.

Monday, May 12th – *Slasher Films Concern Experts*

Wertz started to peel the calendar off the wall. "Sheila Kelly already won the Gaskins pool," Wertz said. "He used up his last two days. He was bitching about being docked when he ran over on the third day, so it's official."

"I guess I came in last," I said.

"She missed by eight days," Wertz said. "I talked her into playing, and she picked the earliest day left in May to be a good sport."

The drive-in had opened for the summer over the weekend. Half the class had seen *Friday, the 13th* there on Saturday. The rest seemed jealous. A girl turned to *Reviews* and began to read: *"Friday, the 13th* is low budget in the worst sense. Another teenager-in-jeopardy entry with six would-be counselors progressively dispatched by knife, hatchet, spear and arrow without building a modicum of tension in between."

"Modicum," a boy said. "Is that even a word?"

"That guy's wrong," another boy said. "You'll see. It will be famous."

"My Dad says movies like this have it right," the McDonald's girl said. "It's a metaphor. You have sex, you get pregnant, your life is over."

Wendy said. "Emergency is behind us."

I'd agreed to be in the delivery room for both miscarried babies, but this time I'd said, "When it's safe." Twenty-eight weeks didn't sound safe. It sounded like special needs. "Thirty weeks," I said. "I'll be ok with it then."

"What's that mean? There's an expiration date for fear?"

"Something like waiting to see if you're going into remission," I said.

"What kind of thing is that to say?"

"It's an analogy."

"I know what the fuck it is," Wendy said.

Both of us, then, were quiet. "Ok," I said at last. "I'm sorry," but she didn't even look at me.

Tuesday, May 13th – *Kitty Hawk Balloon Completes Crossing*

By noon, word had spread that two boys had been caught while calling in another bomb threat. They were using the pay phone in the school lobby.

Wednesday, May 14th – *Love Canal Pollution Sounds Alarm for Nation*

"We need smarter bombers," Wertz said. "There are a couple of pay phones in town. Different pay phones for each call, and we'd be home again."

The bomb threat story was two paragraphs in the local section. No names were mentioned, but everyone already knew the callers' identities. One was a smart boy who'd gotten into drugs. Everybody said "drugs" in a way that told me that it wasn't marijuana, something they found amusing and exciting. The other boy, the students said, had been held back a year and lived in a trailer.

"What's going to happen to them?" somebody asked. "Jail, right?"

Which started ten minutes of discussing what they deserved.

Wendy unpacked all the baby stuff we'd gotten the first time. I'd told everybody during her second month the first time. The gifts had begun to arrive. I'd learned to keep my mouth shut. Even starting twenty-nine weeks, neither of us had said a word. Wendy had barely showed until May. She'd stayed in since then. Our parents lived hundreds of miles away. Now, watching her arrange things, I thought she might be jinxing this.

"Bringing all this out means the baby is safe now."

"You're all superstition," I said. "Your doctor doesn't cast spells and make you swallow potions."

"No. She gives me comfort and confidence. Think on that."

"We can start the Lamaze again then."

"No," she said. "Never." She rearranged a pile of tiny clothes. "Anyway, I remember all that. I don't need you grabbing at me."

May 16th – *Miss South Carolina Crowned Miss USA*

Everyone knew that the trailer-boy had been expelled and the drug-addled boy was going to receive home schooling once his ten-day suspension expired. "How does that work?" somebody asked. "He gets a prize? Ten days of no school and then private lessons?"

"Because he's fifteen until school ends, they have to teach him."

"So, if any of us called in a threat, they'd kick us out for good?"

"Yes. And maybe prosecute."

"What if you hurt somebody? You know. And you were fifteen. What then?"

"That's different," I said, though I didn't know for sure about the school was required to do. When no one spoke, I added, "It's complicated."

"Exactly. Complicated."

I looked from face to face, waiting for somebody to break in. "Yes," I said at last.

"Another Brick in the Wall," a boy said, and three students said "Exactly" in near unison.

"We should role play a trial," the girl said. "You be the judge who asks all the questions. Half of us could be the jury because anybody can be on a jury. The other half could be witnesses and defendants because anybody can have things happen to them."

"Life Skills."

"Dealing with Bullshit."

"We're almost there," I said that night. Wendy hadn't spoken to me with more than phrases and looks for days, and not now either. "When it will be ok. When it won't have problems."

Wendy turned away, but she finally spoke. "Jerry, full-term babies can have problems too. All you are is wishes."

"There's no such thing as wishing too hard."

"You can't ever be happy always asking for more. It's like you're preparing for regret and grief instead of the future."

"That's what wishing's for."

She turned. "Put your hand on me," she said. "You haven't touched me for weeks."

The baby moved as I laid my hand on her. "Are you wishing?" Wendy said, "or are you feeling?"

"Both."

"Do not look away when the time comes," she said. "Don't you dare."

She kept my hand on her. "Yes," I said. "Yes, to everything." Like a litany. An absolution. Sincere.

Monday, May 19th – *Eruption Blots Out Sun, 7 Killed*

"Harry Truman will be a fossil," a boy said. "Ten thousand years from now somebody will dig him up and put him in a museum."

Everybody talked nearly at once for a few minutes before I quieted them down long enough for that boy to break back in. "Wouldn't that be the best way to die? All at once? He was old, so why not die like that and be preserved instead of rotting away?"

"Like those people who die on Mount Everest," the boy beside him said. "They freeze and stay themselves forever."

"Not exactly," I said.

"But almost, right? Enough to stay looking like somebody instead of a box of bones in a hole."

Wednesday, May 21st – *710 families evacuated from Love Canal*

"I already knew that," a girl said. "My aunt lives there with her three kids. One of them is really sick and she's only seven."

The new girl kept her newspaper closed, but half way through class she raised her hand. "My father said he was happy my baby died. He said that out loud."

Friday, May 23rd – *First Woman Graduates from US Service Academy*

"I miss the bombers," Wertz said.

"You could call," I said. "You have first period free. Nobody knows whether you're in that trailer or not."

"You think that's funny?"

"Not at all."

"That's right—not at all."

"Just don't waste that call if I'm out sick that day. Check here first thing."

"Fuck you," Wertz said. "You and your knocked-up harem, too."

Monday, May 26th – *Pac-Man Fascinates America*

"We made it," Wendy said. "We're starting the thirty-first week. I want to go out. I want to be seen. I can walk ten minutes. It's Memorial Day. People are out. Just a few blocks up and back." She wore a blouse that displayed her roundness. She'd thrown away her maternity clothes after the second miscarriage. "Never again," she'd said. "The hell with anticipation. I hadn't argued. Six blocks, we walked. Slowly. Nearly to the school. Then she sat on a wall someone who lived on a corner had built, I thought, because students kept cutting through the front yard. "I'll wait until you come around with the car."

Wednesday, May 28th – *South Korea ends People's Uprising; 2,000 Killed*

Because of the holiday, the papers were a day old, but nobody seemed to notice.

Friday, May 30th – *New Fossils Age Life a Billion Years*

A girl pointed out that the headline couldn't be correct because the earth was only 6,000 years old. I counted six others nodding. "We should talk about something else," I said.

"Yeah, Bible talk is stupid," said a boy who hadn't nodded.

"It helps us when things go wrong," the girl said. "How else do you deal with bad stuff? You know, take care of yourself when it happens."

"You can't," the boy said.

"Two more weeks and I'm never going to read another newspaper, not ever."

"There's a new tv channel that's going on the air on Sunday," I said. "CNN. Twenty-four a day news."

"Like this class, only it never ends? That's like hell."

The secretary knocked on the door. She said, "Mr. Arbus, your wife called. She says to come home at once."

"Home? She said that? Are you sure?"

The girls began to clap. Then the boys. All of them closed their newspapers as if class was over.

"I'll watch them until the sub gets here," the secretary said. "You've barely got started here."

By the time I was outside, the class had crowded the open, upstairs windows. They were cheering. I began to run.

Wendy was ready and calm. "You look so relaxed," I said.

"We're close enough to normal." I hesitated. "Just say yes," she said.

"Yes."

Before I could go on, she said, "Now stop. Be quiet." I kept my lips together. "That's it," she said. "Now say it three times like all those magic spells that work.'

After the Great War, the Future is Furious

Peace
All of the fathers but the boy's have souvenirs from the war--helmets, guns, a bayonet etched, sometimes, in German, Italian, or the strange, unknowable Japanese.

One father has shrapnel in his back. One flings a quick, open hand for failures. One shakes with what the boy's mother calls "the palsy," keeping bottles in his garage and car. All of them carry cigarettes in their hands and depend upon blasphemy for speech.

Though the boy often dreams of them, their apartment has none of those things. Not whiskey. not even the cigarettes and curses. Year by year, his father stays silent, vanished beneath a distant, sealed door.

Because their fathers say *never*, the boys who live nearby point those foreign guns at each other. Because whoever had fired them is dead, they tumble, quiver, and lie still. Because the boy has no weapon except stealth, he becomes a traitor they execute.

Summoned
One afternoon, summer arriving, the boy is lost in the public pool locker room, old enough to know his mother is not searching by methodically counting down the lockers, eliminating one row after another to find him. He is embarrassed, not terrified, not yet, except of admitting helplessness to half-dressed or naked men, their bodies so impossibly hairy or fat that the boy, smooth and skinny, could never belong to them.

The boy's wet suit clings clammy as fever flesh. His mother, who loves to swim, had changed elsewhere before talking his face into the water and lifting his legs into the miracle of floating. When she let go, he had panicked into splash and flounder.

Now, by loudspeaker, the boy hears himself summoned, his name and age repeated just before a voice says, "Your mother is waiting for you outside the door through the blue and yellow wall."

The nearest naked man says, "That you, son?" but the boy shakes his head as if he can't be lost. As if there are other boys alone among the rows of lockers who need to find their way by colors. Head down, the boy studies the floor as he walks away from where his mother waits. He turns into a vacant row of lockers and begins to count. Before long, he is somewhere else, someone not almost seven and helpless while strangers examine him, amused by the happy end of a mother's terror. When he reaches sixty, the boy walks toward the door along the puddled corridor near the open showers where men are busy with their bodies, the rush of spray smothering their hearing as he passes by like a boy who, unashamed, is about to peel off his suit and stand naked among them.

Maze
The boy's school is noise and nuns, as simple as a sidewalk broken by numbered streets, but Mass is an unsolvable labyrinth of soloed Latin. Every day, after school, he creates a maze, each, he tells his mother, a new version of purgatory. When he completes it, he asks her to escape without lifting her pencil.

They live alone, the studio apartment small enough to memorize, the corridors on each floor straight and right-angled, a toddler's puzzle. When his mother struggles, retracing, he imagines her prayer. When she exits, he believes she has managed penance. Always, he times her.

One evening, his mother, the pencil still pressed to the paper, declares there is no solution. Mute, he taps his watch. The apartment is cluttered with hesitation and sighs. When she retraces again, the line thickens until it fills each alley, until it's hell.

Overnight
"You've been here before," the boy's grandmother says, "when your Mommy was carrying you." When he asks where his mother has gone, leaving him behind for his first overnight, his grandmother says, "To the land of privacy."

"There's no such place," the boy says, but his grandmother presses a finger to his lips, nudging him through a bedroom door with her other hand.

"Your Daddy took a nap here right before he left for the war," she says. "Your Mommy woke him when the time came, and then he was gone."

Just like that, the boy thinks, but his grandmother doesn't stop. "Ever since, I've kept it just the same as your Mommy made it back up that early morning. Never washed a thing, the same sheets and pillowcase waiting for him." She takes a breath and pats his head. "Now," she says. "You."

The boy locks the door. He sleeps on the floor. In the morning, before it is fully light, he wakes and unlocks the door to leave for the bathroom down the hall. When he returns, his grandmother is in the bedroom. She says, "My, first thing, without asking, you made the bed as perfect as she did that day. Your Mommy has taught you well."

When his mother returns, she hugs his grandmother and hurries him to the car. After she asks how the night went, he tells her he was afraid. "That's natural," she says. "You're seven. It's something new, and now you'll be fine."

"I locked the door," he says, and his mother smiles.

"Privacy already?" she says. "You're so smart for your age, but I'll tell Grandma about that and next time you won't have to."

"I slept on the floor."

He feels the car speed up as if they have to hurry. A green sign says that within the next six miles there are exits to three towns, two with long names he doesn't know how to pronounce. "What did Grandma say to you?" his mother says.

"This is your Daddy's bed."

"You already knew that."

The boy rubs his thumbs against his fingers. "She said it's never been touched."

"Since then?"

He turns his thumbs so the nails are scratching him. "These are his sheets," the boy says. "This is his pillowcase."

"She said 'is'?"

"Yes," he says. He wants to ask which exit will take them to the land of privacy. He presses as hard as he can, but he can't make himself bleed.

During the Epidemic

The boy brings a dime every Friday to slide into a slot inside a card featuring a smiling girl on crutches. He loves seeing his card fill up. When there are ten dimes, he starts again on a card with a crippled boy. Sister Rose, his third-grade teacher, keeps everyone's cards inside her desk. "You wash your hands, all of you," she says, after the class slots their dimes. "There's no telling who handled those coins. How filthy he was and what you could catch."

Every day, just after lunch, Sister Rose inspects their desks. They need to be clean. No crumbs inside or out, spotless before they have public health, which is, Sister Rose says, a lifesaving class. The contagious, she explains, leave filth that hides on buses and streetcars and seats at the movies. You'll never know who's been there and given you the itch and fester. The contagious never cover their mouths when they sneeze. They wipe their noses on their sleeves where crusts collect like scabs that bleed. They borrow combs and touch fountains with their mouths."

When the boy raises his hand and asks a question, she talks as if he's told her time is up. "You won't know who they are until they carry that filth to you like flies. Look around. You'll see what I mean. Eyes open, class. Keep yourselves clean. Filth is a welcome mat for polio."

When June is close, she says, "Polio" at the end of her speech, snarling it like a curse. She takes a deep breath before she says, "Polio doesn't go away like chicken pox or the measles. You wear braces and use crutches like poor Richard Hartman, who's missed so much school he'll fall a year behind." As always, when everybody looks at Richard Hartman's empty desk, the boy touches his desktop as if filth has returned while he listened.

"Look at this photograph," Sister Rose says on the last day of school, walking up and down the aisles so everyone can see. "Those children are stuck forever in iron lungs. Those children will never do anything but lie inside them so they can breathe." She pauses by Richard Hartman's empty desk and says, "One last time, remember to keep clean."

All summer, the boy washes his hands before lunch and dinner. He cleans his crumbs off the table before his mother sees them. He floats inside an inner tube in the county park lake, careful not to drift where the water would be over his head. Jerry Mushik, who sat beside him all year, splashes and swallows the water as if the contagious never peed there. He says Sister Rose isn't their teacher anymore, but she'll have Richard Hartman again next year and have to shut up about polio every day he isn't absent.

In September, Richard Hartman, wearing leg braces and using crutches, is still with the boy's class. Miss Gardiner, who is younger than his mother, never checks their desks after lunch, but she has new March of Dimes cards for each of them, even Richard Hartman. "The dimes aren't going to help that boy," his mother says. "It's too late for that."

Jerry Mushik laughs when the boy washes his hands after he inserts his first dime. Mushik puts his on his tongue and closes his mouth. "Fuck polio," he whispers. For the next three weeks, Mushik licks his dime. In October, in the cloak room before school, Mushik forces two third-grade boys to lick their dimes, and neither of them get sick.

Boxing

The boy's mother notices that a heavy bag has been hung from a basement beam. "Someone I know would want you to do this," she says, after she buys the boy boxing gloves and has him watch the Friday night fights with her on their tiny television. "See?" she says, but when he touches that bag with the gloves, he inhales as if sinking in sand.

"On your toes," his mother says. "The future is furious, a full-time thug. It wants more than you have, so you must learn to juke and shuffle."

When he hesitates, his mother talks like she's broadcasting. "Jab," she says. "Discover weakness. Uppercut, body blows, the hook from your left instead of the right you too much rely on. With or without brains, tomorrow is a brute."

Nothing is more serious than the speed bag she hangs in their studio. "Again," she says. "Now." His shoes skid where his father's absence lies slick and oily on the floor. In every corner are the things unused for years—vow and promise, faith and joy—each tangled among his father's pre-war clothes.

Fear loiters near the locked door, its glowing cigarette a clock. She tells him to breathe as he shadow-boxes. "Listen," she says, "that voice you will hear is the undefeated singing."

Rehearsals

Early in the first summer of the Salk vaccine, the boy lives with his aunt in New Jersey for a week. It will be summer camp, but free and without the strangers, his mother explains, pointing out the nearby forest and lake, pressing him toward a cousin his age he's met twice before.

His cousin loves chess. "I'll teach you," he says. He squeals and laughs when he tells the boy to tip his king after every game. When they walk in the forest, they follow a path. Whether they enter the woods or not, his aunt, each night, examines them for ticks. After his cousin tells his mother the boy left the path, finding his own way to a creek and an abandoned cabin, they never walk there again. For the week, they share not one embedded tick.

Though neither of them can swim, they go to the lake daily. The water turns their bodies brown. "Like rust," his aunt says. "It washes off." Both of them keep their heads above water. Their lips sealed.

On the last late afternoon, firemen arrive at the lake. With a bullhorn and uniforms, they order everyone out of the water. His aunt says, "They're going to drag the lake," and he watches two of them sling and lower a grappling hook while a man who looks older than his grandfather nudges the boat into tight loops with his oars.

A monthly exercise, only practice, his aunt says, but even with the sun still shining, he and his cousin shiver, dry inside their towels, but a chill clinging to their groins. At last, the firemen bring up a body, its arms and legs limp, lake water pouring, then dripping as they reach to embrace it, securing the dead to applause from the shore.

What ends that week is a bus ride from New Jersey to Pittsburgh, his aunt placing him in the front window seat, closing her goodbye with "Stay put and be quiet." A sailor, moments later, settles next to him with a quintet of comic books, all of them featuring miracles and war. The boy wishes he could tell him the story about floating above the make-believe dead.

One by one, as he finishes them, the sailor hands those battles for countries and planets to the boy. Someone dies violently in every story. When the boy finishes each story, he pages backward to examine the bodies.

At Howard Johnson's, near Harrisburg, the sailor buys the boy potato chips and a Mound's Bar, escorts him to the men's room where nothing happens, that episode so ordinary, the boy doesn't mention it in Pittsburgh.

His mother says how proud she is, how he looks bigger after a week away, healthier, too. They wait for his suitcase to be extracted from beneath the bus. He opens it to prove he's lost nothing she has trusted him with.

"I have a surprise," his mother says. When she parks in front of a row house double, she says, "One side is ours. All your things are already inside."

She guides him through five open doors until she nods at the one that is closed. Inside is a bed and a chest of drawers that fill half the space. "You need your own room," she says, but he shakes his head and backs away. "What?" she says. "All of our furniture is used."

"It's Dad's," the boy says, and there is nothing she can say that convinces him it is not, that she would never do that to him. What she does is drive him fifty miles to see that the bed is still exactly where his father left it, his grandmother saying, "Yes. Yes, it is," like a defendant before his mother drives him back to the bed that is his own.

Tomorrow is his next shot in the Salk sequence, sixteen days until his birthday. Double digits, his mother says, as if it is a difficult milestone, something achieved, with practice, like a column of report card As, something like surviving serious wounds.

Them! . . . and . . . Tarantula!

"Remember this!" his mother says. Across from the Homestead Theater, the sidewalk swarms with strikers buzzing *hell* and *damn* while she buys their way inside where huge ants, within minutes, are screaming at flame throwers, working their claws as they burn. "The End" signals they have entered an hour late, but in minutes, a huge spider stalks the screaming until it, too, is fire-bombed, this time from a jet.

The previews promise two comedies, double westerns, paired romances. When the ants return, his mother mutters, "We know what happens to Them," and tugs the boy to the door beside the screen. Over his head, a woman ten times his size stands hypnotized by a set of enormous eyes. His mother, when he turns, is waving from the lobby.

Outside, at twilight, the strike-closed mill has turned as radioactive as a test-site emptied by the bomb. Lifting their signs, the men spread into traffic. "Them!" his mother says, as if steelworkers were giants, as if an army would soon destroy them all.

The Nuclear Age
On television, the Head Groundsman at Stonehenge trims the lawn with a push mower like the men in the row houses use on their small patches of grass. He rolls up the sleeves of his white Oxford, a shirt like the one the boy wears only on Sundays, freshly washed, starched and ironed. His mother says the Groundsman is making the grass perfect for the tourists who will arrive for solstice.

A month ago, a man who lived across the street had died. Yesterday, the boy's mother had shown him the push mower in the dead man's garage and told him to mow what was becoming a tiny meadow of dandelion, thistle, goldenrod, and milkweed.

Later, when the boy walked the mower into the dead man's garage, his mother had reminded him to store it exactly where he'd found it. "Sweep up after yourself," she said. "Make it look like it hasn't been used."

At Stonehenge, the Head Groundsman says he loves his ancient church. He trims the base of the miraculous construction, meticulous in each shadow. When the crowds arrive, nothing will be out of place.

By now, the boy believes the Bible is only a book of stories. Church is a chore he does poorly. Everything will outlive me is what he never says to the priest.

The next Sunday evening, the boy reads about the villages abandoned in the Soviet Union, the ones whose names have been erased from maps. He knows the villagers are dead or dying in places as mysterious as radiation or ancient relics. By now, the tourists have finished listening for ghosts, leaving behind a clean, well-tended cathedral.

Smart-Alecks

Sister Miriam's desk is in the back of the room so she can keep an eye out. In her black dress, she walks an aisle from back to front, then loops around the row of desks by the blackboard and comes down another aisle. "A good shaking is what some of you need," she says as she walks. She means all of the fifth-grade boys. She uses the shoulder grab and the arm squeeze, the wrist tug and the hand clenched on the backs of their necks. She never touches a girl, but she has a grip for every sort of shake to settle boys down.

Outside, during recess, the boy laughs when Ronnie Tomlin says they should shake the shit out of each other. One boy grabs another and shakes while the girls stare. The boy twists the chains on one of the six playground swings and lifts his feet, spinning like crazy. When a girl says she wants to try, he twists the chains for her and she squeals as she spins.

The next morning, Sister Miriam shows the class pictures of the asylum seats a doctor once built to shake some sense into lunatics. Not so long ago, she says, those chairs hung from hospital ceilings. They shook out the madness. They spun the insane for hours to lessen the blood to the brain.

At recess, an hour later, the boy and five others sit on the swings, twisting their steel chains around and around and tight until somebody shoves, and they scream and spin and thrash like crazy.

"Smart-alecks," Sister Miriam says, when they come back to class. "Know-it-alls," standing so close the boy can feel her breath on the back of his head when she shakes him and the other boys one by one while they sit in their hard-backed seats screwed into the floor. "Do you feel good sense getting into those crazy brains of yours?" she says, standing beside her desk, and all of the boys, facing forward, nod because none of them, they all knew, was crazy.

That night, the boy's mother says Angie Bechtold's mother is on the news. "Ruby Bechtold was a funny one," his mother says. "She had her own ways of doing things."

Angie Bechtold is absent in the morning. The class listens while Sister Miriam tells them to be considerate when Angie returns. Mary Russo raises her hand and asks, "What's *considerate* mean?"

"That's when you act extra nice to somebody because a person she loves has died."

The day Angie returns to school Ronnie Tomlin spins on the swings but doesn't yell anything. Everyone waits for a turn to spin, even Angie. They are all considerate, everybody quiet while they spin and spin.

Marking the Solstice

Because the boy was born the day after his mother's birthday, each year she waits to celebrate with him. Because he was born in the morning and she had been born at night, she says they would have been born the same day in another country. "See?" she says, showing him a map of the world in hours, but he shakes his head. "Never mind," she says, and asks him outside, near noon, to wait for the moment she tells him the sun will pause before its annual slow decline.

Like that sun, everything is crawling toward ice, she says. What will kill her has already begun in her chest, first medicines in the purse that clings to her each time she leaves the house. This June, still twelve years before her death, she hesitates, like the summer sun, in what neither of them knows will be the middle of his time with her, holding her wrist up and squinting at her watch until she says "There, exactly."

Buddy System

A week after his birthday, beside someone named Len he barely knows, the boy drowns himself in the church camp lake, both of them watching each other for panic or surrender while they stand where their heads nearly crown the surface.

No one notices them resurface, but Len is the first to grasp the dock and pull himself up, holding on while the boy counts to eleven before he surfaces.

Neither of them can swim. Carefully, hand over hand along the dock's slippery railroad ties, they had crept to where a white 6 is painted on the highest tie. A flurry of boys who swim had ignored them while they held hands and let go, sinking until they had stood one step from safety.

Now, neither looks at the other as they work back to the white 4 where an orange-beaded rope stretches to the opposite dock. The lake follows them, shy and silent, to their cabin where it puddles outside, waiting to trail them to dinner, lapping at their feet while they swallow meatloaf and baked beans, drink the sweet, metallic orangeade.

Later, outdoors for a sermon surrounded by evening hymns, the lake ripples between them while they lip-sync. When its waves dampen their shoes, they inch closer together, their knees touching. The boys on either side of them sing each verse of every hymn in a falsetto near helium-squeak that sounds trapped as a damaged soul.

After lights out, the lake deepens by their beds. In the dark, it soaks their sheets with stories that begins, "Underwater, the seconds stretch into a scream." Its spray shimmers where thin moonlight seeps through a small, sealed window, its voice now hoarse, then going so thick the words reach them like tongues seeking their bodies to be sure they are not alone.

Two days later, when his mother drives him home, she asks whether he has finally learned to swim, and the boy says, "Yes."

The Scientific Method

In July, its leash twisted by an hour of pacing, a neighbor's beagle leaps off his half of the porch and hangs itself. In August, a sixth-grade classmate, swimming alone, slips under the murky surface of a strip mine pool. In September, the boy is starting junior high in a public school, everybody in his home room a stranger.

Before long, Sputnik says he might soon be a Communist. Before long, the Asian Flu half-empties his classes. By November, the Soviets are listening to Laika, their space dog, until she smothers into silence, circling the earth until she plummets into re-entry's furnace.

That week, the boy crawls into his mother's closet and sits among dresses stacked for charity. With the thinnest negligee, he seals the space where light creeps in and waits for what the air will teach him. For an orbit's ninety minutes, he rides weightless in that capsule.

When he re-opens the door and stands, he sees the speed bag is lying behind a blanket on the closet shelf, but he does not touch it. Downstairs, his mother is still ironing. The radio plays Johnny Mathis followed by Frank Sinatra, both melodies so familiar the boy mouths the words as he descends to earth.

In early December, Chuck Kress, who lives in the double next door, pledges to count only to ninety before he opens the door to the freezer left behind in a nearby empty house. As soon as the boy shuts himself inside, back curled and knees puled tight in a space more suitable for a dog, he starts his own count, concentrating on that metronome for breath.

His heart thrums in his ears, graphing itself against darkness like the strikes of an EKG. He presses one hand between his legs, holding fear, refusing to touch anything but himself while he calculates the mathematics of air. He has reached one hundred and twenty-two when the face of Chuck Kress explains who he has become.

When the boy says he'd counted way past ninety, Chuck Kress says he counted like a launch commander, a man with the job of watching a clock, no longer considering the astronaut who, after all, was only a passenger. The boy slides the shelves back into place as if they are the covers over unmarked wells, ending the experimental age, which he knows wasn't science at all, just the anecdotal evidence of fantasy's tiny risk and the chatter of his senses.

Laugh Track
Once a month, the nearby fire station tests the siren that will signal the world's end. Some nights, in intervals the boy cannot anticipate, the television pauses to high-pitch buzz "seek shelter." Each time, the boy waits for the voice that will say, "This is not a test." His mother sighs and pats his knee. In black and white, the comedies reappear to blink through the snow on the old Dumont's small screen while his mother, even though the boy never speaks, says, "Shhhh." Whatever is funny is sealed behind her lips, not to be opened until the commercials come on.

This year there are programs where each exchange is hilarious, laughter from the audience rising and falling almost as often as breath. It sounds like people his mother talks to after church, the chuckles of men in suits, the titters of women who wear dresses and stockings to shop for butter and milk.

His mother laughs along. She has company now, but he keeps his mouth shut because there is never the laughter of somebody who is twelve. "These shows are funnier now," his mother says. The boy gets so used to the laughter that he can hear their neighbors, too. In their living rooms, there were people like his mother in shorts and t-shirts, dresses and skirts, underwear and robes, who agree about what words and actions are hilarious. Though what he wants to know is what makes all of those people scream.

The Day of the Triffids

The boy turns thirteen, summer stuffed with science fiction movies and books, the unpaved road below the house split along the shoulder, guard-rails slumping level with the gravel. Nearby, a dump deepens with tires and trash, appliances, mattresses. Beyond it, the state game land is a place, when entered, to gather fear like berries. When leaves smother the sky, he is underwater; when branches snap, the played-out mines are graves, his mother's "Never alone in there" insistent as a fire alarm.

In July, he is in love with the Triffids, the alien trees that advance like guerillas after the world goes blind from watching a meteor shower. The forest becomes malignant. The Triffids flourish in the Earth's soil and have an appetite for all those sightless humans. He has watched it twice.

The paths he follows in the game lands are half-eaten by locust and sumac. Just outside of their boundaries, mine entrances are labeled like poisons; a thin canal carries runoff to dunes of silt.

On screen, the Triffids are so easily killed by salt water, they might have arrived from West Oz. The world is saved. Every tree in the woods is rooted or dead. But when August begins, the boy reads the novel, where nothing in the final scenes ends those aliens, even on the last page.

One late afternoon, among a thick stand of pine trees, the boy finds a striped shirt and black socks soaked and faintly rotten as if they have wintered there. The shirt hangs so small in his hands, that whoever had worn it begins to scream. The boy listens hard for heavy steps. He checks the trees for movement.

Although nothing happens except fantasy following him home, he picks up a heavy branch and carries it toward the road, clutching it like bravery. In his room, the novel still lying beside his bed, the boy closes his eyes and sits in his wooden chair that strangers have cut and shaped and fitted into something so common that one would always surround him. He keeps his eyes pressed tightly shut until he cries.

Good Things

Raunchy is a word the boy doesn't recognize, but he is in love with how loud his neighbor Chuck Kress turns up that song on the radio in his spotless used car. Especially the saxophone, what the boy dreams of playing.

Chuck Kress is sixteen and taking him for a spin, two miles up and two miles back on the familiar road that runs so straight and flat, Chuck can reach 100 on the speedometer. "Buried," Chuck says, laughing, though they are down to sixty, their street a quarter mile away, when a car backs across both lanes from a roadside garage. Chuck brakes hard, the Chevy four-wheel-drifting toward a row of junipers that fill the passenger-side window as the boy grips the door handle and braces, the world turning dark green just before it brightens, Chuck's car spinning and stopping so close to the one straddling the road that the boy can see the shape of that stranger's inaudible scream.

Neither of them make a sound during those moments of lost control. *Raunchy* fades into a deejay's voice, but they still do not speak while the other driver straightens and drives away. Chuck, when he talks as he turns into their street, says, "Good thing I knew what to do." The boy says nothing because he has no idea what Chuck has done to save them. To himself, he says, *Good thing I didn't open the door.*

Chuck's dog, chained outside, barks as the boy gets out of the car. "You won't forget this one," Chuck says. "Not ever." The boy doesn't even nod. "Say 'thank you' the next time you see me," Chuck calls after him.

The boy's mother is at work. He creeps to his room and huddles on his bed. Long after the boy lies down, Chuck's miserable dog keeps up with its yammering.

The boy's quiet hysteria gradually fades. Remembering his hand about to yank the door handle, he thinks, *Good thing I hadn't had an extra second to act. Good thing I didn't have time enough to do what was worst. Good thing that lesson was a private one. Good thing I hadn't spouted that wrong answer out loud.* He makes a vow of a future filled with caution, something that sounds, at once, like it has been copied from the answers someone else is writing for an exam he is not prepared for. Like he has been caught cheating, and the teacher is furious.

Just Fine

"SUDDEN DEATH," MY SISTER said at the viewing. "There's no such thing. Gene smoked and drank and carried thirty pounds of flab."

"He drowned," I said.

"After he had a heart attack."

"That's sudden, too."

"You're smart enough to know what I mean," Belinda said. I wanted to argue, explain how the shock of the lake water in April was enough to strain a man's heart into fibrillation, but Belinda had graduated from the Carrie Nation school of righteousness, swinging her heavy axe like a true disciple. "I hope it's got you thinking," she said. "You're sixty-four, twenty-one years older than he was."

"I keep to dry land."

"You think you do, but it takes more than your feet on the ground."

My sister had no children. She had a second husband and a dog she replaced every twelve years. She'd used my son-in-law Gene as an example of foolish behavior and bad judgment since he'd married my daughter Dana during their junior year in college, beginning with, "There's the end of her education" and moving on to "Aren't you worried about him turning her as stump-dumb as he is?"

Listening to Belinda, you'd think Gene had dropped out and taken my daughter with him, but they both graduated, and though his grades were spotty, an overall average of 2.5, there was way worse in that school and a thousand others like it, and no way of Belinda even knowing his grade point except he'd laughed about it once in front of her, reminding Belinda that I'd told him hilarious stories about how I'd suffered from the affliction of unexcused absences and late papers when I'd attended that same college before I managed to get into medical school despite my own stump-like behavior.

But what set Belinda off was hearing Gene admit he and Dana had cheated together on a final exam in World Religions. Gene had bought an old test because a reliable rumor had it the professor changed only one or two of the six test essays each semester and still gave everybody a chance to choose which four to write about. He asked if Dana wanted in and handed her an empty blue book, also purchased from the test seller, when she didn't say "No."

They were getting married in two weeks. "It's not like you, yourself, need to be paying anybody or anything," Gene had told her, and the truth is, he'd explained, Dana hadn't ever agreed. "She didn't even really cheat," he'd said to Belinda when he finally noticed her frown. "She felt guilty, so she only wrote two essays ahead of time, and one of her answers was for the only question that wasn't repeated. She had to smuggle her head-start blue book in and out both. With luck like that, she should never play Russian Roulette."

Now here it was just over twenty years since then, and he was dead at an age reserved for rare diseases, accidents, or bad habits. It was the age you died at in a dozen African countries, but not in the United States, Belinda reminded him, not unless you brought it on yourself.

AFTER THE FUNERAL DANA turned giddy, walking up to people and blurting brief anecdotes with Gene as the central character. It was like she was leafing through an unarranged stack of snapshots, the dates and locations unmarked, and picking only the ones where Gene acted in a way that Dana adored.

The newest story, of course, was the one about the canoe overturning in the lake, she and Gene resurfacing. "Swim for it," he'd said. "I'll drag the boat in." He'd been right behind her, and then she hadn't heard the sound of his heavy breathing or the splash from his kick strokes. She thought it was distance until she got her feet under her and turned to see the unaccompanied, drifting canoe.

The oldest story was about how she'd driven Gene's car into an open space among trees to drink and make out and had sunk it nearly to the frame in mud. Gene was sitting in the shotgun seat with half a gallon of Gallo Vin Rose, staring straight ahead as if he was watching a screen set among the trees. "What if it keeps sinking?" she quoted herself. "What if we can't open the doors?"

When the car seemed to settle another fraction of an inch, she screamed and Gene had put one finger to his lips like a mother before he leaned over and kissed her on the forehead. "We'll be fossils," he said.

After whoever was listening smiled, Dana said, "He was such a boy. If we'd had children, they would have loved him."

That suggested one story she didn't tell, how something had gone wrong with her first pregnancy. A year later, the problem had repeated itself and talk of children had disappeared. Maybe that's what made it more likely that Gene could dawdle. Without children, Dana could work, and Gene's jobs could be intermittent and unskilled. Motivation is a tenuous thing.

Dana worked among men. She kept the accounts at a car dealership. It paid, she said, as well as being the social worker she'd prepared to be, with one tenth the unhappiness. Beyond that, she said nothing about her job, but I'd dealt with half a dozen such bookkeepers at auto dealers, and they were evenly split between women in their early twenties and women over fifty. It was like church, where people disappeared for twenty-five years and returned out of urgency. She had plaques that read five years, ten years, and fifteen years. In another year, she'd have one that read twenty, certifying how exceptions, like lottery winners, can occur. I'd seen them on the wall above her desk the one time, though it was only fifteen miles from where I lived, that I'd visited her at work.

Meanwhile, my sister had turned her kitchen into a replica of our mother's. She'd remarried seven years ago, two months after our mother, who had outlived our father by fifteen years, died and left a house full of furnishings behind, all of which I'd refused.

After we settled the estate, Belinda never served a meal in her dining room, or for that matter, offered a chair in her living room. When I visited, we ate at the kitchen table the two of us had sat at growing up. The same stiff wooden chairs. The cherry table that would outlive us unless her house burned to the ground. She placed our mother's figurines of an Amish family on the windowsill by the sink so it looked like the windowsill in our childhood kitchen. Without touching them, I remembered their weight, the father and mother heavy enough to be weapons, the boy and girl dressed in black and blue, each of them in the same order from left to right that they'd been in for fifty years.

Silverware, dishtowels, pot holders—it was as if she'd never purchased a single item for the kitchen. Even the salt and pepper shakers and the plates. I felt like a boy eating there, like I had to clean my plate, swallowing food I hated like Waldorf salad, Brussels sprouts and stuffed peppers because my sister served the recipes from our mother's vintage Betty Crocker Cookbook.

Her second husband looked old to me, though once, when I visited a year after they were married, I walked upstairs and discovered a set of his college yearbooks and learned that he was three years younger than she was, five years younger than me. He was fifty-nine now, his thin hair white, his posture stooped. But she talked as if she'd married an example for me to follow, telling me, a physician, stories about his regular exercise and fat-free diet. *Healthy* was a word she used often. So was *thin*. She didn't miss a chance to remind me he didn't drink or smoke or eat potato chips and chicken wings, three out of four of which I was dedicated to like a man who had never been educated past third grade. "You know exactly what's going on inside your body," Belinda would say. "Next, you'll tell me you eat lunch every day at McDonald's."

The truth is I love Big Macs but have the self-discipline to eat them only once a month. What's more, I've never smoked and don't touch hard liquor. But, around her, I keep my virtues to myself while I wait for my annual visit to end.

"You've never invited me to your house since Lynne passed," Belinda had said during my last Easter visit, three weeks before the canoe flipped over. "It's been eight years now."

"You're my sister. You don't need an invitation. Did you not visit Mom and Dad unless they invited you?"

"Of course. You don't walk in on somebody just because they're family."

I wanted to tell her that since Lynne had died being a brother had become a performance with me. The thought had the stink of selfishness about it, something I could stand, but listening to Belinda had made me postpone my confession like my patients did their appointments, putting off telling me about loss of appetite and a sore that doesn't heal.

"There's nothing wrong with Gene," Dana had said a dozen times without me asking. "He's just fine."

"Fine is good," I'd answer.

"I mean it, Daddy."

It always took me back a step, her calling me Daddy when she was a grown woman. I felt the same way when Gene addressed me as Dad because he'd married my daughter. "You know, Dad," Gene had said last summer. "I'm only doing construction part time now."

I'd kept my expression fixed. Construction, for Gene, was working for what I called a handyman. Decks. Shower stalls. Baseboards. Anything a homeowner too lazy or ignorant to do that didn't require an expert.

"Part-time?" I said.

"Enough to do my share," he said. "Those other hours are being invested. Twenty of them, say, a week—it'll come back ten-fold, you know, like Jesus explained."

"Jesus was talking about good works. He hated investors."

"I just meant it was an expression, you know, quoting authority."

"So, what are you up to?"

"I found my calling is what I did. Screenplays is where it's at."

"Like hitting a seven-race parlay."

"You bet it is. Dana knows. A dream pays off huge. I know a guy who's getting $600,000 for his script."

"I meant the odds," I said.

Gene had looked downcast for a moment. "Of course," he said. "That only makes sense, but I definitely feel good about this. Definitely. Long odds are what paves the road to riches."

There was an awkwardness between us the rest of the afternoon. When Dana announced she was making a liquor store run, Gene carried a small television onto the deck and turned on a baseball game, something I'd never seen him do. "So I can smoke," he said, lighting up. "This is my lounge. But there's only two stations we can get when the cable's disconnected."

After one inning, he turned off the television and poured two glasses of wine, and I took the change as an invitation to clear things up. "You know," I said, "the kind of work I do you almost always recognize ahead of time what the outcome is going to be."

"Really?" Gene said. "That doesn't sound right. There's medicine. All those prescriptions. And surgery. Right? You send them off to somebody who operates and that changes things."

"When it can."

"I hope that's not true. If it was, I don't know how you could look at another patient being so sure of their future."

"It's what we live with."

"Maybe," Gene said. "The only thing I know is what I can't live without, and first on that list is a woman. I can't imagine being without one." He sipped his wine for a moment, trying, I thought, to read my expression. "Sorry," he finally said, "but I don't know how you do it or else I'm missing something." He twisted his nearly empty wine glass in his hands, the mouthful of wine sloshing nearly over the sides. "I mean what do you do with yourself?"

I looked at the side door, listening for Dana. It was a three-minute drive to the liquor store, and she been gone for twenty. "You know," Gene added, "your desires."

"That's an odd thing to ask," I said.

"My father's been dead more than ten years. He was never old or by himself."

"I'm sixty-three," I said. I finished my wine, giving Gene time to back off or acknowledge that *old* was a sloppy adjective.

"You don't have to be specific," he said. "Privacy is a good thing."

"Yes, it is. And maybe an extra bit of it is sometimes earned."

Gene's eyes flashed toward the blank television and back toward me. "What do you think, being a doctor means you deserve more than the rest of us?"

"*More* can be as various as happiness. Everybody has warning track power when it comes to getting what they want."

"Goddamn, no offense, but you talk like somebody who needs to get laid."

"You still remember what a metaphor is, Gene?"

"I guess some things get packed away in riddles," Gene said. The garage door opened. He swallowed his wine.

"Many things," I said. "A whole goddamned shitload of things gets kept to your own self."

I stood up, and Gene raised his arm as if he expected me to strike him. The door swung open, and Dana paused, staring. "The cavalry is here," she said. "You're saved."

Gene unplugged the television and lugged it back into the house. The only bookshelves they owned were in the room that held that television, a couch, and two chairs. I'd looked at what was on those shelves when they'd bought the house right after Dana had announced she was pregnant. All the books were textbooks from college—sociology and literature. Gene had been an English major, so his books looked more like ones you might buy at a college bookstore—anthologies, individual novels, though all of the writers seemed to be ones I'd read in my three college survey courses twenty years before Gene.

Those books and their arrangement had never changed. Not once. And though I wasn't a reader myself, those old textbooks seemed sad. I'd bought Gene two novels by Faulkner that weren't on the shelf, but I'd never seen them until I noticed both of them, *Light in August* and *As I Lay Dying*, sitting on the back of the toilet in their bathroom. I felt like a thief seeing them there, like I was pawing through a drawer of underwear not my own.

THOUGH NORTH CAROLINA IN late March and April is often warm, like always, when I visited Belinda during that time, we never went outside. She lived with her husband in one of those enormous houses that spring up near golf courses except that it had been built on a lot half the size of a prime fairway location, making the yard look like the kind you could mow by hand. You still see old people using those push mowers along city streets, the front yards maybe ten feet wide, but my sister had a power mower her husband used, I guessed, for fifteen minutes once a week.

There was a deck in the back with patio furniture hidden underneath plastic covers. I'd never seen that table and chairs undraped, but I knew my mother hadn't owned any outdoor furniture, that none of it could be something I'd ever sat on or eaten from.

"You just think it's nice out because it's still snowing in upstate New York," Belinda would say. "If you lived here, you'd learn what nice was."

She was right about winter in New York. It drove you indoors. I'd played racket ball with Gene during the winter just past. He'd smoked a cigarette before each of the three games, but I wasn't good enough to run him.

His hand-eye coordination was amazing. I had to give it to him, he could lay shots down into that six-inch strip near the floor where bounces never came up or toss balls off the walls so they'd arc back into the deep corners. He laughed afterwards, lighting up. "It keeps you fit," he said.

"Or kills you."

THIS MORNING, A WEEK after the funeral, when I knocked on Dana's door, it took her so long to answer I used my key to let myself in. I could hear her moving upstairs. "It's me," I shouted.

It took another minute for her to come down, but I stayed in the kitchen like a guest. I read through the items on the calendar by the phone. On it, for two days from now, was a dentist appointment for Gene. I turned to May and June, but there were no more signs of him.

"I'm sorry," Dana said as she came downstairs. "I was in the bathtub."

"That's what the key is for."

"No, it's not, Daddy."

Though she was wearing a sweatshirt, Dana hugged herself as if she was cold. "Are you sick?" I said. "Were you trying Mom's old-fashioned steaming hot bath remedy?"

"I wish," she said. She sat on the couch and pulled the blanket that lay there like a cushion around her. "I've needed this lately," she said, "but now I bet you want an explanation."

"Strictly voluntary," I said, though by now she resembled a spectator at a December football game, someone already uncomfortable before the kickoff.

"I was just sitting there in the bathtub. You know how when the water gets about half way up it feels right for a bath? Well, I sat there for a minute in that water, and then I reached for the faucet, all cold, and started running water, thinking about Gene as it got up to my chin and all I had to do was stretch out a bit and I would be underwater. I thought I could do that, at least, but I just let the water slosh over the top and onto the floor. Like I was dead, you know. Like I couldn't turn it off and the house would drown with me. And then I got out and the water went down. I stood there in the puddle I'd made and watched the faucet keep running like I could see myself under the surface, and I opened the door so there was a draft and maybe it would shock my heart, but nothing, of course, happened. Nothing whatsoever except I turned off the water."

"It's grief," I said.

"Forty-three," she said. "That's like half a life."

"You don't have to explain yourself."

"Yes, I do. That was yesterday. I left the water in the tub. I turned off the heat in the bathroom and climbed back in three times during the night."

"There's a kind of sense to that," sounding, even to myself, like someone floundering for honest words.

"Is there? Right now, that water's still in there. I'd been sitting in it for half an hour when you knocked."

I glanced at the ceiling as if it might be showing telltale signs of moisture. Nothing was different. My daughter had at least turned off the water once she'd created her laboratory for hypothermia.

"I'm thinking of what he's going to miss," she said.

"What's that?" I said before I thought not to say it.

"Everything else. The next forty-three years. What he would do with himself." I kept myself quiet this time. I didn't want to say a word on this subject.

"Look at you, Daddy," she said. "If you hadn't lived the last twenty-one more years, what would you have missed?"

Disappointment, I thought. *Learning, finally, that the gifts I had were smaller than I needed in order to be happy.* Dana rose from the couch, leaving the blanket draped over the back like an accessory. "You want to go upstairs and watch the real tv with me, keep me out of trouble?"

I followed her to the room Gene had once begun to transform into a nursery by wallpapering it with a design called "Ten Puppies." Fifteen years ago, they'd sent the crib back and replaced it with a large-screen television that stood beside a 100-unit DVD holder. "What do you want to watch?" Dana said, ejecting the disc that was in the player and replacing it in its case.

"Gene loved this movie," she said. "*Titanic.* Who would have thought he'd end up exactly like Leonardo DiCaprio?"

"I bet that's not the part he loved," I said.

Dana smiled. "Of course not. He loved all that king of the world stuff, the big ideas and the high hopes."

"It struck me as a little corny" I said. "Everything was so black and white."

"That's why you never like anything, Dad. You're always looking for doubt."

She replaced the DVD in its slot. The movie above it was *Dirty Harry*. Gene had loved all the old Clint Eastwood detective movies. I kept my hands off it. There was no need to repeat my complaint about how the world was never as simple as these scripts declared it.

Years ago, shortly after her first marriage, I'd taken my sister to a movie when her husband was out of town. An hour into it, she'd walked out, and though I wondered about her after five minutes went by, I hadn't followed her. Forty minutes later I'd found her sitting in the lobby. "Finally," she said. "How could you stand all that gloom and doom?"

"I'd call it tension."

"Whatever you like. Just warn me next time. If I was pregnant I'd be afraid my child would be born depressed if I sat there a minute longer."

BELINDA'S HUSBAND HAD A long commute. He left the house before seven, so that last morning, before I started the eight-hour drive north, I sat alone with Belinda over breakfast until she pushed her coffee cup to the side and left the table, returning with something I thought might be jewelry, something to pass along to Dana. Instead, a sealed bag of hair was in the box, blonde, the strands somehow thinner than I imagined Belinda's hair to ever have been. "My first haircut," she said. "Didn't Mom give you something like this when you left home?"

I shook my head as I stared at the transparent box, which also held what I knew had to be a full set of fingernail clippings, and when Belinda held the box up to the light, I counted ten small crescents, each one so perfect I knew our mother had cut them so carefully with cuticle scissors that she'd finished each nail like perfectly peeling an apple, taking off the skin in complete circles that would lie on the counter like wristbands.

"No," I said. "Maybe she thought of doing it after I'd already had a haircut, something she vowed to do if she had another child."

"Or maybe it's a girl thing," Belinda said. "Did Lynne keep Dana's hair and clippings the first time?"

"I don't know. I mean maybe she did, but I'd have to look around." I reached for the last sweet roll even though I was stuffed. Belinda, for once, didn't amplify my failure.

Minutes later, as I prepared to leave, Belinda passed me in the hall as if we were students changing classrooms. I hesitated, wanting to say a sentence

full of good-natured self-deprecation, something empathetic or even intimate, but when I reached the spare bedroom and entered, I realized what I
wanted was to hear that sentence from her. Belinda was a stranger. I couldn't
remember her at any age younger than twenty when it seemed to me she'd
settled into the body she would live in until I died.

Shaken, I stared at myself in the mirror above the dresser. I looked old
enough to appear ordinary in a coffin. A sister and a daughter, I thought, and
not one child between them.

"YOU CAN STOP PRETENDING to choose, Daddy," Dana said. "I don't think
I can sit still for a movie. I don't know what I was thinking dragging you
up here."

"No problem." Besides the two chairs set facing the television, there was
one tucked under a table that supported a computer and a printer. I didn't
see any sign of paper, blank or otherwise. Nothing in the room had drawers; the closet stood open and empty except for what looked to be boxes of
board games. If Gene had a script, he stored it elsewhere. The computer,
with nothing nearby, looked like a child's toy, something used exclusively for
video games.

"I want to go to the accident lake. Is that ok?" Dana said.

"Maybe."

She tugged at one sleeve of the sweatshirt. "It's nice out, isn't it? You're
just wearing that little jacket."

"It's not nice enough to go without something."

She pulled her hand away and smiled. "Ok," she said. "Give me a minute
and we'll go."

I heard the bathroom door open and shut. In spite of myself, I checked
the top shelf in the closet to be certain nothing was there, and then I began
to name the breeds that filled the parallel strips of varying colors: collie,
setter, German Shepard, dachshund, beagle, St. Bernard, Dalmatian, terrier,
greyhound, poodle. It took me just long enough to remember the tub full of
cold water, and I stepped into the hall, listening.

Within seconds, the door opened. "Ready," she said, though it was hard
to tell what she had done to herself.

Downstairs, she re-entered the room with the bookshelf that never
changed. "Wait a second," she said, and began to fold the blanket until it was
the same small square it had been when I arrived. "There." But instead of
turning, she walked over to the bookshelf and ran one hand across the tops
of Hemingway, Faulkner, Fitzgerald, and Thomas Wolfe, the thick volume

of *Look Homeward, Angel* that nobody seemed to read anymore. She held her fingers up to the light and rubbed them together, and for a moment I imagined her deciding it was important never to dust those books, that she wanted whatever remnant of Gene that was on them to go undisturbed.

I drove. It was less than ten miles, and I turned off the CD player and let her have silence. As we turned onto the dirt road that led to the docking area, she finally spoke. "It was so much work, Daddy," she said, and then she paused for a moment, swallowing, before she added, "You know, marriage, but not the way it sounds."

"It's ok. Gene wasn't exactly steady."

Dana laid her hand on my arm as I parked. "Of course not," she said, "but he never stopped being interesting, not ever, not once." Her voice held the desperation of rationalization, but I took it for truth. A moment later she was out of the car and walking right up to the water's edge.

As I caught up, she lifted the sweatshirt over her head and shook her hair out in the sun. Underneath she wore a pale blouse that somehow made her late April skin-tone look even lighter. She tossed the sweatshirt at me as if it was a football. Her mood seemed lighter now, the bathtub and the forlorn books miles away. "Gene will be like the Kennedys or Elvis," she said. "One of those men forever in their forties."

"'The Summer of his Years,' I said. "Somebody recorded a song with that title when Kennedy was shot."

"Which one?"

"Jack," I said. "He'd turn one hundred this year if he was alive. He'd be an object of awe and sympathy. Elvis would be eighty-one."

"And Gene would be forty-four."

She walked away from me, following the shoreline. "Let her be alone with herself," I thought, not moving even as she stepped into the lake. I was sure she would stop when the water reached her knees, but she kept going, the water to her waist, and then higher yet, enough to make me suddenly afraid she had stones in her pockets like Virginia Woolf, enough to make me begin to follow her.

When the water reached my groin, I inhaled and began to shiver. She smiled as I approached her. "Try a few more steps," she said. "Get up to your chin like me."

"It's freezing," I said.

"Not quite as bad as last week."

"A degree or two."

"Then it's close enough for you to know."

I shook, rippling the water out around my hips. My teeth chattered for a few seconds before I willed them silent. "If we made ourselves stay out here, we could die," she said.

"I wouldn't let you do that."

"Anything's possible, Daddy," she said, and in that moment I thought she was going to swim away from me.

I slogged toward her, the water creeping to chest high. I stood on tiptoes to make myself taller. The breeze felt warm even as it ran through my soaked shirt. It reminded me of all the advice about cold water, about climbing onto the capsized boat because cold air is a lesser evil than cold water. She took two steps back, and I hesitated, terrified.

"I know what you're thinking, Daddy," she said. "I'm a way stronger swimmer than you are. I was a better swimmer than Gene, too."

"Let's go," I said.

"We could last half an hour, Daddy, maybe more. We could get colder and still live for a while." She lowered herself until her head barely cleared the surface. I swam without looking back, Daddy. Not once."

"Once he went into arrest and sank, he couldn't have been saved."

"That's such a terrible lie for a doctor to say. You know what else? Even after, I didn't try to save him. I didn't swim out and dive under and look."

"He was gone already."

"That's no reason not go back and try."

She straightened enough to lift her shoulders from the water. "Let's go to shore," I said and held my breath while she decided.

When she finally moved toward shallow water, she turned and walked backward as if she needed to keep an eye on me. The outline of her bra under her blouse reminded me of wet t-shirt contests, drunk girls winning CDs and concert tickets while guys memorized the size and shape of their breasts. When she reached waist-high water, I wrapped my arms around her. My coat and her sweatshirt were lying on the ground thirty feet away, but we stood like that for maybe a minute, holding each other for warmth and, maybe, I wished, with love, wet and shivering from the same cold water that had locked up Gene's heart.

I want to say I could feel hers beating the whole time, but I was concentrating on her shaking, something without rhythm, stuttering and pausing, shuddering slowly then like she was sobbing. I told myself I'd stand there until she let go, that it was her call how long we'd freeze. If grief wasn't important enough to bear discomfort, what was?

The Year Bobby Kennedy was Shot

JASON CHOOSES A DESK four-seats back in the first row by the window, a good choice, he decides, because whoever is a tough guy in this first period English class will sit behind him in the last two rows, and the boys who are afraid and the girls who aren't sluts will sit in front of him. Everything is important the first day in a new school, especially in ninth grade, when no one else in the building is younger than you are.

As soon as he sits down, Jason notices that this teacher acts like it's his first day, too, writing his name on the board and English 9C as if everybody doesn't already know. And he sees there are fewer black students than his old school, four of them in this class of thirty, all of them girls who sit in the row along the opposite wall. The boys who sit in the back, five of them across the last row, are white, and all of them wear dark t-shirts and blue jeans. Except for one girl, everybody else acts like they pick a seat by accident, dropping into chairs and talking to each other like they're friends. Only the final girl to sit down looks like she wants to sit somewhere else, but there's no other desk except the fourth seat in the second row, right beside the largest of the black girls. "Hunh," the girl says as she sits, making it sound like she's been punched in the stomach.

Mr. Fletcher looks up from a piece of paper Jason knows has their thirty names in alphabetical order. When he hears him say Robert Anders in a soft voice, Jason guesses this class will be one of those where everybody talks and doesn't pay attention. Mr. Fletcher, by the time he gets to Jason Mroz, hasn't spoken any louder; when he says Phyllis Zachs, the girl in the second row says "Yeah" and the boys in back laugh.

"Ok, then," Mr. Fletcher says, beginning to pass out lined yellow paper. "I want everyone to write 200 words for me today." When the groans stop, he smiles. "That means you can fit your essay on one side of this paper. Think of this as you introducing yourself to me. What do you want me to know about you that makes you unique?"

WHEN JASON WALKS INTO English class the next day, he sees that Mr. Fletcher has posted essays on all of his five bulletin boards. Ten of them are on the one labeled 9C, but the bulletin boards are along the wall where the black girls sit, so he can't tell if one of the ten is his.

"We'll be writing three essays during each marking period," Mr. Fletcher says. "That means everyone will be posted once each quarter. Please read them when you get a chance."

After class, Jason walks to the bulletin board and sees that one of the essays is his. The next one says Phyllis Zachs, and as soon as he glances at it, he has to finish.

"Last year something really awful happened to me on a school bus. It was a foggy morning, and I was sitting in the front seat like I always did, minding my own business. A girl named Cindy was sitting next to me and she wouldn't shut up talking about her geography project, some kind of map she'd made out of gunk so everybody could see where the mountains and valleys and rivers and such are in the United States. Shut up, I kept thinking, but she didn't. I looked at the fog. It was pretty. And then there was a big bump and the bus was off the road and going down a hill and it tipped over and everything was crazy. Everybody was screaming but me and Cindy. I was holding my head where it slammed into the window really hard, and Cindy was just laying there with her face all cut and bleeding all over. She looked like somebody who was going to be ugly now with stitches on her face but it didn't matter because she was dead because her neck was broken. You could tell because she looked all crooked and her eyes were funny. I have nightmares now. I don't ride the school bus. I remember the last thing Cindy said before we crashed. 'I'm bringing my map to school tomorrow. It's still drying.' And I remember all that blood. It looked like rivers for her stupid map."

"That's so terrible," Mr. Fletcher has written at the end. "What a thing to have happen to you." Phyllis, Jason notices, spells badly, which always gets you points off, but Mr. Fletcher has just explained that he doesn't give grades during the first half of each marking period. "I don't want to be judgmental," he said. "I don't want to discourage anyone."

Jason has to rush to his next class, but he's glad no one else has stopped to read the essays. His is about getting new contact lenses, how much they hurt the first time the optometrist had put them in. "That sounds so painful," Mr. Fletcher has written on his paper. "But now you can see so much better." Jason hopes nobody ever stops to read his paper. If it was written by another boy, he'd think "What a pussy." His mother has said, "They cost a fortune, bright boy. That's the last thing I buy for you for a year," but Jason hasn't put that in the essay.

When he's leaving school to walk home, stopping at his locker, he sees Phyllis closing hers in the next bank of lockers. She squints at him as she approaches, and he sees that her glasses are thick and make her eyes look funny, but other than that she looks pretty. When she slows down as if she might talk to him, he says, "Yours was the best essay on the bulletin board."

"No, it wasn't," she says. "I get Ds in English."

"Maybe you won't from Mr. Fletcher."

"Yes, I will," Phyllis says. "Schools are all the same, except some are worse when they have niggers in them."

Jason looks around to see if anyone can hear her, and she frowns. "You worried about somebody hearing?" Phyllis says. "I'm not the only one says nigger. Listen to Miss Haseltine. She says the same thing only she says, "chocolate drops." That's what she told Mr. Fletcher. "You have to watch out for those chocolate drops." Phyllis looks triumphant. "New kids should stick together. We're too old to make new friends."

"I hope not."

"What makes you hope?"

"I don't know. I moved once before, in fourth grade, and I made some friends."

"You must have moved to Disneyland," Phyllis says. "I moved last year, and it was just like it is here."

Mr. Fletcher turns out to be one of those teachers who wants everybody to like him. "You're doing fine," he says to each student who gets stuck on an answer. "Take your time and think what you want to say."

Jason is sure this won't work on the boys in the back of the room and some of the girls who sit right behind him. It's still September, and he can hear them whispering to each other, "You're doing good, baby. Take your time."

When Jason shakes his head instead of even trying to answer a question he doesn't know, Mr. Fletcher stops him after class to say, "I want you to know I understand how hard it is to be the new boy when you're fourteen."

"Ok," he says.

The girls from the back of the room are walking by them. Jason hopes they're busy talking about their boyfriends and what they do with them; he can imagine how they would whisper things in his ear if they decide he's somebody to laugh at.

His mother opens the door to his room to tell him she has a new boyfriend, and he is staying overnight now and Jason should know.

"Ok," Jason says.

"Roy doesn't want to scare you or anything if you run into each other in the morning."

"All right."

"He's my friend," she says. "He belongs here too."

She stands in the doorway and looks at how Jason's books are shelved alphabetically in his bookcase, how each of his school subjects has a folder filed by the period in the day. She knows that his records, the 45s he buys, two per month, are arranged in chronological order. "He'll be surprised if he ever comes in here," she says. She picks up his alarm clock and puts it down. "You keep yourself a secret in here, you know." When she leaves, Jason moves the clock to where it belongs.

FIVE BOYS IN JASON'S class, the ones in the back of the room, complain to the principal when Mr. Fletcher, who's walked into the flag twenty times in two weeks, says, "That's enough of this" and lifts the flag from its holder and tosses it into the closet. By the end of the day Mr. Fletcher is a Communist and a traitor according to hallway rumors, and the next morning he apologizes to Jason's class and puts it back up. "I'll just be more careful," he says.

"That's dumb," Phyllis blurts. "We don't even say the Pledge at this school, so why have a flag up there to get in the way like that?"

"Shut up," one of the boys in the back says. "You sound like you're in the Vietcong."

"Yeah," the boy beside him says. "We're all going to Vietnam as soon as we get out of this stupid school."

Phyllis grunts the same "Hunh" noise she made the first day of school. "You're going to get killed there because you're stupid," she says. Jason thinks she's right, but he's not going to argue with those boys. Mr. Fletcher asks everyone to be civil. "Keep talking," he says, "but raise your hand," but nobody says anything else.

BECAUSE JASON WALKS TO school and doesn't have to go to a bus line, he starts to read in the library. The teachers have to stay for half an hour after the last bell, so the librarian lets him sit at a table until she turns off the lights and leaves. By the time he gets to his locker, no one else is ever around. Near the end of September, he notices that the locker next to his, the last one in the row, is ajar. It's never had a lock, the only one like it on his row, and now, after he looks down the empty hall, he nudges the space wider and looks inside.

A pile of shoes is stacked up in the bottom. Jason counts six pairs, two brown, two black, one burgundy, and one red. He closes the locker carefully, trying to leave exactly the same small space that was there before he touched it.

A week later, even though the locker is shut, he opens it again. Now there are eight pairs, another brown and a blue pair added to the pile. When he changes for gym class the next day, he puts his shoes inside his shirt. He's never heard anybody in his gym class complain about his shoes being stolen, but the shoe thief, who has to be in a hurry, would think he was a boy who wore tennis shoes all day and move to the next locker to rob.

That afternoon Jason wants to open the locker next to his and count the shoes, see if another pair has been added today, and for a moment he holds his jacket and stares at it as if it might be remembered in case somebody sees him looking in a locker that isn't his. "Hey," he hears from so close he flinches.

Phyllis laughs when he swings around so fast she knows she's scared him. "You forget how to put on a coat?" she says.

Jason shakes his head and slams his locker shut, clicking the lock and spinning it so nobody will know what the last number of his three-number code is. He wants to ask her where she goes after school if she doesn't leave because he's never seen her in the library.

"I saw Bobby Kennedy get shot," Phyllis says. "His brains were everywhere. My mother worked in that hotel where he got killed."

"Wow," Jason says, but he thinks she might have it wrong, that it was President Kennedy's brains you could see. Jason tries to decide whether to ask her and risk sounding like he doesn't believe her, when she says, "That's why we moved here, because my mother didn't want me to be in Los Angeles anymore."

"I thought you moved here from West Virginia?"

She stares at him through her thick glasses, her eyes looking as big as the plastic circle ones on his little brother's teddy bear Cubby. "Yeah," she says. "We moved there first and then to here. West Virginia was worse than Los Angeles. Even the white people were stupid."

The next morning when Jason looks up from his notebook in class, he watches Phyllis scan the room as if she's looking to see who's whispering about her or who's looking at her. Nobody, he decides, and he opens his literature book and stares at it like it's a palm he's examining, ready to tell a fortune. He listens to Mr. Fletcher because he knows that once during each class he'll be called on for an answer. He hopes it will be early so he can forget about listening. What Mr. Fletcher says is always something he already knows because he's read the assignments.

"Why do the Martians disguise themselves as the space explorers' families?" Mr. Fletcher asks, and Jason says because the humans were far from home and lonely. "Good," Mr. Fletcher says. "And?"

Jason wants to be quiet, but the way Mr. Fletcher is leaning toward him, one hand cupped and pulling toward his tie in small waves, makes him go on. "The space men should have known it was all fake," he says. "Nobody has families like that. If the Martians were really their families, something would go wrong."

Mr. Fletcher says "Interesting" like he does when he wants a different answer. The next two boys he calls on haven't read the story. Mr. Fletcher sighs and tries a new question on a girl named Kristen who sits in front of Phyllis and always wears her cheerleader uniform to class on Fridays.

Phyllis stops him after class. "That sounds like a stupid story," she says. "I'm glad I didn't read it."

Jason tells her he likes it, that he's found the whole book of *The Martian Chronicles* and read it. Phyllis shakes her head. "You're crazy," she says, and Jason thinks she's right, not because he reads, but because he already thinks he's going insane. He wants to tell somebody this, but he's afraid to. He thinks this is a sign his fear is real. If he brags about it, like even the boys who sit in front of him brag about sex, it would all be lies.

He knows he's not like the patients in the movies he watches on television who think they are other people. That's stupid, he says to himself. I know who I am. Napoleon, Lincoln, Jesus—the patients in the stories always pick somebody a little kid would recognize.

In those movies, the interesting crazy people are always quiet. They sit by themselves. They're afraid to be touched. Jason always worries that they will kill themselves before the movie ends. He wonders how those people he likes could do that. Hurt themselves. And more.

Right now, what he is most afraid of is being hurt or getting a disease that never goes away. He washes his hands and cleans his room; he reties his shoes; he says he's sick on days they do gymnastics because he's convinced he'll break his neck.

He wants to tell Phyllis about being afraid because he thinks she's like that, too, only worse. She's like I'll be if I don't watch out, he thinks. He knows what happens to crazy people; they get shock therapy and put in straightjackets. They sit in rooms by themselves and people watch them through tiny windows.

"I WAS HAPPY TO hear you talk the other day," Mr. Fletcher is saying to Jason because it's his mid-term conference. For a week, during the half hour all the teachers stay, Mr. Fletcher talks to each of his students, he's explained, because after four and a half weeks, he has to start grading. "You're very quiet is all," Mr. Fletcher says. "That's not a bad thing, and anyway, you'll get over it someday. There's another world besides this one."

Jason nods like he thinks he's expected to, but he wants to get out of there before he starts to cry because Mr. Fletcher sounds exactly like a minister promising heaven in return for a miserable life.

When a few seconds go by with no one talking, Mr. Fletcher starts to arrange his books like they have to be in a certain order before he can leave the room, but instead of turning and leaving, Jason stands there like he needs to hear a bell.

"I see you've made friends with Phyllis," Mr. Fletcher says then, standing up as he speaks, and Jason shrugs because a nod seems like a lie. He doesn't think Phyllis likes him, but she doesn't hate him like she does everybody else. "Well then," Mr. Fletcher says, "I guess you're going to wait a bit longer to talk to me."

"Yeah," Jason says, and Mr. Fletcher smiles. One of the black girls is standing in the doorway.

"Yeah," Mr. Fletcher says. "See you later then," and this time Jason remembers to leave. When he walks down the hall to the library, all the teachers he sees in their rooms are just sitting there reading a newspaper or a magazine.

"ROY SAYS HE'S NEVER heard of a boy who cleans his room without being told," his mother says. She's moving his radio and his clock, switching their positions. She drops onto his bed and pulls the pillow loose from under the tightly tucked spread. "'Crazy people wash up like that boy of yours,' Roy says. 'He fixing to go to the nut house?'"

When she stands up, Jason goes to the bed and replaces the pillow, tugs the spread tight and wrinkle free. "I had to tell him about you," his mother says. "He's thinking of moving in, and I didn't want you to scare him off." She switches the clock and radio back to where they started. "When you two meet, I want you to set your mind to being polite."

"Ok."

"Roy is a package of his own," she says. "He has his own problems. You'll see right off what they are, so I need you to promise to be good."

"Ok," Jason says again, and then he walks down the hall and outside where the first thing he does, when she doesn't follow, is pull weeds from the flower bed, the one thing around their house that isn't a mess. It only takes two minutes because everything, even the weeds, is shutting down for the winter.

TWO WEEKS AFTER HE first found the shoes, there are eleven pairs in the locker. All of them, Jason finally notices, look like girls' shoes. The next day he leaves his loafers sit out during gym. He worries while they run laps and play volley ball; he ties his shoes three times because he feels like he's going to trip. His shoes are still there after volley ball. There's proof, he thinks, that the thief only steals from girls.

Later, when he stands at his locker, he shifts his eyes to look to see who might be watching before he opens the one next to his to count. He never thinks it will be empty, but now he decides to only look on Tuesday and Friday, always waiting ten seconds after he gets to his locker, so anyone who is checking will show themselves. When nobody ever appears, he thinks he could empty that locker and carry away the shoes without anyone seeing him. He thinks he could steal shoes from the girl's locker room and not get caught, but then he lists five reasons why he would get caught, including a girl coming back in to go to the bathroom and the real thief showing up.

THE NEXT TIME HIS essay is on the bulletin board, it's about having a birthday so close to Christmas it's like not having one. Phyllis writes about Bobby Kennedy being shot. "My mother was in the hotel kitchen washing dishes," Jason reads, "and I was with her because she was working overtime for Kennedy's party." When nobody talks about it, he thinks Phyllis and Mr. Fletcher are the only other people who read the essays. The rest are about playing basketball or being in the band or baby sitting or making a pizza. All of them have as many spelling errors as Phyllis'.

Mr. Fletcher's comments are penciled in beside Jason's last paragraph that says: "'That was some Christmas to forget,' my mother always says on December 30th. 'I was miserable. Your Dad always said you could have waited another two days. Then I could have gotten my picture in the paper and all that free stuff you get for having the first baby of the year.'"

Right beside the very last word Mr. Fletcher has written "How sad." During class Mr. Fletcher passes back tiny pieces of paper with their grades printed on them. Jason's says A-.

As he walks out of class, Phyllis says her birthday is in December, too. "Fifteen has to be better than fourteen," she says.

When he doesn't answer right away, she squints at him. "You're only going to be fourteen, aren't you?" she says. "You're still thirteen."

The black girls, who are trying to get by them, look at him funny, and Jason thinks it's good that they're the only ones that seem like they heard, because here it is the end of October and he suddenly knows he's the only person in ninth grade who is still thirteen years old.

The next day all four black girls turn around to look at him and form a word with their mouths. "Jason," he thinks they're saying, but when they shape the word again, he knows it's not his name. The girl behind him leans forward and breathes on his neck before she whispers "Junior" in his ear. He feels his face go red. What surprises him is the black girls have told the girl behind him. When she leans forward again, she says "Junior High" loud enough for the back row of boys and the black girls to laugh.

Mr. Fletcher glances back from where he is writing on the blackboard, but he keeps writing when nobody says "Junior" again. Jason gets it. He's going to be called "Junior" now, short for Junior High, which is where he belongs if he's only thirteen.

After class Phyllis glares at the black girls when they walk by. Jason hears "Junior" from three different voices as he walks up the hall with Phyllis, who tells him he must have skipped a grade. "Sure, you did," she says, when he denies it. "You just don't want anybody to know you're too smart."

"No. It's because I lived in a state where you could start kindergarten if your fifth birthday came before the end of the year."

"You're the youngest whether you skipped or didn't skip, so you ought to say you did. If people are going to laugh at you, you might as well be special for it." She squints at him. "I got a C- on my paper. I bet you got an A."

Jason begins to see Roy's dirty clothes in the bathroom. A buckskin jacket hangs over a kitchen chair for two days. His mother sits in that chair when she eats dinner with Jason. "Roy had himself the troubles when he was in high school," she says the second night that jacket hangs there, "but he's over them now."

Jason hasn't seen any beer bottles in the trash, so he thinks maybe that was Roy's problem. "Good," he says.

His mother runs her hand down one arm of the jacket and settles back against the chair. "I love this coat," she says. "You know, Jason, some men are better for showing their sorrows."

The following Monday Phyllis stomps into class like she's just learned she has a nickname she hates. "I want my seat moved," she says before Mr. Fletcher gets started.

"Why?" Mr. Fletcher says.

"Because I'm tired of sitting beside this nigger."

Maybe she's just so angry she doesn't remember there are three more black girls in the room, Jason thinks. This isn't like West Virginia or wherever she lived before. Instead, the next phrase she shouts is "nigger bastard," which brings Marcella Grant, who has the shoulders of a man, out of her seat. She closes her fists and shifts her weight through her knees and hips and shoulders, driving her right fist and then her left into Phyllis' face. The other black girls cheer.

"Hold it," Mr. Fletcher says, sounding so thin and uncertain that Marcella doesn't even slow down, slamming Phyllis again. A boy in the back row says, "Punch her lights out." Another one says, "Pound that Commie." And then Phyllis shows she is made of stone because she starts to scratch and claw, sprawling Marcella underneath her and pulling them both down between the desk rows while Marcella says white trash cracker, and Mr. Fletcher is tiptoe-ing up to them like he's deciding if he'll show favorites by grabbing one or the other first.

He pulls Phyllis off by both arms at once, and she kicks the air before he sets her down in her desk. He says, "Settle down for a minute" like he's the world's greatest optimist, and when Marcella sits in her chair, he says, "There, see?" and turns his back to speak to the rest of the class, getting to "Ok..." before the two of them are at each other's throats again, tumbling onto the floor and nearly rolling up the backs of Mr. Fletcher's legs like linemen taking out the ligaments of a quarterback's knees.

Jason doesn't find out what happens after the vice-principal comes to escort both of them away. Boys who fight are always suspended; girls who fight get secret punishments like cleaning desks after school or writing es-says about how fighting never solves anything. Marcella comes back to class the next day. "Where's your girlfriend, Junior?" she says to Jason, but all he knows is Phyllis has stayed home as if she's decided to punish herself.

THE DAY PHYLLIS COMES back after missing a week, Mr. Fletcher grabs a girl right in the middle of class. She sits two rows in front of Phyllis, who watches Mr. Fletcher read questions for a quiz because she doesn't have to take it. After two students interrupt the test by going to the desk to sharp-en their pencils, she breaks off the point of her pencil right in front of Mr. Fletcher and steps up to stick it in the sharpener. His hand is a frog's tongue. He grips her wrist and pulls sideways, snapping the inserted pencil in half. Her eyes widen, but she doesn't say anything. "Sit," Mr. Fletcher hisses, and she does, staring at the white prints which circle her arms while Mr. Fletcher reads the last three questions, none of which she answers without a pencil.

Phyllis shows up at his locker after he leaves the library. She stands by the one filled with shoes. "You see how Fletcher snapped?"

"Yes."

"Him and his head shrinking. Maybe he knows something now he didn't know yesterday." She leans against the locker. "Nixon won that election," she says. "He had Bobby Kennedy killed so he could be President."

"You don't know that," Jason says.

Phyllis smiles. "You know, there's a story that's true I haven't told you."

"Ok."

She purses her lips into a tight, bloodless line. "I want to tell you now, but you have to say you'll believe it."

Jason thinks "No way," but says "Ok" again as if he is one of those dolls his little brother has where you pull the string in the back and it says, "Let's play" or "Night, night" or "You're my best friend."

"I'll tell you anyway. It's really short."

"Go ahead then," Jason says.

"I had a baby last week," Phyllis says.

Jason knows this is a lie. He was eleven when his brother was born. Nobody has a baby without giving it away by being fat.

"It's the truth," she says. "The baby was six weeks old."

Jason nods. He's heard of miscarriages.

"See," she says. "It's a true story and nobody dies."

"Yes, they do."

"It wasn't anybody. It was a mess of blood. You need a face to be somebody."

Jason tries to guess who the father might be, and right away he thinks it has to be a grown man.

When he comes to class the next morning, Jason finds out Phyllis has been suspended for attacking Marcella with a pair of scissors in home economics class the day before. "That white bitch is sure enough crazy," Marcella says.

"Did she try to stab you?" one girl says.

"She just pointed it at me and talked her trash. She's so crazy she probably thought it put the voodoo on me or something."

Jason listens and wants to tell Marcella about how Phyllis walked right back into school after they sent her home, and that he thinks she will come back any time she wants and wait for her if she has a mind to.

It's a Thursday, but he opens the other locker that afternoon, and there are sixteen pairs of shoes inside. He drops a green pair that belongs to his mother onto the pile, and then he takes all seventeen pairs out and puts them in a trash can. The thief will stop now, he thinks, or at least use a different locker. He follows the corridor to where he turns left toward the front door, but suddenly he turns around and walks back to open that locker and check again. He realizes he's expected it to be full of shoes, that this would be the day he knows he is crazy, but it's empty.

AFTER HE GETS HOME he dusts his room, but doesn't vacuum because his baby brother is asleep in his crib. Jason looks at his room and knows it's not as clean as it should be. He pushes the vacuum cleaner into his room and plugs it in, but then he unplugs it and wraps the cord tightly around the vacuum's two hooks because just standing there it makes the room look messy.

He hears the door to his mother's room open, and when he looks out, he sees a man come out of his mother's bedroom wearing only a pair of white briefs. He thinks it is Roy, but then he knows it could be anybody, some other man who doesn't care if he cleans his room every day. The man goes into the bathroom and doesn't close the door or turn on the light. Jason doesn't hear the seat rap against the toilet tank, so he's certain the man pisses without lifting it.

Jason pulls back from the doorway and listens to hear if there are splatters against the seat, but then his mother calls out, "You piss so loud you'll wake the baby," the sound of her words keeping him from knowing for sure.

When the man closes the bedroom door behind him, Jason pushes the vacuum against the wall beside his desk and sits down to read. His brother never sleeps more than an hour. He wishes he could be like Roy wants him to be because cleaning always makes him sad.

THE DAY PHYLLIS COMES back from suspension, she wears a bandage across one cheek. "I was slashed by a gang of chocolate drops who broke into my house," she announces to Mr. Fletcher. Marcella glares.

"We say 'black' now," Mr. Fletcher says. "We try to be considerate of others."

"They were black all right," Phyllis says. "They tried to kill me."

"Were the police called?" Mr. Fletcher says.

"The police are stupid."

"Not as stupid as a girl going to lose that overgrown Band-Aid," Marcella says, and Jason looks at Phyllis, wondering right away whether there is anything under there but her acne.

"WE'RE GOING TO HAVE another little one in the house," his mother says that night. "Roy's the daddy to the one we don't know yet, so that makes him half a father to you." She stands in the hallway outside his door as she talks, the fingers of one hand tapping against it. "He's moving in this weekend. Roy's taking up with us full time, so you'll be seeing him front and center from now on."

Jason waits until the tapping stops to say "Ok."

"His face has had an accident," she says. "You keep your thoughts about it to yourself, you hear?" Jason knows Roy is ten years younger than his mother, who is thirty-three. Whatever accident Roy's face has had is at least five years old.

THE NEXT DAY IS picture day, but Jason hasn't ordered any. "We don't have money for that," his mother says. "If they're your friends, they'll give you a picture anyway."

He sits in his desk and sees only one other boy who hasn't brought a stack of photographs from home room. It's the boy who's ready for Vietnam, nobody he could be friends with.

Mr. Fletcher lets them trade pictures for ten minutes. "That's all," he says, so do it quickly and quietly." In a minute, there are packs of photos fanned out on desks for a kind of solitaire, but nobody is trading with Phyllis, who is wearing a different bandage on her face, something so small Jason thinks he should be able to see at least a red mark outside its edges.

No matter what Mr. Fletcher says, everybody is talking out loud, but suddenly Jason hears Phyllis shouting. "I want to trade," Phyllis is yelling at Kristen, her hand pressing against the bandage.

"You're too ugly. I don't want your picture," Kristen says. Jason can see one of her photos on the desk of the girl in front of him. She's wearing her cheerleader uniform even though, Jason remembers, the pictures weren't taken on a Friday.

Mr. Fletcher looks up, but Phyllis shouts, "I want it" even louder.

"I don't want yours. Take it back," Kristen says.

Mr. Fletcher is standing now, making up his mind. Everybody is watching, so they all see Phyllis take a gun out of her purse. "Give it to me or I'll shoot you," she says, and the dilated pupil of a gun barrel fixes on Kristen's left breast. Phyllis rises over her like a teacher, and she takes all the pictures Kristen has traded for. Mr. Fletcher is fixed on that gun as he moves forward, even as Phyllis puts it back in her purse and takes her seat.

"Please don't touch your purse again," he says.

"Hunh," Phyllis grunts. "It's nothing. I bring it every day for protection from the blacks."

"Ok," Mr. Fletcher says. "Nobody's threatening you right now," and then he asks the class, row by row, to leave, and they begin to file out so straight and quiet they could be doing close order drill. When the first three rows, including Kristen, are gone, Phyllis and Jason and Marcella are all in the new front row. "I'm not shooting nobody," Phyllis says.

"That's good," Mr. Fletcher says, sitting in the empty desk in front of her.

"I got my pictures is all."

"Yes, you did," he says, and then he takes that purse from the desk, tosses it behind him, and grabs both of her arms, twisting them behind her back and slamming her face down on her desk top, scattering that stack of pictures she'd taken from Kristen.

Phyllis doesn't fight back. She doesn't scream or moan in pain even though Mr. Fletcher leans into her so hard her bandage starts to lift off just as he says, "Everybody go now," and the rest of the class gets up and leaves without saying anything, even the boys in the back.

BEFORE THE NEXT CLASS starts, Mr. Fletcher has the two boys who sit behind Phyllis move up one seat. "She ain't coming back," Marcella says. "She and her Band-Aid are off to jail."

"Girls like Phyllis don't go to jail," Mr. Fletcher says.

"They ought to," Marcella says. "For life."

"She needs to be cared for."

"She needs whupped."'

Jason opens his notebook. For once, nobody has called out "Junior" when he walked in, but now that Phyllis is gone, Jason knows he has the worst story to write about of anybody in the room.

It starts with his mother having another baby even though his father hasn't lived with them for five years. But that's not what's awful, he knows, because his little brother doesn't seem crazy even though his mother's old boyfriend Randy had only stuck around for three weeks after he was born before he left.

It's Roy who's the star of this story because an hour before he showed up with a duffel bag and a suitcase, his mother told Jason the accident his face had was caused by the shotgun he'd stuck in his mouth during his senior year in high school. "He tried to kill himself and shot off part of his face instead," she said. "If you look at him from his good side, he's a handsome man."

Jason nodded, remembering the man in the white briefs pissing on the toilet seat. "He's been through a lot," his mother kept on. "He's older than his years. You can trust a man like that."

Jason knows that Roy twisted away at the last second, blowing a hole through his cheek. He's seen Roy now. If you look at his face from the bad side, Jason thinks, you think you're in hell and start touching yourself to make sure you're all there.

HE CHECKS THE LOCKER every day, but the shoes don't come back. Only he and the thief will ever believe they were in the locker next to his for a month. Because everybody else would tell that story to a friend. Because then that friend would open the locker and see the shoes for himself.

He listens every day until Christmas vacation, but never hears any of the girls talk about losing shoes. The thief only stole from older girls, he decides, ones that he never hears because he's in ninth grade.

Or it wasn't a thief at all, he suddenly thinks as he closes his locker for the last time in 1968. Just girls he doesn't know putting a few old shoes in that locker and then laughing about Junior, the new boy, counting them, those girls beginning to add shoes because it was funny.

They could have played a better joke, Jason thinks. They could have talked about the shoes being stolen so the story reached somebody in his English class. The girl behind him could have asked him if he liked her shoes instead of just saying "Junior" in his ear. Or they could have accused Phyllis, because everybody, including him, would have believed them.

Condolences

THE POLICEMAN SAID, "Sorry to hear about this. Our condolences to you and your family." The reporter said, "I'm sorry the occasion brings me here." His neighbor said, "I have your mother in my prayers."

His mother's best friend started a Go Fund Me Facebook page that filled with "Thoughts and prayers" followed by emojis for sadness and happiness and what looked to be anger. The faces on those cartoons looked like the ones on the pain scale poster he remembered from the pediatrician's. Pick a face that matches your pain, the doctor said. He'd always picked one that represented a place just below what he felt. When a diagnosis came, he wanted to be thought of as brave.

In the intensive care waiting room, the television was tuned, each day, to talk shows hosted by women. Someone, he thought, must know the schedule and change the channel to keep a group of women chatting, but then he began to imagine there was an all-talk channel. When his mother, after a few weeks, was moved out of the ICU, the television in the waiting room was tuned to a station that carried real-life unsolved crime stories. Cold cases mostly. Sometimes decades old, friends and relatives of the victims expressing hope.

The night of the hit and run, his mother and her friend Julia had dinner at Mid-Main, two glasses of wine and the almond-crusted trout special, his mother's car parked across the street that serviced mostly local traffic at low speeds.

Somebody gets run down and nearly killed on a well-traveled highway somewhere, there's usually no telling where that car might have been bound. Close by, maybe, but fifty or a hundred miles away is a possibility, that driver on his way to some place besides just down the street to home. His mother had her pelvis crushed and her legs broken on the main street of her small town that has a bypass looped around it for traffic that isn't local. Cars on that street are driven by people who live within ten miles, tops. Mostly within five. Or fewer.

Julia remembered the make and color of the car so precisely a child could find that car. A police department computer did the work. Locally, the choices few. A jeep. White. Three or four at the most within a ten-mile radius of the small Pennsylvania town. One with recent, unrepaired body damage. Not even scrubbed to minimize the evidence. DNA still present. Two days it took.

"If he had stopped," Julia said, "I could at least stand the sight of him."

"At least," he'd thought. "At least Mom's alive. At least they have the evidence. At least there are excellent doctors. At least there's insurance."

Police lab work was necessary. Analysis. Confirmation. Ok, he said, his mother on a ventilator. Ok.

But he wanted to damage that careless, probably drunk driver who sped away. Eye-for-an-eye. Said it to himself. Wheelchair harm. Never aloud. Not yet. At least doing that asshole driver appropriate harm if God or the police didn't step in and do what's right. By the time his mother was released from the hospital. Weeks. Maybe more. Plenty of what he called "grace time," the hospital stay and the rehab center and half a dozen follow-up surgeries, As a gift to his mother, who would never heal, not completely, not ever.

BEFORE SHE LEFT THE hospital, his mother had a lawyer who said coping starts with justice. What's never said is that everyone knows who the driver is. Her friend who was with her when it happened. The bartender at the Mid-Main who served the driver during the hours before the hit-and-run. The police.

THE NEWSPAPER USED THE phrase "a person of interest." Grace, the bartender, told him that particular person lived a couple of miles south of town, that he was a regular at Mid-Main. And still was. He decided that a man who does hit and run has already proved he's a piece of shit. To his mother he substituted "worthless," but both were on the same page in his thesaurus. And for those making excuses, fuck off, that fanciful sort of thinking doesn't float. Only his mother could say that she forgave if she unaccountably chose to exercise that option. For months afterward, no sign of such a thing. "Eye for an eye," he finally said aloud.

"You touch him," his mother replied, "you ruin yourself."

Grace kept him in the know when he ran into her. "I cry sometimes," she said. "That POS sits there with his beer like nothing's happened. And he still has friends who drink with him. It's like they've been infected."

When she was released, at last, from the hospital, a donor presented his mother with a motorized scooter. The donor contacted the newspaper. A photo was taken. The scooter's owner said it had been a life-saver for him once upon a time. In the photo, the donor looked bent and fragile, his hand resting on the scooter as if for balance. In the story, the reporter called it by its brand name Pride Go-Go, a grotesquery.

"How long did they work on that silly name?" he said. "It's the old-fashioned name for a stripper."

His mother let out one of those tiny forced laughs people use when they're making up their minds how funny something is supposed to be in a crowd of strangers. "A lot of those dancers back then didn't completely strip," she said.

"You don't have to end up naked to be a stripper," he said.

"You sound like your father. Mr. Judgment Day, I used to call him when he got like that."

His father had moved to another state fifteen years ago. His mother had moved into his apartment the week before.

He lived alone. Only half an hour from where she had lived, his apartment was large enough for her and her dog. He had literal banker's hours and the rest of his weekdays to walk the dog. He did large loans. The people who wanted them were willing to wait if the dog kept him a few extra minutes.

His mother had always jogged with the dog, a golden retriever who never veered off the sidewalk. Who never needed a leash. She never tripped over it. "You start them off right and they never let you down," she said more than once.

THE DAY AFTER THE scooter story was published, a customer leaned toward his desk and said, "I saw your picture in the paper. Your Mom's the one who got busted up and the police know what's what with the driver."

"Yes," he said.

"Condolences," the man said, "but excuse me if that picture got me to thinking. I bet your mother will be riding around wishing you'd kick that fellow's ass, beat him real good."

"That's possible," he said, but now he was looking more closely at the customer, remembering his face as if he would need to be a witness.

When his mother's lawyer spoke, he heard the voice of mansions. Back at the hospital, he'd offered a free consultation. As someone who sympathizes, he'd said, as someone who could offer a legal take on where things stood.

The people who fired his mother made that call from Colorado. As if misery had no muscle if someone was entry-level and without seniority. She was going to lose a kidney, too. Not that anyone in Colorado would ever check to find out.

For six months, she had worked at the nearby college in a building with a family name on it. "A family with money," she'd said. "Maybe ten million dollars for a name on a building that size."

"And still have some left over," he'd said.

His mother had laughed. "More where that came from, I bet. It's like tithing to them."

Last fall, waiting to take her to dinner, he'd walked across that campus, listening to the girls a decade younger than him talk. Mostly, they spoke into phones as they walked, making plans, saying the names of cities that were far away and even in other countries. He walked with his head down, listening.

After that, he'd always waited upstairs in the library where it was empty or where no one spoke, reading until his mother rode the elevator up from where she was a tutor on the ground floor. Her job, she said, was to save students so they wouldn't leave. So they'd keep paying and fill dorm rooms. "It's bad business if they fail," she'd said.

HIS MOTHER WAS 5'3". She had never weighed more than 105 pounds. A ballet dancer's body. Or a skater's. When he was growing up he'd thought his mother skated as well as the girls at the Olympics. She could spin and jump and land without losing her balance. She laughed when he told her about the Olympics. "This is only one axel," she'd said. "A beginner's jump," and he would go back to working on the real beginner's moves—push and glide, stay standing. By fourteen, he was half a foot taller than his mother. "If we skate on a pond," he'd joked, "I'd be the one to go out and test the ice."

Now he foresaw his mother's surprise at the taboos of handicap, unable to lace up her skates because she had a reconstructed pelvis bone and a fused spinal column. He pictured her taking the first steps of a modest jog, how she would stagger and be stopped by the fear of falling.

His mother had carried keys in one hand and a box of leftover trout in the other as she'd crossed the street between the only two stoplights in town. A block apart. Speed in between unlikely.

Her ninth stride had been her last normal step, about to join the infirm and the crippled.

WHEN A REPORTER CALLED to arrange a first anniversary retrospective feature, lab results had still not been delivered. Any day now had been repeated by the police for months.

His mother smiled at the reporter and thanked all her well-wishers as if they were surgeons who'd fixed her completely. When the reporter left, she hobbled into her bedroom and locked the door behind her. The scooter and walker that had been photographed sat paired in the middle of the living room. Like something you'd see in a senior center, he thought, the last step before bedridden.

Half of the article was about the strange certainty that the white jeep that struck her was parked three miles away. That tests had been run, not to prove anything, but merely to confirm. That the driver remained free.

Slight. That's how the paper described his mother. Diminutive. Like a child, he thought. Like a victim.

The evening after the article appeared, his mother put down a magazine she was reading and said, "You should read this."

"What's it about?" he said.

"These men crossed Antarctica in winter when nobody ever does that, when it's dark all day and beyond cold. There was something they needed to know about the eggs·of penguins. Something so important they did what could have been suicidal."

"The eggs aren't there in the summer, are they?" he said, remembering parts of a movie he'd seen years ago.

"Imagine," she said, "the need they felt to take that risk? In order to be satisfied, they needed to know, to be absolutely sure, and they made it back, so astonishing we read about that journey in the following century."

JULIA, THE NEXT DAY, SAID, "Your Mom has more to worry about than her legs. I thought you should know."

"How much more?"

"Kidneys, for starters. Damage inside her. She won't tell you about the things you can't see."

"Like I'm six years old."

"Like you'll want to hurt that prick worse with all your eye-for-an-eye Old Testament spouting." She paused, listening, he knew, for his mother. "I used to see your mother's spirit all around her when she moved and spoke and even when she listened. She was so lithe and light on her feet. No wonder she skated. Of course, she danced." When his mother, a moment later, stepped into the living room, the space around her was as vacant and ordinary as everyone's, even strangers passing by who he barely noticed.

"Read about those penguin guys while we're gone," she said. "I bet you won't forget them."

He drove the half hour to the Mid-Main. His mother refused to go in that restaurant now. It wasn't the memory, he knew. It was the chance of seeing the white jeep driver. He ordered a cheeseburger and a beer and sat at a table. Grace, when she served a man at the bar, nodded his way. She'd told him months ago that the jeep driver always sat at the bar.

For half an hour, he listened to the driver laugh, sitting between two men who looked to be, like that driver, in their forties, and cheer as they watched the NBA playoffs, never turning away from the television, his friends, and his beer. Somebody like him will never be alone, he thought. Men like him need their pals, company to keep them from looking inside themselves.

When he left the restaurant, he searched along the nearest side streets for the white jeep, but he didn't spot it.

ONE SUNDAY AFTERNOON, HE walked beside his mother on a trail where she had run for years. The scooter was quiet on the packed mulch except when a wheel ran over leaves or, once, a plastic wrapper.

She didn't mind the name, but his mother hated the scooter, too. "It's like those things big fat people ride in the grocery store while they pick out junk food to make them fatter."

"Mom," he said, "they're not all..."

"Enough of them are to make it true."

"You're small, Mom. Nobody would think."

"They should. When I ride through the aisles, all I think about is junk food. Know why? Because I'm as helpless as the fat and the ones crippled by terrible diseases."

HE STILL WALKED THE dog even after she began to use a cane. Before that she'd used a walker. Before that, the scooter, and before all of those, she'd sat in a wheelchair after a few weeks in a hospital bed.

He walked it in the morning, over lunch, after work, in the evening. With a leash. With it tugging and sniffing and tangling itself around his legs as it circled.

WHEN THEY WERE ALONe in his apartment, his mother barely spoke, but when Julia arrived, his mother adopted her cheery voice, the one with a forced laugh at the end of every sentence like a punctuation mark for dishonesty. He listened to his clients at work and discovered they often spoke in that same voice, the one that made everything seem like a lie.

HIS MOTHER READ A lot. "If I start watching television, I won't be able to stop," she said. She read stack of memoirs, using the library's interlibrary loan. "There's so much misery," she said each time he asked what a book was about. "It's reassuring." She didn't laugh when she said this.

Julia drove her to her rehab sessions and read celebrity-filled magazines for an hour before helping her back to the car.

THE JEEP DRIVER, HE thought, must have money, or he'd have been arrested and held until making bail. Everything had been open and shut for more than a year, but the lab work hadn't yet been completed. His own job paid well. If he was arrested, he might be someone the police would protect.

In movies about revenge, it was always life or death, other goals not exciting enough for people to watch. "That's what happens every day to everybody. Nobody will pay to watch a story they're already in," his mother said.

"Hit and run doesn't happen every day," he said.

"It doesn't take a car," she said. "That driver, it's like he was crippled already, and it didn't change him. It's like a birth defect with him."

The jeep, Grace had told him, was garaged two miles from where the driver lived. She said that driver kept an old Chevy in his apartment parking lot, that he drove it to the garage, always on sunny days or clear nights, when he wanted to use the jeep. He thought that would make what he had to do easier. So many things in a garage that burn and explode, but he needed that jeep to live as evidence. So many ways fire could start so far from home, maybe enough reason an investigation would go nowhere. It would be like interest on a debt. He was a banker. Sin could be compounded, too.

He had always been afraid of fire, insisting on nothing but electric stoves, but he researched and took care. The old Chevy burned. Now that jeep would be exposed. Now that prick would know. The police he expected never knocked on his door, incompetent or approving.

THE FIRE, WHEN IT was reported in the newspaper, sounded petty. It felt like a sprained ankle that would heal. There was insurance. Inconvenience was the losing side of some poorly thought out trade agreement.

Because his mother didn't read the newspaper or watch television, he tried to imagine how Julia had described the damage over dinner somewhere, whether his mother had been excited or simply nodded before taking a sip of wine.

HE BEGAN RUNNING, SOMETHING he hadn't done since college, starting with a ten-minute mile, a jog, really. He reached two miles in sixteen minutes, but the increments of improvement had become so small he'd stopped timing himself.

Using a cane, his mother took short walks with the dog. He watched the retriever settle into the slow pace up the street and back. He took photos with his phone. Traffic passed. The dog paced itself exactly to her right, closer to the street, a gentleman according to the history of manners and ancient sloppy streets.

Even if there wasn't a full load, he did his laundry every Saturday. He folded everything neatly and laid it in drawers. He shelved groceries as soon as he brought them into the apartment. He hung his jackets up and closed the closet door, ran the dishwasher and emptied it an hour after it finished running. He replaced CD and DVD cases exactly where he had taken them from. He put the newspaper into recycling just before going to bed. "I have maid service," his mother said, laughing. When his expression didn't change, she said, "I appreciate you trying."

Julia took his mother to dinner every Thursday. Each time his mother came home chatty from a few glasses of wine. "She's such a dear," she said.

Julia told him, "Think of it as your night off" until he wanted to scream at her. Every Thursday he ate chips and dip while he drank beer, putting all of the empty cans except two into the dumpster behind the apartment house. He left those two in the recycling bin beside the sink for his mother to notice.

HIS MOTHER STOPPED GOING to rehab and did her exercises at home. For the three months before the second anniversary, she talked about moving "back where she belonged."

He'd never been in a fight, had never even thrown a punch, but now he'd fished his old metal baseball bat out of an oversized cardboard box he kept stored in the laundry room. He hefted it a few times and stuffed it halfway back in, but he began to study the anatomy of knees, how best to shatter a kneecap or destroy something equally crucial to walking normally.

He came across dozens of references to assault with a deadly weapon, remembering the phrase from television cop shows. In a couple of episodes, the weapons had been the fists of trained fighters. The only assault on a set of knees he found was the Tonya Harding and Nancy Kerrigan case, and Kerrigan had skated in the Olympics anyway. Crippling would take some doing. He had to be more thorough than the idiot who'd smacked Kerrigan and ran off before finishing the job.

The lawyer had long ago stopped calling. If it comes, justice is a miracle, his mother told him. She worked part-time now. From his apartment. She didn't have to stand for hours. Or sit for long.

ONE THURSDAY EVENING, HIS mother out again with Julia, he waited in the parking lot where the jeep driver kept his replacement car that he didn't worry about being stolen, broken into, or splashed with mud. He checked his watch and lapsed into thinking about how he'd never learned to swim, afraid of water deeper than chest high. How the nearby river, from time to time, coughed up a body, what accident might account for it if another year passed without a lab report.

While he checked his watch for the fourth time, something rapped on the passenger-side window. A policeman he thought, panicked, but the door opened and his mother dropped onto the passenger seat with a soft thud, her cane striking the dashboard and falling from her hand. A set of headlights beamed on behind him, and his mother said, "Julia, the stealth driver." She picked up the metal bat, turning it over in her hands as if they were a lathe. "You used to be so careful about putting everything away exactly in its place that I thought you might have a problem with the OCD."

"I was like eight years-old then."

"This can't do anything like the damage a car can do unless you expect to bash his head with it," she said.

"Just his knees," he said.

"I thought as much," she said, "but that's enough now, the being here, the bat."

"It won't be enough even with."

"Julia told me about your love for Leviticus. You know they cribbed all that from Hammurabi, the eye-for-an-eye thing."

"Or everybody, no matter where they live, knows it's the way it should be."

"Maybe, but just remember that all those old timers who talked about God's will and justice, they only took it seriously when the victim was a man, and even then, the injured guy needed to have money."

"Times change," he said, and she tapped his thigh with the bat.

"I've been counting empty slots in your beer cases," she said. "What do you eat with all those ones you dump somewhere? Delivered pizza? The boxes tossed somewhere? You haven't cooked for yourself on Thursdays since forever."

"Bean dip. Salsa."

"And the chip bags?"

"Always with the bottles."

"Help me move," she said, and for a second, he thought she had hurt herself dropping into the car seat. "There's an opening in the same apartment building I lived in, the ground floor."

"Perfect," he said.

"Better, at least," she said, and lightly poked his ribs, smiling. and whether or not that was a reprimand or a thank-you, it hovered between them until she dropped the bat and steadied herself, pushing against the door, then to her feet, taking one barely-aided step, then two, before leaning on the cane and turning back to face him. "You know," she said, "a man like that one would say he was within his rights to beat you to death with that bat if he came up on you and took it. He'd make himself a martyr." She turned again and hobbled two steps. "Think on that," she said, not turning this time. When he did, he thought his mother had told Julia to call that driver and keep him busy until they drifted into the lot with headlights extinguished. He might ask her, a few days from now, as he carried her things into the new apartment.

THE NEWSPAPER DIDN'T MENTION his mother for the second anniversary. A week later, when she was rushed to the hospital for surgery while he was at work, it was Julia who told him. "Your Mom said, 'See you on the other side of this.'"

"They're fixing the kidneys? Why now?"

"It's more than that."

"How much more?"

"That's what the surgery is for."

HE VISITED FOR THREE days. One kidney had been removed. The other, the doctor said, would be monitored. Dialysis was a possibility. His mother seemed lethargic. She seemed to pant rather than breathe. Her blood pressure, the doctor said, was troublesome.

During the fourth afternoon, he was at work, when Julia called. His mother was receiving antibiotics. There was more possible surgery. Sepsis, she said, but didn't elaborate.

By the time he arrived, his mother was dead. "They waited too long to treat her," Julia said.

The doctor started with "Her body attacked itself." He said "compromised" and "weakened" and "all we could."

That night, he read about the men in Antarctica. They had nearly died for something shared with a very few. How his mother had seen things, he thought, trying to go back to what her normal had become. Not satisfaction, but acknowledgement, what, now that she was gone, he could not live with.

HE WAITED UNTIL AFTER the funeral. He waited through the newspaper coverage. He waited one more day before knocking on the murdering prick's door. "Sentencing you in person," he said. "Making sure you heard first hand."

"You had your fun already. Any more, and it's you that does time."

"Eye for an eye," he said. He kept his hands in his jacket pockets and his eyes fixed on the prick's face, but nothing changed. His color stayed the same. His breathing was steady. He looked undamaged, or, at the very least, expertly repaired.

"Not if you plan it. Not pre-meditated."

"Condolences," he said. the word spilling so easily from his mouth that it sounded as if it came from such a faraway place he might not even have said it

aloud.

"I don't get you."

"Think 'pre-need,'" he said, and then, just for an instant, as he pulled his hands from his pockets, the prick's eyes flicked back and forth and his mouth opened slightly before he straightened as if he'd noticed a scratch that was small, yet so deep that it couldn't be rubbed out without delicate, expensive reconstruction, let alone his thumb.

Fool's Mate

UNCLE FRED WANTED ME to use something he called a thirty ought six to shoot across a pond on his farm at a target he'd constructed out of hay bales and a bed sheet. "Use the sight," he said. "Steady yourself like you're taking a picture of your girlfriend."

It was late April 1970, just over two months until my sixteenth birthday, when, my mother had promised the summer before, to buy me contact lenses. Since sixth grade, while the world gradually turned to soup, I'd never worn my glasses anywhere except for emergencies like spot quizzes on the blackboard or playing baseball. I'd stopped wearing them altogether when tenth grade began. The only spot quizzes all year had been in history where I sat up front and squinted hard. Facing a curve ball had made me give up baseball. But by July, I'd be practicing for my driver's test, seeing clearly required.

Now, while Uncle Fred watched from just at the edge of my peripheral vision, I pointed the rifle, pretending I could see something besides a blur of white and a hazy hint of red from where he'd pinned a crimson circle of cloth in the middle of the sheet. I fired, feeling the stock recoil into my shoulder. "High," Uncle Fred said, which meant, I decided, that he hadn't seen a sign of the bullet striking the sheet or the ground anywhere near it.

I lowered the barrel by what I imagined was the tiny fraction of an inch that would make me lucky. What I didn't want to do was miss so short that the bullet would strike the pond, which ended twenty feet from the target. If I was short, Uncle Fred would see how far off I was, maybe a ridiculous ten yards, whereas no mark could mean I'd missed by only a few feet. "High again," Uncle Fred said. "Squeeze the trigger so you don't jerk the barrel up when you fire."

I needed to hit something. I squinted like I always did on the vision tests in grades school until that didn't help me get past the first three lines. Finally, I thought I saw red and squeezed. "Low," Uncle Fred said, disdain creeping into his tone, and I looked so blankly at him he frowned. "Maybe your Pop should get your eyes checked."

"I'll let him know," I said. I needed to hit the surface half way across the pond to even see a splash.

"You're not letting the gun do the work," he said. "It's made so you don't have to do much thinking."

I passed it to him. "I'll try it again next time." I imagined looking through the sight wearing my contact lenses. If it was easy as Uncle Fred claimed, the red cloth would be so clear I couldn't miss.

"You think too much is your problem. You wait until the army gets you. They'll straighten you out. You know what I'm saying? There's war going on."

Uncle Fred had fought in Korea and wished, every time that war was mentioned, we'd gone after China and taken care of two birds with one H-bomb. When I didn't answer, he said, "Your Pop let it slip you went to that protest downtown."

"For a social studies project," I said, spouting the words so quickly, Uncle Fred must have thought I'd made up that story while I was still standing by the capitol building in Harrisburg.

"Those draft dodgers need the business end of this rifle. You get me?" He was breathing hard, like voicing his contempt and anger was like running uphill.

"I'm not old enough to dodge," I said, but he aimed and fired. The sheet flapped. "Good shot," I said, and he turned, his face so close to mine I could see his pores and sweat. He twisted away, set himself, and fired again. The sheet with the red spot didn't move, but when he grinned and nodded as if satisfied, I felt myself go empty inside as if I'd imploded. A breeze stirred the high grass in front of us, but when I squinted, the sheet with the red spot kept hanging limp and still.

UNCLE FRED WAS A straight-shooter, no patience with fools who, as he put it, "weren't worth a hoot in hell." But out of six choices, he was my favorite uncle, and he'd returned the favor ever since I could remember. True, I didn't have a brother and only had three cousins on my father's side who were boys, but they were the sons of Fred's sister Eileen, all of them in their twenties by then and, in Uncle Fred's phrase, "not much to speak of." I figured I was the last hope of a man who was childless and no prospects of that condition changing because my Aunt Clarise had suffered three miscarriages and a hysterectomy since I'd been old enough to understand what all of that meant.

Aunt Clarise wanted a son to dote on, too, giving me presents without Christmas or my birthday on the calendar. Like the chess set she gave me when I visited months before my tenth birthday. "Fred says this is the game every boy should learn," she said. Uncle Fred arranged the pieces for me and moved them around, explaining what each was capable of. "You read up on this," he said. "You practice for a while, and then I'll give you some pointers."

When I followed my mother to our car, I held up the chess set box so the old couple who lived next door could see. They smiled and waved from their yard. Like Uncle Fred, they rented out most of their property to a man who raised corn, the farming taking place on the other side of a thin stand of trees. Uncle Fred always complained that they didn't take enough care of their property that wasn't farmed, but it was mostly, I knew, that except for that one house and yard, there was nothing but fields of corn behind them and open space on either side. Fifty years ago, he'd told me, two brothers had split the fifty acres of property and put their houses right beside each other, one on either side of where they divided the property. "Like fools."

A month later, I carried that box back inside his house and told him I was getting good, that I'd beaten a neighbor boy who was twelve and had a set made of wood instead of plastic. Uncle Fred said, "Show me."

It took him twelve moves to checkmate me. "Try again," Uncle Fred said. I lasted eleven moves. He said, "Once more."

Panicking, I decided to open by sending my pawns out in an unusual way to confuse him. This time he beat me in three moves. "That's called the Fool's Mate," he said. Then he stood up and walked away. The neighbors were outside, but I kept the box under my arm when I walked to the car.

My father said, "Fred has his ways. You're old enough to understand."

My Latin teacher had her ways. She reseated twenty-eight of us after every test, from best score to worst, announcing the numbers. Because I'd never been seated anywhere but the first two seats, I loved that class, though sometimes, waiting for a test to be returned the next day, I'd lie awake worrying that I'd fall back to the third seat or, nightmarishly, the second row. For sure, I didn't brag to Uncle Fred about how much I knew. "Latin is for priests," he said. "Everybody knows the kind of men priests are."

Besides remembering all those rules and memorizing the words for everything, I also got to sit near Becky Smarsh because I'd never been anywhere but first or second chair, and neither had Becky. "You two, the teacher said. "If you were a couple, you'd end up hating each other." For months, I'd been hoping to have the chance to prove her wrong. After class, we had started talking to each other while we walked to biology, where we were separated by the alphabet, S and B four rows apart. I kept thinking I needed to hurry that couple-promise along because once April ended, my opportunities would begin to wind down just like school.

For sure, April was my father's favorite time of year. The birds returned, and my father loved to identify them from a distance. I barely saw movement and flight. Spots on the branches that were close. He called out names and

I looked as if marveling. "They're beautiful," he would say, and I hoped he
would soon tire of looking and naming like some sort of Adam.

My father was proud of his eyesight but wouldn't correct his hearing.
Fred seemed to be able to overhear my thoughts, but he wore glasses every waking minute. I'd inherited my eyesight from my mother, but she'd
been dead for eight months by then, and my father, always what my mother
called "reluctant," had lapsed into entire days of silence, leaving my personal
habits for me to figure out. "Your Pop always thought wives do the indoor
things," Aunt Clarise said, who started buying me sweaters to wear over my
wrinkled shirts.

Uncle Fred rephrased her. "Your Mom, before she died, didn't let you
dress like a hillbilly and eat like a pig. Listen to your aunt. She's the only one
you have within shouting distance."

My father's other brother and his wife had moved to New Mexico a few
years ago. On my mother's side, there were only aunts by blood, but all three
lived in Missouri where my mother had grown up and didn't do anything but
send a card for birthdays and Christmas, and all those were signed by my
aunts, two of them still folding a five-dollar bill inside each time. Uncle Fred
and Aunt Clarise lived twenty miles away, what my mother had always called
"a hop, skip, and a jump."

When I was twelve, Uncle Fred bet me five dollars I couldn't swim
across his pond. "It's not far," he said. "You can throw a rock across it, no
problem." What he wanted to know was whether I could manage the first
ten feet without panicking and sinking. "Your Pop never learned," he said,
"and it looks like he's never going to make sure you do, so here's your chance
to catch up to all the boys." We were in the old rowboat he kept for fishing
for the trout he stocked the lake with each year. Just then, we were drifting
in the deepest part, and as he finished his short speech, he had me stand
up. "Ok now," he said, "we're jumping when I get to three and don't you be
a pussy."

I was still thinking that over when Fred said "Three" and pushed me. He
followed, but instead of helping me stay afloat, he paddled by the boat to make
sure I didn't grab it. "Don't panic," he said. "Let yourself go. You can't drown
unless you lose your mind and flap around like some limp-wristed pansy."

The first Saturday in May, at the Roaring 20s class party, I was excited
because Becky Smarsh flirted like a flapper in a thrift-store slip dress and a
string of pearls. "Don't you love feeling like it's long ago?" she said. I cinched

my grandfather's vest; his silver watch chain sparkled. "Maybe next year we can have a Victorian party," she said. "Or even a medieval one."

"In armor?" I said.

"A codpiece," she said, laughing while I forced the grin I guessed I was supposed to flash.

Our Latin teacher was the class advisor. She played a recording of the Charleston to get all of us into the mood, but when only a dozen girls tried dancing with each other like they were in a black and white movie, she gave up and let the student dj play the songs we loved. Becky held her arms out like an invitation. When we began to dance, she pressed against me until my arms wrapped around her like we were going steady. "I hate biology," she said. "Freitag makes the Bible a book of fairy tales."

During lab that week, along the classroom's smooth black counter, I'd watched her, from three stations away, completing the same experiment Rob Baker and I were doing. The one Pasteur had managed years ago to refute the old-timey belief in the presence of "life-force" in air. Now, she laid her head against my shoulder and told me that she loved the recipes of ancient biology that Mr. Frietag recited, expecting us to laugh. "My father says science makes us small," she said, and then she stepped back, the music still playing, and asked, "Do you like this dress?" Couples moved back and forth around us as she gave me a chance to stare directly at her body. I didn't say anything. "I guess you do," she said, rewrapping her arms around my back.

A few songs later, our Latin teacher said, "Look at you two" as she did a chaperone weave across the high school gym. She didn't tell us to unclutch.

"Mrs. Glick approves," Becky said. "Let's go out next Saturday. I have a license now. My father never goes anywhere but work and church."

"Go out where?" I managed.

"A surprise," she whispered.

SATURDAY NIGHT, BECKY DROVE slowly on the back roads near her house until we reached the state game lands and parked. "Surprises are fun," she said. "Are you ready?'

She flicked the headlights on, then off, sending some signal into the trees, creating, she said, the evening and the morning of the first day. "My father would worry we're as alone as Adam and Eve," she said, reciting the passages about God's simple, yet perfect recipes for births from clay and rib. "Kiss me," she said. She flicked the lights again as if she wanted God's finger pointing at us as I leaned toward her.

She was breathing hard. "Imagine being Adam," she said, "after you ate that apple. How you would see Eve now." She unbuttoned her blouse. "Just look, Chris. Don't touch." The pale blue bra she was wearing left most of her breasts exposed. Then she buttoned her blouse again while I tried to remember what I'd learned in Sunday School about dirt and bones. "Surprised?" she said. And then she started the car. "Now, let's go get something to eat besides an apple."

My father relied upon indefinite nouns and the absence of direct objects. "What do you think you're doing?" he said when I slept in Sunday morning and missed church. Then he relied, as always, on the silent treatment, not speaking to me until I apologized. It was worse than being hit because it left things up to me to make the punishment end.

"He'll burst a blood vessel someday keeping all that anger inside," my mother sometimes told me. But her own body, it turned out, was verifying that feeling. When I was ten, she'd been hospitalized with blood pressure so high a doctor expected stroke.

"Just a scare," my father said, "just a scare," repeating himself until, five years later, my mother's aneurysm translated his phrase to "We've lost her."

A WEEK AFTER THE funeral, Aunt Clarise had called and said, "Your Mom mentioned those contact lenses to me once. I'll make sure they're taken care of."

"They're expensive," I started.

"For your birthday, just like she promised. But this will be the last time for a gift that's a thing. All you need from now on is money, just like the rest of us, and it goes into a college fund so you have a little something when off you go to be a doctor."

It sounded as if sixteen was the age of consent for the end of celebration.

ON MOTHER'S DAY, AS if Uncle Fred thought my father would be mourning like it was a wedding anniversary, he carried two six packs of tall boys into our house, sliding one into the refrigerator and setting the other one on an outdated *TV Guide* on the living room coffee table. After he passed one to my father, he handed me one. "Take your time with this. You need to learn." My father, without speaking, took a sip of his beer before placing it on the carpet and walking down the hall to the bathroom.

"That's your Pop, right there," Uncle Fred said. "Taking a pass. It goes all the way back to missing his chance to serve. He'll never know how he'd measure up, and now everything that feels like a battle chases him away."

"He was ready," I said. "The doctor stopped him."

"I was a junior in high school, not much older than you are now, when he got called. When he came over to the house to say he'd failed the physical, your Granddad and I could tell he was happy even though he tried not to show it."

"That doesn't mean he'd run away if he'd gone."

"War is opportunity," Uncle Fred said. His glasses reflected the light in a way that made me squint. "I don't have to explain myself, do I?" He held his stare until I nodded. "Good. When perspective calls, be sure to listen." He lifted his beer to his mouth, but both of us knew my father must have heard that last part coming back in the hallway. Fred narrowed his eyes then, giving me the once-over. "Your boy needs a haircut," he said, but I could tell my father was stuck in silence mode. "That Kent State thing is only the beginning. The Guard showed the way."

Opening his second beer, Uncle Fred looked so unfamiliar I almost expected his next sentence to be spoken in a foreign language. My father stared out the window as if his good ear was clogged with wax. Whatever I had to say to Uncle Fred could wait until I was an adult. Whatever my father needed to say had less than another minute to be uttered. Anything would have done.

WHAT MY FATHER DID, after Fred polished off the living room beer, leaving the other six-pack as a gift and promising to drive slow and careful, was try to explain from his spectator's point of view. "Your uncle came home in one piece on the outside, but there's more to it than that. Pour the rest of that beer in the sink. Let's go for a ride and I'll show you a few things."

In ten minutes, we were on the street where he'd grown up, but we weren't there, he said, to stop in at Granddad's. He parked on the next block. "Ted Delo's house right here," he said. "Ray Tolley's over there." I'd heard those names before and guessed he was trying to shore up who he wanted me to see in himself.

The houses were on opposite sides of the yellow-bricked street, but I thought you could switch them and not know which was which. "Ted Delo died in Italy. Ray Tolley died in France. Ted's mother has lived here twenty-seven years more years without her boy and a good chunk of that without the husband she lost to the bottle by the time Fred was off to his war. She's been on a walker for the last eighteen months. There she sits on her porch."

My father called out, reminding her who he was. I said hello, and she raised a hand a few inches before she looked confused and rested it on the arm of her chair. An oxygen canister sat nearby. "Lung troubles," my father whispered.

A door slammed across the street where Ray Tolley had lived, and a couple, both with shoulder-length hair, hurried down the stone steps to a blue VW. After they pulled away, Mrs. Delo clucked her tongue. "We have hippies now," she said, as if they were a disease. She rocked forward and sat back as if concentrating on breathing. When she sat up again, she said, "I remember you from when you were newborn. Your Grandma, may she rest in peace, was still on her feet then."

As we walked back to the car, my father said, "Ray Delo and I took our physical together. We'd have gone in together, but he passed and I didn't. You wouldn't be here if it wasn't for my bum ear."

"It feels as if I've just been born when I sunbathe naked outside," Becky said. She propped herself on her elbows and laughed. "Don't you look like a lost puppy. We have that high fence around the backyard. My Dad likes privacy so much that nobody can see me but God."

She wasn't naked, but we were at the county park, not in her backyard, and the pastel-green bikini she wore gave away most of her to whoever cared to look. "Just to be sure," she added, "I've checked the expression of the man who lives next door." The sunlight was so bright I had squint. "There's a poet," she said, "who says tanning is like being fucked by God," and I felt as if I'd become weightless, vanishing like the cream I'd rubbed slowly into nearly every part of her flesh, how she protected herself like someone preparing for a future of being adored.

"What's her name?" I said. Her tan was already so deep it seemed, just then, to absorb the light until I could stare, eyes wide, without blinking.

Instead of telling me, she said, "Think about that. God can watch any girl he wants."

Becky's father made no secret that God watched everybody, regardless of their age or gender. Becky said he was tracing the "begats" through every century in the six thousand years since we had sprung from dust, everyone a cousin descended from a pair of parents. So far, he had the most recent sixteen spread across rolls of butcher paper, working back to the ones listed in the Bible, expecting them to fit them together like the transcontinental railroad meeting up perfectly in Utah around the time his great-great grandfather had been born.

Becky's father was in the room with us as we unrolled that thick, tan paper across the perfectly polished kitchen floor. "Have you been saved, son?" he said.

"Dad," Becky started, but his expression didn't change. "You consider on that, son. There's nothing more important than that."

"I will," I said, which was the truth. He had me thinking about how I didn't expect to be saved whatsoever. Becky, too. And him, for that matter. Someday, when English was dead and gone and being taught like Latin, a classroom full of fifteen-year-old kids would be translating the stories about God and Jesus and all the rest, wondering who would have ever believed such myths.

MR. FRIETAG SPENT THE last two weeks of the school year on heredity, showing charts of plant and animal family trees that I thought would crush the fantasies of Becky's father. As if she heard me thinking, Becky said, "My Dad's not the only one, but Frietag would lump them all together as fools."

"Next year is chemistry. Maybe there's nothing for him to get worked up about."

"Yes, there is. And he'll miss Latin. All that faith."

"So will I. I'll miss sitting in the desk we've earned."

TWO SATURDAYS AFTER SCHOOL ended, I earned 20/20 vision by enduring the pain of having plastic contact lenses inserted on my eyes. The optometrist hadn't exaggerated, not even a little bit, about what he called "discomfort," but when I managed to keep my eyes open, the world was so astonishingly clear that I felt reborn.

Every morning, my father would look at my face as if he thought I was going blind, but after a week he lapsed into repeating, "Make sure you're extra careful when you put your eyes in. Your aunt paid good money for them."

Uncle Fred, when he saw me, said, "So you can see, but you can't keep your eyes open?"

"Something like that."

"When's that squinting going away?"

"Soon," I said, something I hoped was true.

When I saw Becky, her body, even from across the room, was so clear that she looked like someone I'd never seen before.

THE WEATHER, IN MID-JULY, turned awful, the rain heavy and lasting for two days and showing no sign of ending. My father didn't let me practice driving. "Another week will be good for you," he said. "That test can wait until August."

The four lawns I was cutting could wait, too, so when he went to work, Becky drove over, showing up while I was watching flood story news on television news. "Just think," she said, after I turned the TV off, "what could happen if it kept up?" With the drapes shut and the lights not on, the living room was so dark that it seemed like her voice came from far away. "Your house is up high," she said. "Which animals would you allow to shelter here?"

"That's not going to happen," I said.

Becky laughed. "Of course not," she said, beginning to undress me. "Everybody thinks they're so smart. Rainbows are just refracted light until you decide you need them to finish a story."

"I like how this story might end," I said, lying back naked on the carpet.

"Look at you," she said. "You know the whole story, right? After the rainbow disappears, Noah ends up being seen naked by his children."

Her blouse was open now, her skirt hiked up. Right then, seeing her with corrected vision, I wanted her to stay half-dressed, even her face staying partially hidden in the darkness.

"That poet had it wrong," I said. "God would want to fuck you on a cloudy day. He'd like a little mystery."

"Chris," Becky said, her voice sounding as if it came from beneath the floor. She took my hand and guided one finger inside her. She began to move, humming, and when she touched me, I came immediately.

"I HAVE AN IDEA for your boy, and it can't wait," Uncle Fred had said to my father on the phone before he invited us to meet him at a tavern far enough out of town it had an RFD address. As soon as we sat down at a table, my father acted as if Uncle Fred would start in on how he should use the last half of my summer vacation as an introduction to boot camp, but all Fred seemed interested in was the grease-stained menu.

"These are the best fish sandwiches you'll ever eat," he said. "Never mind the smoke and the hillbilly music." Above the bar, a maroon flag covered most of one wall. A braided gold trim ran around the edges. There were no emblems or designs, just the embroidered words, in the same gold thread, GO TO HELL VIETNAM DEMONSTRATORS

The waitress slapped a pitcher of Schmidt's and two empty mugs on the table. "And here you go," she said, carefully placing a glass of Pepsi in front of me.

"So," Uncle Fred said to me, filling the two mugs, "what are you doing different with yourself now that you can see?"

"I don't know. Cut grass until I go back to school."

Uncle Fred shook his head and drank his beer straight down while my father sipped. I swirled my ice cubes, hoping the waitress would come by with a refill. Uncle Fred poured himself a second beer. My father looked as unhappy as Uncle Fred claimed.

The fish sandwiches, as huge as promised, spread beyond the perimeters of the plates. For a few minutes, all three of us dug in until Uncle Fred, his sandwich half-finished, lifted his mug, placed his elbow on the table, and held it in a practiced way a foot from his mouth. "I have a story for the both of you," he said. He drank off half the beer and kept the mug in that ready position. "A blind beggar minds his own business until some boys start bothering him," he began, and my father's expression lapsed into what looked like sorrow. "They mock the way he moves, which he can't see, but all this foolishness draws a bigger crowd. And then they mock what he says, yell things at him, touch him, finally, and goad him into swinging his cane."

I saw where this was going. It sounded like *King Kong* or *The Hunchback of Notre Dame*, but Uncle Fred took a time out to finish his beer and take a few bites of sandwich before he dropped back in. "They dodged his cane while he swung harder and harder, going by sound, until he happened onto a target, the skull of a girl who was just passing by on her way to go shopping. Ka-whop, she was down and bleeding. The blind man thought everybody was quiet because they'd finally wised up and were going to leave him be. He dropped his cane, and then they rushed him and beat him senseless."

"Did the girl die?" I said.

"That's up to you. That's as far as the story goes."

Uncle Fred pushed his plate away and filled his mug to the brim. When he tipped the pitcher over my father's mug, there was barely a trickle. The waitress, as if she'd kept an eye out, walked our way to ask if we needed a refill, but Uncle Fred stood, dropping a twenty-dollar bill on the table. "I've got this," he said. With only a one breath pause, he polished off his beer. "Slow and careful," he said, shuffling toward the door like he could use a cane of his own.

"Finish up," my father said, after he'd added three one-dollar bills to the twenty and the waitress gathered them. For a minute, without touching what was left of his sandwich or his beer, he watched me eat. When my plate was clear, he said, "Drive us home." He didn't speak again until we were parked in the driveway. "Well done," he said. "Let's get you that license this week."

Once we were inside, my father watched television for over an hour while I listened to the radio in my room and counted down the time until Becky would rescue me. I heard him go in and out of the kitchen three times. A bunch of snacking or a lot of restlessness, I thought. He was there for the fourth time when the phone rang, so he picked up before I made my bedroom door. After he didn't call me, I decided to head to the bathroom for a fresh-up shower.

I wore only fresh underwear when I turned the corner and re-entered my room. My father was sitting on my bed. He didn't stand; he turned off the radio. "That was your Aunt Clarise. Fred hit someone with his car on his way home." He looked slowly around my room, investigating each wall as if he'd just realized where he was.

"And?" I said.

"A child," he said. "Fred told her a boy ran out from between two parked cars like they do sometimes chasing something." His pause was shorter this time. "A ball. A dog. Another boy. She didn't say because that's when Fred took the phone from her and right off, said the boy was at least school age."

"Six?" I said. "Seven? Eight?"

"Old enough to know better, maybe."

"Uncle Fred said that?"

"No, he just said 'school age.' And then he said he did what he could for the boy while he waited for the police and the ambulance to come. The cops gave him one of those breath tests they do nowadays. He passed, he said, but he told them he'd had a few at the fish sandwich place, that they could check his story with the bar."

"What's a few even mean to the police?" I said. "How much does a pitcher of beer hold?"

"At that place? Quart and a half. Fred didn't say anything about them checking with us. After that, he didn't sound like himself."

"What's left to tell? Is the boy hurt bad? He always goes slow when he drinks."

As soon as he looked away, I knew things were serious. "The boy died. We haven't heard the end of this."

I called Becky to let her hear the news. Then I walked three houses down to where a policeman lived and asked him about the drinking while driving numbers. "Someone you know in trouble?" he said, glancing up the street as if he expected to see my father.

"It's for school," I said. "For biology class."

"It's .15. Close to a six-pack in an hour for a man of ordinary size."

"Thanks," I said.

"Put in your report that anybody but a fool thinks that number should be reset down to .10."

When I got back to the house, my father, who I'd never seen having more than two beers at one time, seemed surprised at first by those numbers. "Really?" he said. "Well, in that case, Fred is safe. He wasn't in the wrong." When he didn't move, I thought he was recalculating, and I walked to my room to do some rethinking of my own.

Twenty minutes later, the phone rang. Though my door was open, my father began to talk so softly I couldn't hear what he was saying. I sat up straight on the edge of the bed and waited until I heard him drop the receiver into its cradle. He was still standing by the phone when I entered the kitchen. "More bad news," he said. "Fred shot himself."

"How bad?" I said.

"In that patch of woods on the far side of the pond," my father said. "Where it was private. I have to go. You make do here."

I MADE DO BY calling Becky and blurting the news. "My parents are at a church meeting," she said. "Can you get here somehow?"

"On my bike," I said.

"Like a little boy," she said. "Do it."

In her room, as soon as I arrived, Becky said, "Your uncle decided to go Biblical. He did what he needed to do to get out of hell."

"The one right here on Earth," I said.

"The other one, too. The one that never ends. Can you imagine him there?" For once, though she'd told me we would be alone for two hours, her blouse wasn't half open. Her skirt stayed extended half way to her knees. "Go ahead," she said. "Try." She twirled her hair on one finger, looking at the floor as if she'd spotted something crawling. As if she was thinking of allowing its legs to find her bare calf and climb. As if she would welcome six, eight, or a hundred legs.

I sat back, thinking she was testing me, and what I wished I could do was close her wide-open door and lock it. Instead, I examined the floor, found nothing, and believed, suddenly, that she was imagining the geology of hell, a fault groaning beneath us while her hair twirled and the one lit lamp flared into brilliance, its weather swooning through my nerves until I moved toward her. From outside, from that only nearby yard, somebody started a lawnmower, its roar approaching and receding until the engine stalled. Whoever was mowing pulled the cord, the engine catching, then stalling again. Three more times, the cord was yanked, each pull and release promising less, then not even that.

The Geography of Ridicule

"First agenda item is the loyalty oath," Mr. Gloff said. It was 8:01, the morning after Labor Day, and I stood with fifty-five other teachers at Liberty High School and raised my right hand. The oath was a repeat-after-me, a wedding vow for allegiance to the United States in our words and deeds while our students could see and hear us. I said the phrases out loud, and so did everybody else.

The second item was the time clock, new this year because the sign-in sheet didn't work the previous year. "Some days there were thirty signatures at 7:59," Mr. Gloff said. "We all know that's impossible."

Nobody objected until after the meeting. "It's a factory now," an older man walking in front of me said to the woman beside him. "Everybody knows why."

She nodded like she knew. When they passed a pair of guys my age, the man said, "Happy now?" to them, but kept moving.

"Draft dodgers," the woman said, and I slowed down before I had to pass them and hear myself, the new teacher, judged by a pair of strangers.

The second week of school, a few seconds after every teacher in the faculty lunch room finished laughing at Steve Wharton's "LBJ's still not running" joke, Fred Stepnowski smiled. Not like somebody a little late to get it, but like he was drunk or simple-minded or telling himself a different story altogether, pleased by a secret punch line. I was happy to polite-laugh, relieved to have my job, and it was easier to oblige lousy jokes and lunch time gossip than to let somebody know I was as bored as Nixon choking out "Sock it to me" on *Rowan and Martin's Laugh-In* because his campaign manager thought it would make him look human.

It was Stepnowski's first year, too, so two weeks of seeing him smile late like that at the lunch table was teaching me how quickly somebody could be tagged an oddball. Worse, he kept to himself in his science classes. Students said he taught on mute. "You know," they said. "His lips move, but he doesn't say anything."

He was the first new teacher to get a nickname that stuck. *Chemo*, his students called him, and that name swept through the school, all the way down to the ninth graders I had for English. Students laughed at the name in unison. I had enough of it after two days. "He's not teaching chemotherapy," I said.

"But it's perfect," a girl in my best class said.

High achievers were what Liberty called her and the other twenty-nine during second period. I was grateful for them. My other five classes were two middles and three lows because I had all 176 ninth graders. "Anywhere but in here," I said, the first thing I'd demanded since school began. But every day during the third period study hall duty I shared with Stepnowski, boys blurted that name aloud from the back of the room, sounding as if they were calling a dog.

I had the front for my share, two thirds of the room to watch over because of where the break came among the rows, so I left it up to Stepnowski to deal with it because those voices always came from the last four rows. Stepnowski never spoke. He stared at the forty seats he patrolled in a way that didn't focus on anyone, and then he'd open one of those super-size candy bars the band sold, peel the foil, and break off two squares at a time to hold in his mouth like a chocolate cough drop.

I figured that chocolate for going soft in the pocket of his sport coat, but he never wiped his fingers, so I decided he kept them refrigerated in his lab. Sooner or later, I thought, students would tell me they'd discovered his cold cache of candy the way they told me they knew Miss Blatty, who taught seventh grade math across the hall from me, kept a flask in her top file drawer that was always locked. What I couldn't figure was why those shouts of "Chemo" stayed spotty, only once every ten minutes or so during that forty-five-minute study hall. It was as if five boys—never a female voice—had a plan to each shout once a day.

But by October I'd heard so many "Chemo" shouts, the number creeping up to eight or ten different voices per period, I started to worry that our study hall was being secretly observed, that Mr. Gloff could listen through the speaker system supposedly meant to send messages one way. I thought of how I'd be evaluated after bursts of "Chemo" were never reprimanded. Somebody eavesdropping wouldn't know which part of the room those voices came from. For all Gloff would know, I was standing close to those shouters and letting Stepnowski be humiliated.

There was something on every teacher's record called "large group discipline situations." Half the questions Mr. Gloff had asked when I'd interviewed had been about discipline, my ability to punish and make those punishments stick. I didn't want a "must improve" penciled in on my form. In the fall of 1968, I needed the teaching deferment. "Sweetness," Alex Cole, a second-year teacher, told me the first week, and I nodded my agreement. Stepnowski, five seconds later, smiled.

Mr. Gloff had recommended Miss Blatty to me during orientation. "You talk to her, and she'll set you straight," he'd said. "Take it as in-service. Rely on the judgment of a long-time teacher you have the good fortune of being across the hall from."

Miss Blatty was short and gnarled and a veteran of thirty-six years of seventh and eighth grade math, beginning, she told me, in 1932, "When you didn't have to put up with any lip."

She was a stickler for the female student dress code. She measured skirts for the number of inches they rose above the knee; she examined each new style to insure the design was really a skirt, and when she noticed a threat, she acted. In October, one of my high achievers, dressed in culottes, was dragged out of her chair by Miss Blatty before the bell rang. "If you won't do your job, I'll do it for you," she said, while I regretted not slapping her face in a great gesture of relinquishing my protection from the draft. That girl left my room in tears; she reappeared, just before the end of class, wearing a skirt.

I'd seen worse spinelessness than mine in the face of Miss Blatty's wrath. The second day of school, when I'd settled into a chair in the faculty lounge at the beginning of fourth period, Miss Blatty walked in just as Wharton lit up. "Just because there's smokers in here the rest of the day doesn't mean there's smokers in here now," Miss Blatty said. "You can't wait, you go to the men's room."

"And then what?" Wharton said.

"You'll think of something to keep you busy," Miss Blatty said, and then she laughed one of those cackles belonging only to witches and spinster school teachers.

Wharton looked at his cigarette as if it might counsel him on what to say next. "Maybe I should have my schedule changed," he said at last. He flicked his lighter on and then off, stood, and walked out, leaving the door open as if that was some sort of statement.

The word about my study hall got around. Miss Blatty, after I kept showing up to sit with her and Mrs. Benn, the ninth-grade history teacher, asked me about the "Chemo!" taunts. When I told her about the geography of ridicule, she snorted. "Can't let it fester," she said. "Whatever you do, you do it right away on the spot."

"It's better to be tough right off the bat, and then ease up," Mrs. Benn agreed.

"Or don't ease up at all," Miss Blatty said. "That Stepnowski fellow should crack one of those smart asses across the back of the head. That would be the last time he'd hear Chemo spoken aloud."

Mrs. Benn shook her head. "Some men are like that. They can't raise a hand to anybody."

"Not like yours," Miss Blatty said.

Mrs. Benn went back to her book, but I'd already heard the stories about her husband, how every year, on the first day of class, he stripped off his coat and challenged his students. "Anybody who thinks he's tough enough, you walk up here now and take your best shot," he said to each class. Because he taught general math to juniors and seniors, he had almost all of the worst students in the school. But no one, twenty years and running, had stepped up.

I'd seen the proof. Walking into an assembly with him the week before, the auditorium filled with a thousand students talking among themselves, I'd heard the room go quiet row by row as we moved from the back to the front, every one of those students shutting up as we passed. I knew they weren't going quiet for me.

The school had a no t-shirt rule, and Miss Blatty paddled boys in her classes for wearing them before she sent them to the office. "Somebody from home brings them a change of clothes, or they sit down there all day," she said. "You want me to smack your t-shirters? And the ones with hair over their collars—they get a day to be rid of it. It's in the rules for those who give a damn." She looked at me in a way that declared I was one of those who didn't.

That was the week of the first Men's Marching and Chowder Club meeting, the Saturday before Halloween. The night was full of beer and spaghetti and a choice of gambling games like pool, poker, or shuffle-baseball. By the time we'd finished eating, I'd poured from half a dozen pitchers. When each of the new teachers was told to stand up and say something to introduce himself, I joked about my Mr. Chips premonition, that I'd be sitting here with a beer in my hand in 2008 as long as somebody forty years younger went to the bar and got it for me. Everybody clapped, and Mr. Gloff jumped up and declared that this was his thirty-first season, and what made his job so wonderful was being able to see, each September, "all those young tits walking toward me." Everybody laughed. Stepnowski, sitting three tables away, smiled when Gloff sat down. By the time things settled, nobody remembered to demand his new-guy's speech.

ON MONDAY STEPNOWSKI FELL into step with me as soon as study hall ended. "You married?" he said.

"No," I said.

"Good for you." A group of girls in tight sweaters coming toward us made me think of Mr. Gloff. "My mother always checked me for ticks when I was a boy," Stepnowski went on. "She thought they were up to something."

We'd received a memo that morning about a head-lice scare. Maybe Stepnowski was using it as an icebreaker. "My mother thought telling me to stay out of the woods was preventive medicine. There are two kinds of ticks, did you know that?"

"No," I said, beginning to believe this had nothing at all to do with head lice, that Stepnowski had saved this up to test my good will. A moment later I began to decelerate because we were nearly to the intersection in the hall where I'd turn to the faculty room and Stepnowski would head straight for his next science class.

Stepnowski didn't slow down. He was already three steps away when he said, "Ticks are all deaf and blind, but both kinds smell you coming."

The next day, during study hall, a girl's voice squealed "Chemo!" A minute later, a second girl called out. I watched to see if I could pick the next girl out, but that was it for the day except one boy near the period's end. When the time came, I'd tell Stepnowski which seat, and he could deal with it or not.

As soon as I stepped out of the room, Stepnowski was beside me. "Ambush ticks and hunter ticks," he said, re-entering the story as if the arm of a record player had been raised and held overnight before dropping back into the groove from which it had been lifted. "Ambush ticks just sit there in the weeds and wait for something to brush against them," he said. "Hunter ticks track you down."

"Really?"

"Makes you think, doesn't it?" Stepnowski said. "You know how many ticks grow up to be adults?"

We were coming up on my left turn to the faculty room. "No idea," I said at once, because I wanted to know the answer before the next day.

Stepnowski kept walking, taking six more strides before he answered, "One in a million," making it sound like the odds for the success of our students.

STEPNOWSKI WAS ABSENT FOR the rest of the week. With a substitute in study hall, there was more chatter, but nobody shouted "Chemo!" for three days. The woman who was filling in paced around her forty desks so quickly I started counting her rotations. Thirty-seven, I got to, and I added on three to make a round number because I hadn't counted until she picked up speed. The second day, she slowed to thirty-five.

Two minutes later, instead of going directly to the lounge, I went back to get the anthology I used for my middle achievers. I closed the door, walked to my desk, and laid my grade book down. Then I stood right there to watch Miss Blatty through the windows of our two closed doors because she was fishing in her file cabinet. It was all I could do to keep from pressing my face to the glass, hoping to see her unlock her file drawer and drink from a hidden flask.

What she did was lift out what looked to be a folder of pre-printed tests, the sort of exam a professional agency uses to see how students match up all across the country. She slid that folder inside her grade book and turned so quickly, looking my way, that I had to open the door at once to keep her from knowing I was spying.

I was eight steps down the hall before she called out to me. "Forget something?" she said, and I immediately touched my sport coat as if I could forget I was wearing it. I stopped and looked back, substituting gesture for my voice because I thought it would crack. She patted her grade book, and I smiled, walking back to retrieve it. "You get more than a wrist slap for that," she said.

Because she didn't wait, I had to follow her up the hall and open the door she closed behind her even though she must have heard how close my footsteps were. "Young Corey Gillis here just about committed a mortal sin," she announced to Mrs. Benn.

Mrs. Benn looked me up and down. "Grade book not in his possession?" she said, and Miss Blatty cackled.

"I had a mind to steal it off his desk when he left it," she said, staring at me instead of looking at Mrs. Benn. "But then I thought I'd give him grace this once."

"Listen," she went on after I sat down. She dropped her voice, but didn't move closer. "Do you want to be a fool for kindness?" I had to tell myself not to lean toward her as she nearly whispered. Mrs. Benn didn't look up from the newspaper. "Psychology," she said, "is for those who can't fend for themselves."

I held myself still. It was up to her, I thought, to insert significance into the lecture. "Bob Benn," she said. "Ralph Dutton." She paused. "Got those? Now listen. Tom Vargo, Len Grace. What do you think?"

"I don't know," I mustered, and she snorted.

"Yes, you do," she said. "You go stand outside their doors and listen. You'll hear what I'm saying. There's teachers and there's pansies."

Mrs. Benn looked up. "Kate means those last two can't control their students."

"I counted four t-shirts in your first period class today, and two with hair as long as mine."

THE NEXT WEEK, WHEN Stepnowski returned, we walked out of study hall together, but he didn't offer another nature lesson. Half way to where I turned left, though, I heard Chemo being called from behind us. "Cheeemo," I heard. "Cheeeeemo." This one a girl's voice squealing it. There were only another ten steps before I could turn, pretending I didn't hear whoever was calling. Stepnowski kept his eyes focused directly ahead. I started to expect him to reach into his pocket for two squares of chocolate.

I wheeled and looked straight at a boy who not only had hair over his collar, but wore the start of a mustache. He was walking between two laughing girls and pitching another "Cheeeeeemo!" when I laid both hands to his chest, grabbed his shirt, and drove him back against the wall.

Surprised, he stumbled, and his head smacked into the cinder block with the sound of dropped melon. His eyes teared, and then he swung a round-house right, my extended arms just long enough to have his fist drive through my paisley tie, snapping the tiny chain of my tie tack.

I slammed his shoulders this time, bending my arms for leverage. If he had a mind to drive his fist into my stomach or under my chin, he had the opportunity.

His arms dropped. "I don't even know you," he said.

The girls were gone. "Let's walk," I said, but I didn't let go, pushing him backwards through a small, gathered crowd. When we cleared the circle, I dropped my hands, and he turned to walk ahead of me, not another word between us, even after he sat down in Mr. Gloff's office before I told him to.

"Mr. Gloff will be back in half an hour," the secretary said. "I'll keep an eye on your problem child."

In the faculty room, I told my story and asked Miss Blatty and Mrs. Benn how my case looked to them. They were sympathetic. "I've only lost my head one time in thirteen years," Mrs. Benn said, "and all over a silly dance."

Miss Blatty sat up like she'd heard this story before. "I walked in and this little black boy Jerome was dancing beside his desk even though there wasn't any music."

"They don't need music," Miss Blatty said.

Mrs. Benn took a breath. "'What are you doing?' I asked him, and he answered, 'Doing the Mashed Potato,' his feet still sliding, so when I grabbed him they went out from under him, and I went down right on top, slapping his face with both hands."

Miss Blatty cackled herself into a short bout of coughing, but Mrs. Benn didn't smile. "I don't know," she said. "I think it was the name. The Mashed Potato. I thought he was making fun of me somehow."

Mr. Gloff came to my door while I was clearing my desk at the end of the day. He closed it behind him, and I could see Miss Blatty move into her doorway as if she had to check hinges. I told my story to Mr. Gloff, who nodded throughout and said "Ok" three times.

"You give out punishment now, not take it," Mr. Gloff said. "You can personally intervene when you see fit."

The next day, Stepnowski left as the bell rang, slipping out ahead of the students. He left quickly the day after that, and I understood, the following Monday, that he meant to avoid walking with me, that he must have turned and watched me grab that boy. That maybe he hadn't smiled five seconds after I'd disappeared down the hall. What I did know was that not one student called "Chemo" on either day.

WITH NIXON WINNING AND Johnson on his way out, nobody talked about politics at the next Marching and Chowder Club party. Instead, every new teacher had to pay two dollars to enter the shuffle baseball tournament to fill out brackets and boost the winners' share. "You're with Chemo," Cole said. "See you in the losers' bracket."

We took our three warm-up shots, the first time either of us had ever touched the smooth plastic discs players directed by hand. All three of Stepnowski's dove off the end of the board into the trough labeled OUT. "You'll learn," our opponents, two guys with cigars, said. Stepnowski didn't smile. He filled two cups with beer and carried them to where the game stood, drinking fast from the first as if he he'd swallowed bugs that needed drowning.

By the time I got the feel for distance, Stepnowski and I were down seven to one, fourth inning of a five-inning game. He slid his discs carefully, but he aimed only for the tiny home run that was so unlikely to be hit, it was for desperation that came with two on, two out, down three. Or for the single-minded.

I had the top of the fifth inning to play for our team, at least, and I bunched three singles and a double, another single before there were two outs and I had one shot at the home run, leaving my disc just outside the target where OUT lay large and definitive. By the time it was our turn again an hour later, I couldn't find Stepnowski. "Too bad," Wharton said, claiming the forfeit. "Tell Chemo he owes you two bucks."

I stepped outside to breathe something besides second-hand smoke and found Stepnowski standing at the curb, holding a cup of beer in each hand. From where I hesitated in the shadow of the entranceway overhang, I could see one was nearly empty, and I used it as a clock, figuring him for being out here maybe five minutes. "How come you're not married?" he said without turning. "You find out about girls before you got trapped?"

"What?" I said, but I stepped up beside him.

"You know what I mean. You should have grabbed the bitch that was screaming."

"I knew the boy was shouting. I didn't know which of the girls had."

"Bitches know they're immune. You know that, right?"

He drank off the rest of the first beer and tossed the cup aside just as a car pulled up alongside him. "Here we go," he said. "Twenty miles of bad road." He lurched off the curb as the driver-side window rolled down.

A woman leaned out, her dark hair tumbling down the side of her face. "Fred," she said, "don't bring that piss in the car."

He stopped, took a swallow and poured the rest on the hood of the car, holding the empty cup upside down and aloft so long I thought she might jerk that car forward just enough to nudge his knees to buckling. Instead, the window rolled up and Stepnowski dropped the cup and opened the passenger side door, saying something that began with "Next time" and ended with a door slam.

Stepnowski's wife, I figured, and she must have dropped him off and then come back for him as a safety valve. She'd made what sounded like a for-ty-mile round trip twice in one evening or else sat in a movie theater waiting for whatever hour they'd agreed upon. I tried to imagine doing that trip even once in an evening because I didn't trust someone else to drive.

THE DAY SCHOOL REOPENED after Christmas vacation, I heard Miss Blatty yelling at a boy in the hall during first period. "Jail's too good for you," she said, but I didn't hear the smack of her paddle. A moment later she walked him through my door and sent him to an empty seat in the back. She looked my way and nodded before she left.

The boy had let his hair begin to creep over his collar during our two-week break. He was wearing a t-shirt that said Summer of Love above a peace sign, and I wondered if he had an older brother or sister who'd given him the shirt for Christmas or maybe just handed it down after they'd found out the truth. He listened as I played the recording from the newest movie version of *Romeo and Juliet*; he moved his desk close to a girl who was reading along, following the words as if he'd just joined our class.

Just before class ended, he raised his hand. "Can I come back tomorrow?" he said, getting a laugh loud enough to bring Miss Blatty to her door.

By the time I reached the lounge for free period, Miss Blatty was already complaining about "peace boy." "You can't enforce those dress codes anymore," Mrs. Benn said. "I know that boy. As soon as good ones like him come to school with long hair and silly shirts, that's the end of it."

Miss Blatty stood up and walked out, leaving Mrs. Benn and me together. "It's so hard to be like that," she said. "My Bob grew an ulcer from it."

"He never gets off work," I said.

Mrs. Benn laughed. "That's funny," she said. "I'll have to tell Bob you said that. He'll get a kick out of it."

"Or take his coat off the next time he sees me in the hall."

I expected her to laugh again, but she seemed to darken. "That's just it," she said. "It's having to be the person you're expected to be." She glanced at the door and then back at me. "Like Kate," she said then. "She's been hateful so long she doesn't have a choice anymore."

In February, the Marching and Chowder Club held an over-the-hump party to celebrate passing the half way mark of the school year. There were some frowns among us during the night, older teachers worrying about contract troubles, the talk of a possible strike in the spring, and by the time we'd pushed back our emptied spaghetti plates, the beer had loosened up everybody, even Stepnowski, who seemed to be interested in the union talk.

Wharton was laughing. "You know what Frank Manucci called the strike talk? Manure. Can you believe it? Like a wood-shop teacher from the city who couldn't tell a cow from a horse would say manure instead of shit."

"You're forgetting Manucci's been here so long he came on horseback when he started," Cole said.

Not smiling, but holding only one cup as if he was trying to diet, Stepnowski interrupted. "You know what some fertilizer can do besides make your garden grow?" Nobody said a word while I counted to five. "Blow up the school, if you had a mind to."

"Sweetness," Wharton said, and laughed like something funny had been said.

Stepnowski looked at his beer so long I expected him to pour it on Wharton as if he was the hood of a car, and then he put the half-filled cup to his mouth, waited a moment, and swallowed it down in one gulp before walking away.

"Fucking Chemo," Cole said and looked straight at me. "A basket case, right?"

"Maybe," I said, not sure what to say next, but then all of us saw Stepnowski stop because his wife had just come inside as if she'd overheard us. She lifted the cup from Stepnowski's hand and tossed it in a trash barrel. After he followed her out the door, the voices and laughter seemed louder, as if everyone had watched and had an opinion that needed to be heard.

By March the strike threats from both the school board and the teachers' union had taken on the tone of college campus war protests. Six hundred dollars was the distance between settlement and the school's first ever teachers' strike. Not much for a thirty-five-year veteran like Miss Blatty, but that difference was ten per cent of my current salary.

Just before the end of the month, the strike promised for April 15th as if tax day was a symbolic deadline, Mr. Gloff called "all draft-eligible teachers" to the lunch room for a meeting at 3:30. "There's talk," Mr. Gloff said at once, "that the school board will refuse to sign the forms for your draft deferments if the union goes out on strike."

Gloff had everybody's attention. I was weighing the $600 more we were asking for and the $300 more we would probably get against having to look for another job where the school board would rubber-stamp my draft papers. Nothing about the war had slowed down since September. "What does 'There's talk' mean?" I said.

"'There's talk' means they've made up their minds already."

It sounded like the equivalent of contract negotiation biological warfare. It sounded illegal. It made me eager to vote against the strike. Gloff waggled his head as if he was trying to express sympathy. "The board thinks young male teachers are behind the strike threat."

I watched Stepnowski slide a chocolate bar out of his coat pocket. "Sweetness," I heard myself think, the word disappearing into a maze of tracer fire, and then he said, "I'm voting to strike."

"Ok," Mr. Gloff said, as if he'd just heard something reasonable. Stepnowski crammed what looked like four squares into his mouth, crumpled the wrapper, and smiled.

After the meeting ended, I walked back to my room to close up and get my coat. It was nearly April, but winter hadn't slacked off yet in western Pennsylvania. I lifted my coat off its hanger and heard somebody follow me into the room. When I turned, I saw Stepnowski toss the candy wrapper into the wastebasket.

I thought he'd come to ask me what attitude I had toward the draft, but he stayed quiet while I pulled each window blind to half mast, lining them up like every teacher did at 3:30 unless you wanted a note in your mailbox the following morning. I waited for him to get around to what he'd come for, but he acted interested in the bulletin boards I'd covered with student essays, slipping from one to the other as if they formed a gallery. There were six cork boards, three of them across the back of the room, and by the time he passed them all, finally stooping to stare through each half-covered window, he had me thinking about looking for a weapon in his hand.

"Cole and Wharton and those others, they're fools," he said. "Nobody needs to care what happens to fools."

Stepnowski pivoted away from the last window. He stopped by the first bulletin board and peered at the essays like a father at open house. I gathered papers and books as if it was important to stack them neatly, letting him decide why he'd chosen my room to haunt. "They're fools, but you're a fucking cunt," he said at last, turning and walking through the doorway. When I looked in the wastebasket, I saw the wrapper was for a candy bar filled with almonds, something that made me think I hadn't been paying attention.

THE FM ROCK STATION I listened to before I began my half mile walk to school didn't bother me with news, so it was my home room students, the following Monday, who told me Stepnowski had killed his wife the night before. Beaten her to death. "Chemo offed her," a boy said, and the girls told him to shut up.

"How could he do that?" one said.

Because he was drunk, I thought at once, but I kept everything I had to say about Chemo to myself even though both of my morning classes couldn't stop talking about it, arguing the details they'd learned from the radio or the newspaper. She was heavily bruised. Bones had been broken. A fractured skull was likely, but an autopsy was scheduled to decide that. Only one boy suggested Chemo hadn't meant to kill her, that all he'd done was smack her around, and maybe she'd hit her head when she fell. The girls screamed at him. "He was kicking her," a girl insisted. "That's how you kill somebody." The boy looked around a room of nodding heads and shut up.

When I went to study hall, I expected a substitute for Stepnowski, but nobody showed up. I circulated, the only strategy I could think of, but study hall had never been more orderly. The students whispered to each other when they talked, and when I approached, they stopped. *Large group discipline*, I thought. I wanted Miss Blatty to see how I could handle a room. I hoped Mr. Gloff had the speaker system on two-way.

Wharton was sitting in the lounge when I walked in after study hall. He'd lit up a cigarette as if he had a point to make, but Miss Blatty wasn't noticing it.

Mrs. Benn had a copy of the local newspaper, and she acted as if she'd been waiting for me before she read it aloud, finishing with "According to a police spokesman, 'Alcohol does not seem to be involved.'"

"Sweet Jesus," Miss Blatty said. She waved a hand in front of her face as if she'd just detected Wharton's smoke. "Some things deserve a beating," she said. "We don't know his side of it."

Wharton stared at his cigarette. Mrs. Benn folded her newspaper and began to roll it tight. "Nobody hits somebody without a reason when they're sober," Miss Blatty went on. "All these years, and every one of those pipsqueaks I've hit deserved it." She looked at all of us. "Go ahead. Tell me I'm wrong."

The long ash on Wharton's cigarette broke off and fell to the floor. "Well," Mrs. Benn said. "We'll never know her side, will we?"

She glanced at me as if it was my turn to offer something sensible, but I kept quiet because what I wanted to know, right at that moment, was how Stepnowski's expression had changed. What he looked like just before he took the first swing at his wife.

He'd been gripping her arms, twisting bruises into them, and what I imagined was his spitting chocolate as he suddenly screamed at her, spotting her blouse with stain specks she'd looked down at, disgusted, ignoring his threats, saying something like "This won't wash out, Fred" just before his face turned the mottled red of rage, his mouth working soundlessly until he stepped into that first punch, shifting his weight so her head snapped back and her legs buckled. The rest, I agreed on with my student, was him kicking her until she stopped moving.

Of course, what did I know about rage? All I knew, so far, was saving face, intent on not being a man who could be humiliated by teenagers, regardless of whether they were good or bad.

Whiz Kids

"WHIZ KIDS," CHARLEY'S FATHER said. "You boys think you are, but you don't know the half of it."

"Which half?" Charley said, but his father wasn't slowing down.

"You'll see. Go look it up somewhere. There was this show on the radio when I was in high school called 'Whiz Kids,' and these boys could answer everything. Girls, too. They didn't have to go to college to get any smarter."

Charley Rhodes and I had placed top thirteen, state-wide, in the Exceptionally Able Youth Contest, guaranteed scholarships as long as they were used at a Pennsylvania college. The Lieutenant Governor had announced the top thirteen in order at a ceremony in the auditorium by the Carnegie Museum in Pittsburgh, and we were #4 and #13, but all the money was the same as long as it didn't exceed tuition, room, and board at any state-related school.

I was ok with that because I was set on majoring in history at Penn State, following that with law school, but Charley had applied "science undecided" to the most expensive places--Swarthmore and Haverford and Penn-- where the difference would have to be made up in loans because his father had trouble keeping a job let alone saving money.

Charley kept saying he didn't care about the money. Instead, what pissed him off was how the awards were reported. "People think I'm in last place the way they say it," Charley complained when he saw the write-up in the *Pittsburgh Press*.

"We're one half of one per cent of the best," I said. "2600 people with SATs over 1300 took that test." Those were the figures the Lieutenant Governor had mentioned in his speech at the ceremony on what turned out to be Groundhog Day, but the newspaper didn't say a word about any numbers besides one through thirteen, ignoring what I thought was the real story, how two guys from the same school had scored so high.

"I'll say one thing," Charley's father said. "This here makes Penn State more than a dream."

Charley's expression didn't shift, but I knew that he'd lied to his father about applying to Penn State and starting out by commuting, in order to save money, at the two-year campus that had opened a few years ago across the Ohio River near Monaca. We both lived with single fathers—Charley's mother had died in a car accident, mine from cancer, neither one living past

forty-five. We were practically twins about some things except Charley had
two older sisters who'd gotten married right after high school and had three
kids each in less than five years.

When I asked my father about the Whiz Kids, he said "The Philadelphia
Phillies in 1950, the year before you were born—Robin Roberts, Richie
Ashburn and that gang." I had to ask him if there was another bunch of
Whiz Kids to get him to say, "You mean the Quiz Kids? The ones everybody
said were geniuses?"

"That sounds more like it," I said.

My father brightened. "One of them was James Watson. You know who
he is, right?"

"One of the DNA discoverers," I said, and he nodded as if that meant
we could keep talking. "Charley's Dad called them Whiz Kids."

"The show was on the radio for all the years Morris Rhodes and I were
growing up. You shouldn't forget a thing like that, but a man like Morris
Rhodes talks and talks and thinks if he uses enough words he'll happen on
to what he means."

My father, a real estate agent, was always saying things like that about
other people, the tone of his voice so even you'd think he was reading from a
book. It was a voice I listened for in myself, afraid I'd grow into it.

FOUR MONTHS LATER, ALPHABETICAL by last names, Charley and I sat beside
each other at graduation. We both were singled out because the high school
principal announced things like scholarships and test successes at graduation.
A school board member even announced the twelve guys who'd enlisted, and
I noticed that every one of them was listed as being in the vocational track.
But when he called us up to receive our diplomas, the superintendent of
schools mispronounced at least nine names, including mine, saying William
Reeser instead of finding out about the i-sound of Reiser. Charley nudged
me. "Who is this guy?" he said. "I never saw him before."

That night, drinking at a party that an old girlfriend, Ellen Vollmer, was
allowed to have in her downstairs rec room, Charley kept calling me "the
mispronunciation." "You get to be top dog like that guy on the stage and you
don't have to give a shit about knowing anybody one bit," he said.

"There's no consolation in knowing everybody you hate is an asshole,"
I said.

Charley snorted. "Reeser," he said, drawing it out like a strand of mozza-
rella. "You know there's some. You know there's enough."

"It doesn't seem as if there's ever enough consolation," I said.

"Fuck you then," Charley said. "Fuck you twice." And then he shut up the way he did when he was tired of lying.

I shrugged and wandered back to the keg as if my half-filled plastic cup was empty. Ellen Vollmer smiled when I passed her, but she was leaning against a guy from last year's senior class, so I knew she was absolutely taken. Before I turned back toward Charley, I took a long time filling my cup and taking a few small sips. I knew how to measure the space we both needed. Throughout that last year of high school, I'd convinced myself I knew every "fuck you" and "fuck you twice" Charley spewed my way showed a sort of love, that his getting in stride with me the next day was an apology that I could accept by never mentioning what he'd said the day before.

To be honest, I was more of a studier than exceptionally able, somebody who read every assignment twice in order to succeed, but Charley was a genius, somebody who could memorize just about anything put in front of him. Back in November, just after we'd taken that EAY test, Charley was the only one in our English class who'd memorized more than the fourteen lines of poetry Mr. Little required everybody to stand up and recite.

Instead of picking a sonnet, exactly fourteen lines with end rhymes to help out with remembering, Charley had chosen "The Death of the Hired Man," a long poem by Robert Frost without end rhyme, plunging right in with "Mary sat musing on the lamp-flame at the table/ Waiting for Warren," but when he finished line fourteen, he kept going, not stopping until he'd finished thirty-three lines that I followed in the book to see if he was getting every word correct.

Mr. Little sighed twice during those extra nineteen lines, and then he said, "That's enough, Charles," as if he was afraid Charley would do the whole thing.

For a few seconds Charley stood in the front of the room without moving, and it was hard to tell whether he'd stopped at the end of line thirty-three because that was as far as he could go or because Mr. Little had sounded bored. But then he said, "There's more," and I didn't doubt he wanted to keep going.

"Yes, there is, Charles. A good bit more," Mr. Little said, and I could see my classmates opening their books to remind themselves. When Charley didn't return to his seat, Mr. Little sighed again and seemed to be deciding something before he finally said, "Give us the home business then. That's a way to ice the cake you've baked for us."

"'Home is the place where, when you have to go there, / They have to take you in.'" Charley said, but he still didn't move.

"Thank you," Mr. Little said.

"'I should have called it/ Something you somehow haven't to deserve.'" Charley added, and then, before Mr. Little said anything else, Charley sat down. There are 176 lines in that poem. I counted them while the girl who followed Charley stumbled through a sonnet by Shakespeare.

That night I told my father about how angry Charley was. "Anger," my father said. "Sometimes it lets people do extraordinary things, and certainly that boy's always been mad about something."

"He didn't learn that whole thing from being mad."

"You know," my father said, "there's a difference between reciting and learning. Don't I remember you telling me that his one A- was in world history because the final exam was nothing but essay questions?"

"Charley's pissed at being salutatorian," I said, "but not because he had one A ."

"Second out of 300? What did he miss out on except giving a speech?"

"The valedictorian, Sue Gerhart, did you notice in the program she was listed as 'commercial track'? She stopped being in our classes after ninth grade. She never took chemistry or physics or calculus."

"Still," my father said. "It's a wonder your friend grew up to be as smart as he is without encouragement."

"It's just luck how we're born, isn't it?" I said.

"But that luck is less likely from the likes of Morris Rhodes."

"Charley's going to Swarthmore," I said, angry now and using the ammunition Charley had spoken into my ear as we worked our way back to our seats after receiving our diplomas.

"Then he's in for it."

"He's as smart as anybody else who's going."

"That's not what I mean. Smart only goes so far."

"Smart's smart," I said, and my father gave me a look filled with so much disappointment that I felt a rush of pressure in my bladder.

I DIDN'T SEE CHARLEY for a few weeks. He'd gotten a job as a stock boy at the Giant Eagle, but I was cutting lawns the way I'd been doing for three summers to earn money. When he'd started in on making fun of me for doing boys' work at Ellen Vollmer's party, I'd promised to show him my tan in two weeks and said, "By then you'll be losing IQ points from doing that grocery store work."

Charley didn't laugh. "That's exactly right," he said. "You do stock boy for a year and you're that guy people wonder what happened to."

But when I finally caught up with Charley, I didn't mention our jobs because the first thing I noticed was he'd shaved his head. He'd had collar length for two years, but now he said right off, "It's to keep my hair from falling out. If it's really short it won't comb out like it's been doing."

I knew what he was worried about. Charley's father had been bald for the twelve years I'd known him. Slick bald. His father, when we were kids, had always used the line "a big brain doesn't leave room for hair," but once we knew about heredity and the odds it accounted for, he gave up on that.

"Like a beard," Charley said now, "how you shave it and it gets thick."

"I don't think so."

"Easy for you with your old man having a full head of hair."

"You'll scare everybody at Swarthmore," I said, meaning it, because Charley, who was thick and muscular through his chest and shoulders, seemed somehow swollen with a shaved head.

I expected Charley to pick up on that line, give me the old "Fuck you, fuck you twice" routine, but he acted as if pulling his old Plymouth into McDonald's took full concentration. We were eating hamburgers and fries in the front seat before he said, "We're moving."

I waited for a few seconds, but Charley's silence forced me to ask, "Where to?"

"Not far."

"Then why?"

"There's houses in our plan that have sunk. There's old mines underneath all around us. Everybody knew, but that made the lots cheap back when. Now there's cracked foundations and a sinkhole or three."

"It's going to be hard selling if your neighbor's house is lopsided."

For once, Charley smiled. He stuffed the last of his second burger into his mouth and swallowed before he said, "The old man's moving the house."

"The whole thing?" I said like I was the one who was losing IQ points mowing lawns, and when Charley nodded as if that was the perfect question, I added, "I'd like to see that."

"You will if you can get your ass up early next Tuesday, meaning ready to go when I pick you up at six a.m. There's no lawn needs tending to that early."

We ended up driving to a street called Strawberry Lane less than a mile from Charley's house. The lot was bare, so muddy from Monday's all-day rain that I made sure I stayed on the board that stretched toward a hole in the earth that looked too small for a house to fit on, but I could see there was a foundation ready and waiting, cement poured, everything in that about-to-be basement looking like Charley's cellar emptied of all its trash.

"That's right," Charley said, "exactly the same."

"Amazing."

"No, it's not. If it wasn't perfect, this whole thing would be fucked."

A half hour later, when the house rolled up sitting on a flat-bed truck, it didn't look like any house I'd want to live in. Ripped from the ground, it looked more than tiny enough to fit on the foundation, and I remembered that if it hadn't been for Charley and I always hanging out in the basement, we'd never have had a space farther away from his father than a whisper could travel.

Charley's father was right behind the house in the used Mustang he'd bought the summer before, and he called us over. "You boys help me celebrate," he said, passing a fat bottle of Gallo Vin Rose our way at 6:35. Charley didn't hesitate. He took a big swallow and handed it to me.

"Housewarming," he joked, but he was watching as I lifted that bottle to my mouth, and I had to take three sips before I thought he was satisfied.

Charley took another drink, and when his father waved him off, he kept the bottle and moved back toward the lot. He looked excited, like he'd been the one who'd done all the calculations and preparations. He slogged into the muddy lot and disappeared around the back of the house, leaving footprints so deep I expected his shoes to be sucked off. I stayed in the street. And so did Charley's father, who stood beside me smoking as the house was situated. He ground the butt on the asphalt before he spoke with his eyes on the settling house.

"Ain't this here a miracle now?"

"Seems that way," I tried.

"Seems is for Bible magic. This here you see with your own two eyes."

He shook another cigarette from his pack of Lucky Strikes and lit it with a match he tore from a book that read "Learn Plumbing at Home."

"Somebody smart like you boys figured this here out," he said. "Those fellows at Penn State won't know what to make of the both of you."

Just then Charley reappeared, circling around from the other side, standing in the mud so close to the house I half expected him to break the Gallo bottle over the paneling and give that house a name. "I know this," Charley's father said after he let out a slow breath of smoke, "those whiz kids I was telling you about, they was a hell of a lot smarter than the fellow who was asking the questions. And listening to them talk like that made me wonder if they had any friends."

Before I could conjure an answer, Charley's father drifted off to talk to the movers, and I started checking my watch because I was scheduled to make up one of yesterday's rained-out lawns at 8:15 before my Tuesday customers at eleven and one and three. Charley scraped his shoes against the curb, getting the worst of the mud off. "I'm never going back to the old place," he said. "Fineview Street is strictly taboo now."

"It's up to you," I said. It felt like an easy thing to agree with. There were other classmates who lived in Charley's plan, but I didn't know any of them, and without Charley's house to visit, there was no reason for me to be anywhere close.

I thought he would pass the bottle to me again after he took another swallow, but he held it upside down and said, "Dead soldier" before he opened the passenger door of his car and motioned me inside. "I hear you took out Claire Schaeffer. You get any?" he said a moment later, the empty bottle nestled between his thighs as we pulled out.

"We went to the movies and McDonald's."

"She signed up for the Miss Bridgewater Boat Club contest?"

"That was her sister," I said. "That was Missy who had the Playboy Bunny body."

"She doesn't have to win like Missy, but she should enter so you could at least check her out in her two-piece," Charley said, but then his expression changed and he lowered his voice. "I'm taking Sue Gerhart to dinner at Ghezzi's next week. Ask Claire. I need some back up."

WHEN CHARLEY PICKED ME up, he had a beer in his left hand as he drove. "At least have one," he said, so I knew he'd noticed me glance at the empty half-quart in the cup holder. "I have twenty-four pounders on ice in case I find out I want to share it with Sue, but it just might be all I want to share is her television for the moon landing tonight."

"I don't get it," I said, but I fished out a beer and opened it, counting on Charley to take his time so we could finish and toss the empties into the cooler that would surely go into the trunk until after dinner.

"Her old man owns a 25-inch RCA," Charley said. "There's only one first step on the moon, and I want it as big as it gets, not on that shitty seventeen-inch black and white my old man sits in front of every night."

"Claire and I get to see the big screen?"

"Absolutely. And that jackass Ted Kennedy and all that Chappaquiddick stuff had better not steal any more of the moon's headlines."

I swallowed fast when I saw we were already turning into Claire's street. "He's lucky there's a moon-landing two days after to push his story onto the second page."

As soon as we stopped, Charley hopped out and dragged the cooler off the back seat. "The fucker," he said. "He's all drunk and probably driving that girl some place to fuck her and then he gets her drowned and runs away." I half expected him to open a third beer and have it in his hand when I got back to the car with Claire, but he was empty-handed and smiling, the front windows wound down as a natural air freshener.

Big-screen tv or no big-screen tv, I thought Charley had asked Sue Gerhart to dinner then asked me to come along because he wanted to embarrass her somehow and have a witness, but Sue acted as if Charley's gleaming skull was ordinary, and it was Claire who said, first thing, "Wow, you look spooky with no hair."

"Maybe so," Charley said, and I felt myself relax.

I'd never been in a real restaurant with a girl. It was always fast food and movies or drive-in theater food between features. Ghezzi's wasn't high class, but we ordered off a menu that had half the words in Italian, and somebody refilled our water and brought more bread when Charley and I had finished it even though neither girl touched it because it was already buttered and garlic flavored.

"I'm going to modeling school," Sue said after our main courses arrived. "Power's. In Pittsburgh."

She was tall and thin, I could see that, the kind of body that maybe might get her noticed, but all I could think of was "valedictorian" and take a glance at Claire to remind myself how she measured up as a possible Miss Bridgewater Boat Club, focusing on the breasts that would catch the judges' eyes when they were lifted and squeezed by a tiny tight top.

For sure, I was relieved when Charley didn't pick up on "valedictorian modeling," but the silence that settled in made Sue try again: "I bet the Class of 1970 will have moon landing pictures in their yearbook."

Ours was coming out in a week, published at the end of July so everything from the whole year could be included. There was always a pick-up day when everybody got theirs and passed them around to be signed. Claire had worked on the staff, so she started to chatter about Bobby Kennedy's killing coming too late for last year's yearbook and how this year's would have him and a repeat of Martin Luther King, Jr. so it wouldn't seem like we were playing favorites.

"Like either one went to Beaver Falls," Charley said.

"So everybody remembers fifty years from now," Claire said.

"Are we going to be retarded then?" Charley said.

"Hey, what song did you say was your favorite while we were in high school?" I asked Claire to get something started besides an argument.

"'To Sir, with Love,'" she said right away. "When Lulu sang it in the movie I started crying. It was so beautiful. One of these days my children will see it under my picture in our book, and I'll play it for them."

"How about you?" I said to Sue. "What song title is under your picture?"

"'Abraham, Martin, and John,'" she said, and I was surprised Charley didn't say a word about Dion putting doo-wop behind him to try and revive his career by singing a plaintive folk song.

A few minutes later, though, Charley looked at Sue, then at her plate, and said, "You wasting that?" and I could hear his father's voice in those words, how, the two times I'd eaten dinner at his house, Mr. Rhodes had spooned food from every bowl onto my plate as if I were five years old—peas, corn, stove-top stuffing, and a turkey roll he sliced, the pieces falling apart as soon as they were freed, dark meat pressed together tightly inside a circle of breast meat.

"There's way too much," Sue said.

"Somebody worked to make that."

I saw Charley look at her as if he were evaluating her would-be model's body in a medical way, her thin arms, her small breasts. While we were walking into the restaurant he must have noticed she was his height, maybe slightly taller at 5'10".

"Food shouldn't be wasted." Charley's plate glistened where he'd wiped up the remains with the last slice of our second basket of bread. Sue poked at the ravioli with her fork, and for a moment I thought she was giving in, but all she did was separate each piece and announce "Six. You want them?"

"No, they're yours," Charley said, and I realized that Mr. Rhodes had never touched Charley's food, that he'd had to sit and finish or never be allowed to leave the table.

"Well, then," Sue said, and she laid her fork across her plate.

No one said another word until the waiter took dessert orders, and though Sue said she wasn't interested, she let Charley feed her two spoons of tiramisu. He and Sue even laughed together as she had to lick her lower lip to keep that dessert from dripping off her chin, and I knew Claire and I would be seeing the moon landing better than just about everybody who lived in Beaver County.

A half hour later, as if we were back in junior high, we all sat in separate chairs in Sue's living room, and for once, Charley was quiet all the way through Neil Armstrong's chosen words.

It was late, but after Charley dropped Claire off, blowing the horn as I kissed her by her front door, we rode around drinking the beer he'd stowed in the cooler that was now filled with water. "You're not getting any tonight either," he finally said, "but there's shit going on you need to know. I'm now a United States Marine."

"Bullshit," I said, knowing I wouldn't have laid a hand on Claire even if Charley had parked his car in the woods and gone for a walk.

"I'm fucking serious. I'm tired of kid shit," Charley said. "Answering questions as if anybody gives a flying fuck." You know what? The more answers you get right, the more people hate you. Some whiz kid can have my scholarship."

"I think it's too late to hand it down to #14," I said.

"Then fuck #14. Let him pay his own way to Penn State. Or better yet, one of those cheap-ass state colleges like Clarion or Edinboro."

Charley passed me another beer from the water-filled cooler. Two hours later, we had it nearly emptied, and we were parked among a small cluster of cars outside an all-night laundry where the customers gave us something to talk about besides Ted Kennedy, the moon and the Marines. "You could walk in and shoot the last person inside there and nobody would ever know who did it," he said. "And you can bet anybody doing laundry past two in the morning is nobody the police are going to spend a long time looking for."

"That makes no sense," I said, but I was past explaining why.

Charley crumpled his empty can and tossed it into the cooler. "We're about fucking empty here," he said, handing me a fresh one and pulling the tab on his own.

"That's ok. I'm totally beat."

Charley seemed to be studying the customers inside the Laundromat. "What if it was you inside there and you had a gun of your own? If I shot you in the leg or someplace like that, would you shoot back and maybe take a bullet in the head or just suffer that wound and hope I'd stop?"

I took a swallow, trying to get past Charley's tone, but the beer felt like it was going to come back up if I managed one more mouthful. "That's never going to happen," I said, and then, before Charley could keep his hypothetical slaughter going, I added, "1480 SATs—you'll be the smartest guy in Vietnam."

"Or at Penn State."

A man as old as our fathers walked toward one of the nearby cars balancing two laundry baskets of folded clothes. "When do you have to report?" I finally said.

"August 15th. Maybe Ted Kennedy will be in jail by then."

"Maybe not," I said, and Charley, for once, laughed and started the car.

"'Abraham, Martin, and John,'" he said. "The fuck."

Charley, I thought, was drunker than Ted Kennedy had been a few nights ago, and I was staring at the road as if that would help him drive. I'd never revealed my favorite song from high school at Ghezzi's, but suddenly it was on the radio as we drove, and I fought the urge to tell Charley this was what would be under my yearbook senior photo. I wanted to spell out G-l-o-r-i-a, Gloria with Van Morrison and pound on the dashboard like I was fourteen and thrilled to be riding in a car driven by somebody besides my father.

I'd listened to that song hundreds of times, maybe half of them with Charley Rhodes close by, and now I was wondering whether Charley would say I was a fucking idiot for wanting to turn it up. That I was still into kid shit, but the last thing Charley said that night as I tumbled from his car at three a.m. was "Watch yourself. Once you're a lawyer, you'll start in with the politics, and before you know it, you'll be Senator Reeser-Reiser. I hope you at least keep it in your pants."

AFTER I TOLD MY father about Charley's change of plans, he acted as if he'd expected that announcement. "Your friend already uses the vocabulary of a Marine," my father said. "He'll be more comfortable there."

"Vocabulary is just a convenient persona," I said.

"Which enables its master," he said at once, grinning as if he were welcoming me to a secret society for the pretentious while everything Charley had amazed me with in high school turned small. Even the day in American History when Miss Hartley, in mock despair, had said, "Sometimes I think no one remembers any of the Presidents except the ones carved on Mt. Rushmore."

"Lyndon Johnson," somebody had shouted out to laughter.

"John Kennedy," someone else said, and no one laughed.

"Dwight Eisenhower," Charley said then. "Harry Truman, Franklin Roosevelt, Herbert Hoover" and all the way back to Washington.

Miss Hartley said, "Bravo, Charles," but Charley wasn't through.

"Hubert Humphrey, Lyndon Johnson, Richard Nixon, Alben Barkley," he began, taking us through the Vice-Presidents in reverse order, something even Miss Hartley had to accept on trust because who had ever heard of William Wheeler, Henry Wilson, and Schuyler Colfax. The only way a Vice-President could be remembered was if a President was shot.

WHEN I CLIMBED INTO Charley's car a few nights later, he said he had a surprise for me, something that had to be done before he reported for duty.

We crossed into Ohio, and worked our way near Youngstown before cars parked for a mile along the shoulder let us know that a crowd-pleaser was close. I expected Charley to drive past the open field that was parked full and find a spot a mile down the highways, but he pulled in as if he'd seen a spot open up. We wove through the cars for so long I knew we could have parked a mile away and hiked back by then, Charley's fingers drumming on the steering wheel, the radio off as if he needed silence to see better. "Get out," Charley suddenly said, and when I hesitated, he pointed at a narrow space we'd passed twice. He worked the car so close to the passenger side that flies wouldn't be able to escape from the door I'd used, and then he slid out and side-stepped to where I was waiting. "Our neighbor will just have to crawl across the front seat," he said, and we were off to what I could see was a carnival bigger than the one that set up in the abandoned strip-mall parking lot a mile outside of Beaver Falls every summer.

I followed Charley past all the familiar rides and booths full of greasy food until we reached a plywood fence decorated with bear head decals, every one of them with bared teeth. "Bear wrestling," Charley said. "How cool is that?"

"You boys eighteen?" the ticket taker said, and we nodded, all the proof he seemed to need. "Enjoy yourselves," he said, and we paid the two-dollar admission to pass through a thick curtain and watch.

The bear wrestling cage looked small, a space where it would be hard to hide for very long. The bear, whose name, according to the sign was Max, was busy with a middle-aged fat guy in a Cleveland Indians t-shirt as we found a spot in a makeshift second row to watch from, but seconds later, the guy was down and out. While Charley followed the motions of the bear, there were three more takers, men willing to pay $10 to see if they could last two minutes for a $100 payout. Big guys egged on by their drinking buddies. Guys who outweighed Charley by fifty or even seventy-five pounds, none of them with shaved heads. None of them lasted a minute because that bear just slapped them and wrapped them.

It was uncanny how well that bear was trained. But it wore a muzzle and its claws had been trimmed down to fingernail length like people do with cats. Charley said, "Pussy" after each gave up, smothered under the weight and "pinned" according to the promoter's referee. When he raised his voice after the fourth victim, some heads began turning our way.

"Go ahead, tough guy," somebody called out.

"Pussy," Charley said, and it was unclear whether it was meant for the wrestler or the spectator.

"Fuck you, baldy," the man said and Charley smiled, and I thought he was deciding who to fight.

Five minutes later Charley was in the cage with the bear and the handler. Charley didn't circle and stall like the others. He charged that bear and hit it like a tackling dummy at football practice. Except he couldn't wrap the bear up, and aside from a muffled grunt, the bear held its ground.

Charley plunged in again, and the bear wrapped him up like the others but Charley slipped down and out like some Bear Cage Houdini, and there were a few cheers and something like a small roar when he rushed the bear again, this time swinging his fist, even the beaten guys whooping and hollering.

Only this time Charley ended up with just one arm free, and he thumped that bear twice up high on its chest, and before anybody managed another shout of "Git 'im" the bear whirled Charley away with such force we could hear the bone break as Charley spun into the bars.

Charley's face went ashen. His arm dangled. He snagged a bar with the hand on his good arm and tried to hold himself up as the handler moved in to calm things down with the bear. It was a minute later when I learned everybody signed a waiver about injuries, but I was so sure the whole thing must be illegal that I encouraged Charley to ask for money for medical expenses.

"It was fair," Charley said. "I got no beef with the bear."

"The bear always wins. There's no fairness to that."

"They'd put it down if I raised a stink."

What Charley got was a ride in a golf cart the handler produced in order to ferry him away without the fanfare that might reduce the line of men who wanted to bet on their wrestling skills. I was left with nothing to do but work my way back to the car on foot, a few minutes of reverie in the deepening twilight.

We exhaust ourselves on lies, I told myself. All of us. And then we scramble to put one deceit in front of another until betrayal makes us tumble. I could have begun to make a speech with those thoughts, but instead I took the keys from Charley when I reached his car and began to drive without speaking. Charley shivered for the first mile, but then he clenched his teeth and set his eyes on the dashboard, and that kept him still. Forty-five minutes later I watched him walk inside where his father, for all I knew, would set that arm himself as if they lived in a wilderness where self-reliance was essential.

It turned out the break was clean. His arm would heal. The Marines would wait a bit, but two weeks later, when the original reporting date went by, Charley shifted somehow, always asking me to meet him at Ricci's, the bar I could walk to where we'd been drinking underage for a year. Charley was always drunk when I arrived, as if he'd been sitting there alone for a few hours, as if the days that had opened in front of him needed to be filled with something besides waiting and healing. Or maybe it was just because it wouldn't be long before he would be alone in Beaver Falls in September.

A week of that and Charley stopped asking me to drink with him. By then what I did know was that Charley had chosen Swarthmore because it was the most selective college in Pennsylvania and one of the most expensive. Once he'd been accepted, he could begin to plan for something else to do in the fall than attend college. The EAY scholarship didn't come close to covering the cost.

"Fuck you," he thought he was saying when the deadline for a deposit passed. "Fuck you twice," and because Swarthmore wouldn't forgive him, he was free to settle for the Marines and the war where his bitterness and anger would carry him straight into the heart of the present.

What changed things was Charley's father calling, the week before I was off to Penn State's main campus, to tell me Charley had disappeared. "Three days now," he said. "I was thinking maybe you could stop by when you have a minute and take a look around, see if maybe you can tell what he's up to."

"I could try," I said, though it seemed as improbable as moving a house from one place to another on a flat-bed truck.

I waited another two days, giving Charley whatever chance he might have to do his version of the Prodigal Son, but when Mr. Rhodes called again, I said I'd be right over and meant it.

I borrowed my father's car, promising to be back in an hour, but I had already turned into Charley's old housing plan before I remembered the house wasn't on Fineview anymore. I made a left into Overlook, the first cross street, in order to turn around, but then I stopped because Overlook ran parallel to Fineview, and since it sat higher on the hillside I could look between houses down to Fineview. There was the vacant lot, of course, but what surprised me was that all the neighboring houses looked normal, not a For Sale sign in sight. Every house had lights on. Instead of turning around, I drove along Overlook until, two blocks later, I could spot damage. Maybe Morris Rhodes had bonded the homeowners. Maybe he'd saved his block and the next one, too, by sacrifice like some follower of a primitive homeowner's cult. But what I was sure of, just then, was that Mr. Rhodes was afraid Charlie had chosen the Marines the same way he'd picked Swarthmore, as if risk and cost needed to be high enough to allow him to refuse.

Two minutes later I knocked on the door of Charley's house for the first time since it had been moved. His father let me look around his room as if I were a cop come to decipher clues. "He didn't take much of anything, so he has to be close by," Mr. Rhodes said, hovering like maybe he expected me to know where a note of some kind would be hidden. I knew Mr. Rhodes was thinking Canada and disgrace rather than dead somewhere, that his son was maybe a whiz kid and nothing else and whether or not he could live with that.

The only thing I noticed was that Charley's yearbook wasn't in his room. I'd written in his book first thing during signing day. He hadn't said a word about King and Kennedy then. He'd told me fill up the whole inside front cover and run over if I had to.

I'd kept it inside the lines, filling one page exactly and ending with "Fuck CHARLEY up in Vietnam" as if I believed that coincidental name meant he could make a difference. After he'd done mine, I'd gotten busy with getting notes from classmates, even girls I'd barely known who wrote "Good luck at college" and "You were always so smart."

I'd seen Charley reading my page full of anecdotes and a few minutes later, when I looked around, I hadn't seen him. He was there at the end of the hour though, the book under his arm. "Claire Schaeffer write she wants to fuck you?" he said.

"No."

"Herb Jackson write that?"

I thought of Herb and the rumors about him, and I'd laughed, but even then, I'd known Charley had disappeared for an hour, that he hadn't asked anybody else to sign his book, especially not Sue Gerhart, who'd signed mine with a simple "Friends forever" on the page with the photos of Martin Luther King and Bobby Kennedy.

Mr. Rhodes finally said, "What?" as if he understood I'd finally learned something he hadn't. Maybe, for instance, that Charley couldn't forgive others because he couldn't forgive his own weaknesses.

"Nothing," I said, and the look that settled on his face, somehow close to weeping, made me hurry past him and down the stairs, opening and closing the front door so carefully he might have expected me to be waiting in the living room when he followed, ready to reveal where his lost son was hidden.

After the Locks are Changed

Home

After the locks are changed, after he stops cursing and pounding on both doors, he hurls his key against the kitchen window while McCartney, her German Shepherd, yips and whines. Still, he calls several times each week, always after midnight with slurs of pleading punctuated by threats. When she puts her phone on mute at ten p.m., his texts bloom like algae. Each morning, his messages begin with "Let's meet" before they skid from sentimentality to rage.

One night, McCartney stiffens and growls. Her daughters, thirteen and ten, sit up from their books, alert and listening. She hears scraping from the bathroom and knows he's remembered the window with the warped frame that makes it impossible to lock. She taps 911, gestures the girls to her side, and leads them outside to her car. From the kitchen window, as she pulls away, he displays two middle fingers. She doesn't hear barking. She doesn't see a strange car parked along the street, so she drives only a few blocks before turning left and then u-turning before parking, headlights extinguished. When the police pass by within minutes, she tells the girls, "He won't even have time to steal anything. This one will cost him more than an overnight and a warning."

She calls 911 again. "We're safe," she says. "Thank you."

In a voice barely above a whisper, Renee, the older girl, says, "No, we're not." Darcy, the younger, stares straight ahead as if she expects her father to appear.

The First Time

The five women are teachers, the husbands five different things, the party DJ'd by the IPod of the hosts. Twice, he turns up the volume. Twice, a woman, not the homeowner, turns it down. The third time, he dials the volume to jackhammer, and that woman's husband turns it off, the party on pause. He finishes his drink while she apologizes to everyone. He hears her repeat it as she asks for their coats. "It's not your house," she says when they are outside.

"Really? Like I don't know that? You act like I'm six."

"Not six. Drunk."

"You know what? You're a sponge. You suck all the joy out of the room, you and all the rest of those lightweights. That wasn't a party. That was a PTA meeting."

"Some of those lightweights have children waiting for them at home. They have baby sitters they have to drive home. Adult things."

"We don't have kids."

"Yes, we do. And a babysitter, too."

"We have a fucking sponge is what we have. This adult can drive it home."

"Not hardly," she says, showing him the keys.

For six miles, he is quiet. For a full day, she does not speak. "I'm supposed to say I'm sorry, right?" he finally says. "Ok, I'm sorry. Happy?"

She stares. "No, I'm not happy. Are you?"

"It's not like I touched you. It was just words."

"That's not an excuse, that's a deflection. If you ever touched me, it would be over."

"Ok," he says. "I get it."

"I'm not sure you do."

"I'm really sorry," he says. "See?"

New Year's Eve, Los Angeles

At 7:30, after taking Darcy to her friend's sleepover nine blocks away, she and Renee walk home together. Nearly there, they see an empty car double-parked, the driver's side door open, its lights extinguished. Here, after dark, fifty yards from home, their street always feels dangerous, alley-like, badly lit. Budget apartments sit below on one side instead of single-dwelling houses and duplexes like the ones set into the hillside on the other. She notices Renee veer right, and she drifts her way as subtly as she can muster. The next bend takes them into the street's deepest shadows just before the flight of stairs to their door.

"Those apartments are sketchy," Renee says, after they are inside and McCartney welcomes them. In the bedroom Renee and Darcy share, Renee chooses a record her grandfather has sent her for Christmas, one of the eight used albums of his he's guessed she'd love—Queen, Judy Collins, Linda Ronstadt, Harry Nilsson. She plays an entire side of *Nilsson Schmilsson,* singing softly along. The dog, instead of settling, is restless, pacing to windows. He doesn't bark.

An hour of music, and then she and Renee begin a second trip—another sleepover, the girls three years older for New Year's Eve five blocks away. As soon as they walk around the bend, they see two police cars by the double-parked car, its door still open, but now a girl is inside. Except for the policeman who waves to invite them past, whoever arrived in those two marked cars must be inside the apartments. "What you looking at, little bitch?" the girl says. The policeman's wave shifts into demand. "That's it, keep walking, little bitch," the girl calls as they pass him. "Fuck you, little bitch," she yells as they clear the scene.

"I wish I hadn't looked," Renee says when the street turns wider on the next block. "Did you look, Mom?"

"Yes."

"But she only talked to me."

"You're nearly as tall as I am already. You'll never see her again."

They have only three more blocks, both on the other side of an avenue where traffic is constant. They stand at the intersection, three streets intersecting the main highway, a series of left turn lights extending the wait. Down the sidewalk on their side, they see a small crowd has gathered where the apartments have a lower entrance.

"McCartney knew, didn't he?" Renee says, after they cross.

"Yes, he must have sensed when the police arrived."

The new year is less than three hours away when they reach the sleepover house. Both of her daughters will stay up for the bells and sirens and fireworks from thousands of yards spreading toward the city. "What do you think she could have done?" Renee says. "She didn't look much older than I am," whispering as if it were a secret.

Pentecostal

McCartney becomes a nuisance for unwelcome sounds. Car door slams. Voices passing on the street below. The wind driving a deck chair against the sliding, glass door. But he is security for the threats she does not hear. She reinforces McCartney with a motion sensor. Though coyotes, some nights, rouse the dog to barking before frightening her floodlight to brilliance. Renee and Darcy mostly seem to sleep through her double alarm. After a while, the coyotes, as if they have memorized where light begins, pace at the edge of darkness while McCartney does his extended solo.

One night, long after the coyotes have retreated, McCartney is so dissatisfied, she leashes him and steps outside. Across the highway and from beyond the hillside houses that end in wilderness, the glow of the latest wildfire has lengthened the radio's menu of languages. Fuego salvaje. Chay rung. Incendios. Smoke has drifted into the neighborhood. Evacuation is unlikely, but possible.

The vacant lot next door has been cleared of brush and damaged trees to lessen the chance of attracting embers. As if emptied, every nearby house is darkened, the ordinary and the reasonable already elsewhere or at rest. Although she sees that it's him at the edge of the light, McCartney is a lunge of howls.

The spotlight scorches them. He has something in his hands that looks like an axe handle or baseball bat. "I'll kill that dog if you let him go," he says. The girls, holding hands, appear behind her but do not speak. He crouches like a gargoyle, four steps, then three, close enough that she sees what he is carrying is the bottom half of his cue stick, what he hefts slowly from left to right and back again. "McCartney will hurt you first," she says. Renee begins to scream. He backs away and disappears.

Darcy says, "Why did McCartney bark at Dad this time?"

"McCartney's not stupid," Renee says. "He knows Dad is dangerous now."

From somewhere close, a car alarm begins to moan inside a garage like a steady pulse. From house to house, barking has erupted. Each flaring light translates their speeches, not into salvation, but, for now, reprieve.

Across Country

He sends a text to her about a shooting in the Pennsylvania town where they once lived. A jealous ex-husband has killed his former wife and her new boyfriend. "Asshole," she sends back. "You, too."

When he doesn't answer, she puts her phone away. At breakfast, Renee says, "Dad texted me a story from where we used to live. A shooting."

"Did you know those people?" Darcy says.

"No," she says at once. When she Googles the full story, she learns that the shooter used a homemade gun. That the victims sat at an outdoor table so the shooter had no doors to open before and after he fired. A customer who conceal-carried burst through the restaurant's door and shot the killer twice. "A hero," one witness said, though both victims were dead and the killer managed to get back in his truck and drive away.

The girls have read every word of the story. "She wasn't doing anything wrong," Darcy says. "They hadn't been married for over a year."

"That restaurant wasn't there when I was growing up," she tells the girls. "It wasn't there after you two were born. I don't even know where it is." She does not tell them she went to high school with the woman who was killed. She says she didn't know either victim, which is true, at least, because she barely ever talked to that girl back then.

"Everything is so random," Renee says.

The Worst Time
"We're out of beer."

"You can't drive."

"I'm not drunk. It's three miles."

"You don't have a license. Remember why?"

"She's sleeping."

"Not for long."

"You think a few beers means I can't watch a sleeping baby?"

"And now she's awake."

He picked up the baby. "I'm carrying her. See? It's not hard."

"Put her down."

"I'll hold her until you come back. Fifteen minutes. Holding a baby isn't hard."

He walks with the crying baby to the balcony of their second-floor apartment. "Bring her back inside."

"You think I'll drop her?" He extends his arms over the railing. Darcy kicks at the air.

Now she is crying too. "My God. Please."

When he pulls her in and turns, she rushes at him and takes Darcy from his hands. He doesn't resist. "You're so OCD. I never knew that until this second one. You act like you never had a baby before, like Renee never happened and you're starting over." He opens the refrigerator and pulls out the last beer as she leads Renee and carries Darcy to the car.

"Hi, there," he says, when she reappears the next afternoon. "Look, I cleaned up. I vacuumed and did the dishes," but she walks into the bedroom to gather things into an overnight bag. "Look, no beer in the fridge," he says, but she passes him without speaking.

He calls down from the balcony just before she slams the car door shut behind her.

"Never again," he says, which he repeats when she returns in three days, which holds true for eleven days.

When Darcy is Five

The cookie in her daughter's self-illustrated book has long hair cut into bangs so much like hers she says, "The gingerbread man is a girl," but Darcy explains he is wearing a wig. Her cookie runs out the kitchen door and escapes to run and play, but on the last page, that gingerbread man is trapped inside the three-dimensional, pop-up mouth of a scarlet fox, the wig gone in the final picture, lost, perhaps, in the struggle, and when she asks why he is smiling as he's being swallowed, Darcy says, "Because he only has one face."

When Renee is Eight

She draws twelve pages about a princess who needs to be saved. The door to her red-brick tower is chained shut for a dozen sunny days, her hair tightly curled and long, but nowhere near what would welcome a prince to climb. One line per page, this princess sings an abridged "Over the Rainbow." Bluebirds dot every clear sky. Lemon drops sparkle, then fade, but as she finishes, the prince, arriving on horseback, applauds and stays mounted. The rest of the story, Renee whispers, is a secret-secret.

The Mermaid Cemetery

For her eleventh birthday, Darcy asks for a trip to the mermaid cemetery near the ocean. The cemetery is surrounded by a fence with an ornate gate that says, "Welcome to look, but not to touch." Someone tends these graves. Someone has carried kelp and seaweed to vases brimmed with water Darcy tests with her fingertips. Renee says, "Stop," but Darcy licks her fingers, tasting the salt. Renee opens the brochure and begins to read the captions under the photographs that describe the histories of the mermaids who are buried beneath them. The girls follow the mulch trail among headstones shaped like fish, becoming mourners. Aloud, they both wish themselves transformed, wanting to change in order to have bodies that can live in water, scales swallowing their skin until their legs fuse, light and land abandoned, so deep below the surface, they will be impossible enough to be worshipped.

On Location

Renee tells her that Emma Stone played tennis for a *Battle of the Sexes* scene on a nearby Los Angeles court. "Down by the fountain," she says, meaning the Riverside courts. Meaning not too far.

Renee has played three times and plans to use her fourteenth birthday money to buy a vintage outfit like the one Emma Stone wears in the movie. Renee wants to swing her racket like Emma Stone, who had never played before she'd taken the part, but she thinks it would be hard to play with a wooden racket, so strange and heavy, its sweet spot small.

She drives Renee to the Riverside courts. They stand where Emma Stone pretended to be Billie Jean King winning a tournament held in San Diego. Less than 100 yards away a row of power lines towers up from where they follow US 5 and the roar of traffic.

Renee asks her to watch *Battle of the Sexes* again. They sit side by side on the couch. concentrating as if they haven't already seen it. At last, Renee says, "Look, there it is, right where we were standing," and they watch Emma Stone run across the court, swing her wooden racket, and deliver a winning forehand as Renee leans against her.

Art School

One late afternoon she waits for a student's father who is late picking up his daughter from her art school. Renee and Darcy, who do their homework every day in her school office, are impatient, already packed to leave. From the upstairs classroom, they watch both the front and back street for the father's car. The downstairs doors are locked.

When the pounding on the back door begins, Renee says, "It's Dad. He saw me at the window."

"Your Dad is here," Darcy calls to the student. "He's out front."

"Lucky," Renee says, but she steps back into the middle of the room while the student leaves through the front door.

As soon as she is alone with Renee and Darcy, she cracks a window and says, "Don't make your daughters see you get arrested."

"I'm not doing anything," he says. "There's no law against talking to my wife and kids."

"It's only six o'clock and you're drunk."

"You don't know that."

"The girls won't be talking. None of us are coming out until the police arrive." She holds her phone to her ear so he can see.

"You bitch," he shouts. "Fuck you," he yells, slamming his shoulder into the door. When it holds, he says, "You cunt" and walks away, but instead of leaving, he climbs the set of stairs to the parking lot and opens a car door.

Despite her warning, the girls are at the window now. "Whose car is that?" Renee says. "Why does he have a car?" He raises one arm and points something dark at the window where they stand. She is mesmerized, but Darcy drops and rolls into the office, Renee drops to her knees and follows her sister by crawling. Once they are inside, she runs into the office, locks the door, and taps 911.

"We do that drill in school," Darcy says.

"That's for elementary," Renee says. "Nobody in middle school will roll on the floor except weird kids. You'll see next year."

In less than a minute, a police helicopter hovers overhead, but by the time the police arrive by car, he is gone. There are security cameras outside the building and above the parking lot. "We need to confirm it was a gun," a policeman says.

"We're not crazy," she says. "The girls have been drilled. They both dropped as soon as he raised his arm," but the police say they need to study the object in his hand.

"Maybe it's a phone. It would be hard to tell," one says. "We have the make and model of the car. We have the license plate. We'll get the video enhanced and call you in for confirming things."

Minutes later, in the car, Darcy says, "Daddy could have shot all of us."

Renee says, "He just wants to shoot Mom."

The following day, she returns to the church where her art school for children, four to fourteen, is housed. This week the mediums are water color and acrylic painting, projects arranged by age and experience. Two of her students live on the same block. News has spread. There are queries about security. A mother mentions the homeless served lunch by the parish; a father asks who controls the weekly AA meeting held inside a downstairs room. Someone lingers to suggest she consider a location dedicated exclusively to art, testing, as he speaks, the strength of the studio door, the challenge of its lock. Nobody says a word about the source of the disturbance.

The day after that, a policewoman pauses the video where he's inside the car, his arm extended. "It's a phone, not a gun," she says. "See there?"

The girls crowd closer, but she stays distant as if the image could materialize in the room. As if the policewoman is wrong. "We understand your fear," the woman says. "It would have been impossible to tell in the moment. You could still press charges for the threatening gesture."

"Good news, then," she says.

"Pressing charges? Yes, you could call it that."

The Last Time
Because school has just started, her art classes as well, she and the girls don't fly to Pennsylvania for his father's funeral. Because he wants to hang out with old friends, he flies to Las Vegas instead of home. "I need a ride," he says on the phone.

"No," she says to herself. "Why?" she says aloud, and he short-lists, "You don't have school. Neither do the girls. It's not that far. My friends took off. My card is maxed out." As if Las Vegas is a field trip. As if it's about her guilt.

Darcy says, "How far is Las Vegas?" Renee says, "Why can't he ride the bus?" She says, "You'll see."

The trip takes nearly four hours. As he wheels his suitcase toward the car, she nods at the paper bag he carries. "It's barely noon," she says. "We have another four hours in front of us."

"It's not open," he says, something worse, because she can smell it on him before he displays the full bottle and unscrews the cap. He nurses the vodka for a few minutes before he asks her to stop at a KFC as they are leaving the city behind.

"Nobody else here eats that," she says.

"Is that right, girls? You don't want any extra crispy?"

Renee grips Darcy's arm to remind her not to answer. He comes back to the car with a bucket. "Did you at least bring napkins?" she says. He settles in on a drumstick.

An hour later, she and the girls have to pee. When he lifts the bottle in salute, she sees it is nearly empty. They are gathering a few snacks in the convenience store when Darcy looks out the glass door and shouts, "Daddy's sick." He's sprawled on the sidewalk; Renee begins to cry. Outside, they both hold back while she shakes him, but he doesn't respond.

"Your husband?" the store manager says from the doorway. "I've already called. I can't have that here."

"The police?"

"He doesn't need a cop. He needs a doctor."

Even with the windows down, the car is torrid in mid-afternoon. She sends the girls back into the store. Customers turn their heads as they pass. Some loiter by the large front window. On their way out, they look in another direction. Before long, the EMTs start an IV and load him into the ambulance. She tells Renee to dump the rest of the chicken and the empty bottle into the trash can that stands just outside the entrance. "Where are you taking him?" she asks the driver.

"Las Vegas," he says.

"We're on our way back to Los Angeles. That's like starting over."

"There's no help between here and there," he says. "You must know that from being on this road before." There is nothing to do but follow. In the hospital cafeteria, while he is "under observation," their early dinners are so bland, they are hard to swallow.

Near twilight, he is wheeled to their car. "It was so fucking hot sitting in the car while you were pissing. I got myself out, but the fucking parking lot gave me a knockout punch." She stares straight ahead and drives. In the back seat, the girls pretend they can still see to read. After it is full dark, he says, "Route 66 is out here, girls. Where everything was cool once." Nobody speaks. "You're right, girls. There's nothing to even see here. No wonder nobody lives here. Fucking desert. It just puts you to sleep." A few houses blink by at a crossroad. "Somebody's awake there, but not for long, I bet. Nobody sleeps in Las Vegas because it's cool inside and the lights stay on. If we were there, we'd all be awake and talking where they know how to live in the desert without boring people into a coma."

As they pass into the city, he says, "So, nobody's talking?"

Rollover

In the third year of drought, her house foreshadows ashes. For several days, the texts and phone calls cease, but then a police-woman calls. "From the art school dust-up," she says. "I recognized your ex's name at the scene. I thought I could give you a head's up."

"Your father was in an accident," she tells the girls. "In that car we saw at the art school, with the woman who owns it."

"A bad accident?" Renee says.

"A rollover. The car's a loss."

"Is he dead?" Darcy says.

"No. He was driving. The passenger side door took the full force of a large tree."

"She's dead?" Renee says and begins to cry.

"Not yet."

"Was he drunk?" Darcy says. "Did he fall asleep like that time in the desert?"

"Yes, and maybe."

"So, he goes to jail?" Renee says.

"Probably."

"I hate that word," Renee says. "That and *maybe* and *hopefully*."

"And *'we'll see'*," Darcy says. "Like we can't see anything right now. Like we're blind."

"Like we won't know what's happening until it's over," Renee says. "Right, Mom?"

The Past Tense of the Census

In the national census year, before they moved to Los Angeles, she had sought part-time work, self-designed hours convincing her to canvas the county of farms and quiet, well-zoned streets. There were heads to count, assessment questions, and not every house, she soon learned, was welcoming. House trailers were rare and always alone, set so often on barely landscaped lots that she was surprised by one site's borders of high wooden fence, a lawn weed-infested, yet closely mown by somebody, she thought, who was taking whatever care he could, not a man who, before she reached the door, opened it and stood naked, except for sandals, two steps above her.

Once exposed, she thought, a man might be capable of anything. She backed away, saying nothing, fishing for her keys. She kept her eyes on him, but he didn't move. She drove back to the house they rented where he was babysitting, four weeks out of rehab and two months sober. Darcy and Renee, three and nearly six, skittered around the fenced-in back yard. Twilight settled in. They stood beside the deck rail so the girls could see they were watching. Their neighbor's Black Lab barked longingly at its fence gate as she began, hushed and intimate, to speak.

Was that guy drunk? he asked. *I don't think so.* What did he say? *He was soundless.* What did he do? *He picked his teeth, spit, and showed himself.* How close was he? *Arms' length. Pounce distance.* And right there her story ended as if she was willing to tear only one page from her notebook of memory. By then, all she could make out of their daughters was movement. "They're getting hard to see," she said.

"Just wait," he said. In a little while, they'll disappear."

About the Author

Gary Fincke has published twelve collections of stories, including Sorry I Worried You, winner of the Flannery O'Connor Prize and The Killer's Dog, winner of the Elixir Press Fiction Prize. His stories have appeared in such journals as The Missouri Review, The Kenyon Review, Black Warrior Review, CrazyHorse, The Idaho Review, and Cimarron Review. A recent essay "After the Three-Moon Era" was reprinted in Best American Essays 2020, and he has won the Bess Hokin Prize from Poetry Magazine as well as multiple Pushcart Prizes for his work in three genres.

Acknowledgments

Billie Holiday, Sylvia Plath, the Weather Each Morning	*Valley Voices*
Roustabouts	*Green Hills*
From the Heart	*Willow Springs*
Gun Comfort	*Santa Monica Review*
Something like the Truth	*Green Hills*
The Probabilities of Timing	*Valparaiso Fiction Rev.*
After the Great War, the Future is Furious	*Green Hills*
Just Fine	*Southern Indiana Rev.*
The Year Bobby Kennedy was Shot	*Idaho Review*
Condolences	*Laurel Review*
Fool's Mate	*Beloit Fiction Journal*
The Geography of Ridicule (as *Sweetness*)	*Green Hills*
Whiz Kids	*Santa Monica Review*
After the Locks are Changed	*Pithead Chapel*

Printed in the USA
CPSIA information can be obtained
at www.ICGtesting.com
JSHW022355170624
64783JS00005B/14